KILL-A-

AND OTHER STORIES

The new head arrives at Davenport Secondary just at the beginning of the 'Kill-a-Louse' campaign. Soon the whole school is in uproar – can it be that rebellion is as catching as nits in the hair?

These fourteen stories introduce a lively collection of school characters. The two basketball stars Dave Petrovic and 'Goliath' Gillespie are rivals in sport and for the attention of glamorous Melanie Fish. Then there's Jeanie, who writes a poem called 'Ode to a Spot', and Abdul, whose days seem dominated by his teeth and his search for the identity of the mysterious voice on his CB radio. Will Mr Timpson, the student teacher, be able to control his blushes when provoked by Meena Patel and Sharon Marriott and will Fergie Fish finally meet the dreaded Davenport Kipper at the school Fancy Dress Disco?

Susan Gregory's highly entertaining stories follow her earlier collection *Martini-on-the-Rocks and Other Stories*. 'Very, very lively. Good fun and good quality' – *Guardian*

Another book by Susan Gregory

MARTINI-ON-THE ROCKS
AND OTHER STORIES

SUSAN GREGORY

KILL-A-LOUSE WEEK

AND OTHER STORIES

PENGUIN BOOKS

To Toni, Mathew, Ant and Em

PENGUIN BOOKS

Published by the Penguin Group
27 Wrights Lane, London W8 5TZ, England
Viking Penguin Inc., 40 West 23rd Street, New York, New York 10010, USA
Penguin Books Australia Ltd, Ringwood, Victoria, Australia
Penguin Books Canada Limited, 2801 John Street, Markham, Ontario, Canada L3R 1B4
Penguin Books (NZ) Ltd, 182–190 Wairau Road, Auckland 10, New Zealand

Penguin Books Ltd, Registered Offices: Harmondsworth, Middlesex, England

First published by Viking Kestrel 1986
Published in Penguin Books 1988

Copyright © Susan Gregory, 1986
All rights reserved

Made and printed in Great Britain by
Richard Clay Ltd, Bungay, Suffolk
Filmset in Monophoto Bembo

Contents

Kill-a-Louse Week
7

Spot On!
21

2 Young 2 Go 4 Grils
37

Goliath and Dave
48

The Davenport Kipper
67

The Bacon and the Rose
84

Yella Custard
103

Eye! Eye!
116

Abdul and the Vampires
131

Rubber Plant
147

Contents

Pantomime Horse
162

Skegness, or Bust!
176

Uniform
193

Fergie Finds Out
206

Kill-a-Louse Week

The new head arrived at the beginning of Kill-a-Louse Week.

He came to 'hold the fort' at Davenport Secondary after seven years of retirement. He had to come because Mr Joseph, the usual head, had been rushed into hospital on the first Saturday of the autumn term, right in the middle of refereeing the third year rugger match. The third year rugger team had had plenty of horror stories about how the attack had taken Rugby Joe ' 'E went green as slime and choked on 'is whistle.' ' 'Is eyes went round and round and 'e give this 'orrible 'owl.' But they were sorry to see him carted off on a stretcher and pressed in close to get a last look.

The first the school saw of the new head was in Monday's assembly, when Miss Roberts, the biology teacher, was telling them about Kill-a-Louse Week. 'One child in every fifteen,' she told the anxious-looking faces lifted towards her, 'feels *lousy*. And that's because the child *is* lousy, that is, has lice. Such a child is also a "nit-wit". He or she has nits or louse eggs in their hair. So don't go calling your best friend a nit-wit, now you know what it means.'

'And now,' she said like a conjuror about to draw forth a rabbit, 'for a *picture* of the louse. Usually a louse is too small to be seen with the naked eye *but*,' and she held

7

up a ginormous photograph of what a louse looks like under a microscope. The picture was so fearsome that Terry Tindale pulled down his eyelids, rolled up his pupils till you could only see the whites of his eyes and let his neck twist sideways and loll, his hands twitching as though he hung from the end of a rope. When his mate, Fergie Fish, who had been scratching thoughtfully and not looking at the louse, glanced round and saw him, he received such a shock that he fell over backwards in a dead faint.

The new head leapt to his feet, cutting Miss Roberts off in the middle of her horrorbag description of a louse's blood-sucking mouth parts. 'BOY!' he bellowed, so loudly that the front row of cross-legged, knicker-peeping girls rose and collapsed like a wave. 'YOU, BOY, OUTSIDE MY ROOM HEREAFTER FOR A LIBERAL DOSE OF THE CANE.' The second years around Fergie Fish gently slapped him on the chops to revive him and whispered the glad tidings. 'Yer to 'ave the cane. That New Sir said so. Yer to 'ave it 'ereafter. I 'spect that's on the bum.' Fergie Fish groaned and looked as if he might keel over again. The second years propped him up.

The teachers had already had a bellyful of New Sir. He strode into the staff room at quarter to nine for a staff meeting as if his hush-puppies were seven-league boots. He took a roll-call and made a note of all the staff who hadn't turned up yet. Then he fixed those present with a look. 'On my way through the building this morning I caught several pupils CHEWING. It is my intention to STAMP THIS OUT. I expect everyone to SUPPORT ME TO THE HILT. I do not take kindly to back-sliding and I crush with my heel any snakes in the grass.' He ground his rubber sole into the carpet and regarded the card-school in the corner with a terrible eye.

So twenty minutes later in assembly the second years had every reason to look worried. Not only was Fergie up for the cane, but the first lesson every Monday morning was R.I., taken by the head. Usually this was a laid-back sort of lesson when the head explained to the second years how God had favoured the school during Saturday's match or unaccountably taken against it. He told tales of tries that were 'little miracles' of grace and drew diagrams on the board showing the exact position of the boy scoring the try (very close to God in the headmaster's scheme of things), the boy who passed him the ball (the son of God) and the flailing and failing Opposition (the Holy Spirit Incarnate).

The second years lined up outside room four in doleful mood after assembly. Fergie Fish had taken himself up to the secretary's office. Mrs Peters was as kind as Rugby Joe and gave him a pitying look. She told him to sit on the wooden chair New Sir had placed just outside the door. When she peeped out a few minutes later Fergie was in sorry conversation with a piece of string. 'It's cruelty to humans,' he informed the string gravely. 'It is, honest. In a civilized country it wouldn't be allowed.' Mrs Peters hurried out to give him a reviving draught from her coffee cup but at that moment New Sir burst through the swing doors and tut-tutted at Mrs Peters, waving her into her office. Fergie tottered to his feet, shoving the understanding piece of string into his pocket. 'Wait till I flash,' snapped the head, gown flapping like a vampire bat. Fergie couldn't help staring. The school had never seen a *gown* before. And New Sir was going to *flash*? Then he noticed the traffic lights outside the head's door. They'd been put in before Rugby Joe's day, but he'd never found a use for them. His door was always open except on those days when he was over-due with the Governors' Report. Then the door was kept firmly shut and you could hear the sound of Rugby Joe groaning and shredding up paper. Usually, though, the door was not only open but Rugby Joe was outside it, laughing with Mrs Peters, hugging a coffee cup, and resting his bum on the radiator.

The eye of the little green god flashed and Fergie gloomily made an entrance. There were three sharp gasps followed by three sharp yells and he shot out like a pin-ball, crashed through the swing doors on to the staircase, ricocheted from wall to wall down two flights of stairs and exploded into the bottom hall, slamming the door behind him. Mr Mortimer, who taught basketball, was knocked sideways by the blast. He lifted his eyebrows at Fergie who gulped, 'Sorry-Sir-but-I've-just-had-the-cane-Sir.' Mr Mortimer's eyebrows rose higher. 'Might one inquire what for, Fergus?' 'Faintin' in assembly, Sir.' Mr Mortimer's mouth went straight. Fergie was well known for his chronic anaemia. Fergie Fish threw faints like some people throw parties. Mr Mortimer nodded and strode past Fergie in the direction of the headmaster's staircase. He laid an absent-minded hand on Fergie's shoulder in passing. 'Just remember, mate. We shall overcome.'

Meanwhile, the second years were waiting in a ragged queue outside room four. A third were tugging combs through their punk hair styles because Miss Roberts had said lice enjoyed improper grooming. Another third were sifting through one another's thatches in search of louse eggs on the side of hairs. And the final third were giving their heads a bit of a rub and wondering if they'd had lice for three months and were just getting to the itchable stage. They thought they might just wash their hair tonight, if nothing more exciting cropped up.

Ten minutes later they were still waiting. The only things that had happened during those ten minutes were that Mr Mortimer had charged through the doors from the head's stairs, moving faster than any louse, and had galloped across the bottom hall without pausing to give the girls' ears a friendly tweak or to pull a few noses from passing boys. And Fergie had had an idea.

Half of Fergie's idea came to him when Mr Mortimer said, 'We shall overcome,' and the other half when Tez put his arm round his shoulder and said, 'Sorry, Ferg. I didn't err-um think. I'll make it up to you, though. Honest.'

At that moment the new head strode into the hall. He gave the second year a look of deep disgust. Then he snapped in their direction, 'HIGH TORDER.' The second year looked at him blankly. 'HIGH TORDER, HIGH TORDER,' repeated New Sir crossly. He stamped his toes with each phrase. New Sir was not pleased. Mr Mortimer had threatened him with a union meeting because that stupid child had received the cane. Who did that upstart of a P.E. teacher think he was? 'HIGH TORDER,' he bellowed for the fifth time and the whole of the second year twitched like a snake in spasm.

Fergie Fish was racking his brains to fathom it out. New Sir was fixing the girl at the head of the line with his pale eye. It crossed Fergie's mind that perhaps he knew this girl and was informing the class with some violence that he'd taught her – 'I taughd 'er.' Behind Fergie's left ear Tez was also trying to winkle out a meaning. 'I tord I taw a puddy tat?' he whispered to Fergie who shoved his neck forward like a tortoise in an

attempt not to be on the hearing end of this witty little
attention. For he didn't wish to be on the receiving end
of the head's attention again either for some time if he
could possibly avoid it.

Too late. New Sir came india-rubbering up the line
to where the two boys stood. Roughly he pulled out
Tez (very small) and Fergie (very tall), shot-putted
Fergie to the back of the line and dragged Tez to the
front, largely by a lobe. 'There,' he said, casting Tez to
rest at the very front of the line. '*Height* order, and look
sharp about it. By the time I clap to ten.' The claps
rang forth like pistol shots as the second years hurried
and scurried and darted back to back in some vastly
complicated folk dance and finished up in a line de-
scending by approximate degrees. The head grunted.
'Very well,' he said as the last clap crackled round the
hall. 'You may proceed, second year.' At the back of
the line Fergie quickly penned a note to the mate who
had ensured his treatment as a guided missile. Tez could
pay for it now! 'Dear Nit-wit,' he wrote, 'I shall be
humming. When I stop, you start.' He dropped this
cryptic message on Tez's desk as he slid past.

The second years shuffled into place as New Sir rose
and fell, heel toe, heel toe, at the front of the class. (He had
left the door of the classroom wide open. He was one of
those teachers who pride themselves on an absolutely
silent classroom and require the rest of the staff to pride
them on it too.) 'I intend today,' he informed his pupils
with a grimace, 'to take an Old Testament story. The
Egyptians did evil in the sight of the Lord.' He gave
Fergie Fish a terrible look. 'And a visitation of
PLAGUES descended upon them. There was a plague
of BOILS and a plague of FROGS . . .' Fergie Fish
stared back at New Sir, a look for a look. Very, very

softly, so softly that you could scarcely hear him, Fergie
started to hum.

> '*We shall over-co-o-ome,*
> *We shall over-co-o-ome . . .*'

The head looked faintly puzzled. He tugged at his nose
and then he rubbed his ear. 'A plague of LOCUSTS,'
intoned New Sir a little louder, as if to hide his own
doubt. Fergie turned up the volume somewhat, looking
desperately in the direction of Terry. New Sir had started
to walk down Fergie's aisle to check out what he thought
he'd heard. He pretended great interest in a chart showing
the life cycle of the warty toad. All was quiet. New Sir
left the toad and moved slowly to the front. Very very
softly from an entirely other part of the room came the
limpid strains, 'We shall over-co-o-ome.' They came and
went like perfume on a breeze. No one could have said
for sure whether they were in the air or no, and then they
died quite away. New Sir rolled a finger round the inside
of his ear and droned on.

Meena Patel was bored. What was a plague anyway?
She stuck up her hand. 'Please, Sir, can't we do Krishna
now? We sometimes do with Rugby . . . Sir.'

New Sir could not believe his ears. A child telling a
Head what they did and did not do? A pupil putting in a
request, for all the world like Housewives' *Choice*?
'Rugby Sir? *Krish*na?' replied New Sir in tones of deep
mystification and pique. In the bottom hall Mr Mortimer,
practising at the basketball net in a rare free period,
stopped shooting to listen. 'This is *my* school for the time
being, and a Christian school in a Christian country.
While *I* am its headmaster, there shall be no Krishna
here.'

Meena shrugged her shoulders as New Sir swung away

from her, and settled down to write a letter to Rugby Joe on his hospital bed. Carefully she removed the middle page of her R.I. exercise book for the purpose. 'Dear Sir,' she wrote, tongue out of the corner of her mouth to keep the letters on the line, 'I am writhing to tell you that we miss you verry verry much and are verry verry sory about your appendicks. You are a wonderful marvellouse teacher, Sir, and I can't think of anything else to say as no word good enough has been invented. Lots and lots and lots of love from Meena. S.W.A.L.K.'

Meanwhile New Sir had reached the point where he wanted the class to read about the plagues in the Bible. He turned to pick up a stack resting waiting for him on the radiator. Immediately the humming started again, to the power of two. New Sir whipped round. The children were staring accusingly at one another, astounded. 'Who was *humming*?' roared the headmaster, beside himself. He couldn't believe it. Nobody hums for a Head! 'I distinctly heard a humming.' The children recovered themselves and stared innocently back. Katerina Wainwright took a deep breath and spoke up. '*I* didn't hear no humming, Sir.' The others shook determined heads. No, they hadn't heard any humming either. Perhaps Fergie and Terry hadn't *realized* they were humming. Nobody hums for a *Head*!

The head recovered himself and thumped and banged round the room, dealing out Bibles. The rush of air past Meena's head swept up the letter to Rugby Joe and caused it to flutter to the ground. New Sir fell upon it, like an eagle on a chick. 'What *have* we here?' he inquired, rising up with it between his talons. 'Dear Sir, I am *writhing* to tell you . . .' New Sir read it aloud in a mock falsetto, then snorted and ripped the letter into tiny pieces, letting them trickle through his fingers into the waste paper basket. 'Detention throughout break,' said New Sir to Meena Patel.

At that moment there was a noise like a river bursting its banks and the fifth year boys stampeded past room four on their way from biology to the changing rooms. The head flung himself from the room and roared at the fifth year to come back but they were already through the bottom hall and the only answer to his elephant-like trumpet was the slamming shut of the swing doors leading to the lobbies. Then the bell went. The second year heaved a sigh of relief. The head gave them a look. 'I believe you have geography next period?' 'Yes,' replied the second year, round-eyed and with dread in their hearts. 'I have a message here that Miss Bickerstaff telephoned this morning to say she is unwell,' said New Sir. 'She gave instructions as to the work you are to undertake, and I shall remain here for another period to supervise you.' The second years' shoulders heaved and fell in a corporate sigh.

There was another loud clatter followed by a great thudding as the fifth year bounded into the hall bouncing their basketballs. The first five minutes of every lesson were spent on manipulative skills. The very building seemed to shudder as the fifth year pounded round and round, bounce bounce bounce and bounce, thud thud and thud. Under cover of the noise Fergie and Terry started to hum. After a moment Meena Patel joined in.

New Sir was rummaging in a large black folder for work sheets and he looked round sharply. There was nothing to be heard, however, but the blonk blonk blonk of eighteen leatherette balls. New Sir lost patience. He charged over to the door and leant out. 'Mr Mortimer, a word if you please. The second year cannot be expected to concentrate on the Amazon basin with this racket going on. Please to start your game and stop all this infernal bouncing ABOUT.'

Mr Mortimer's mouth went straight again. 'I wouldn't question your choice of lesson content and I'll thank you not to question mine, *Sir*. If the noise troubles you so much why not close your door?' New Sir was beside himself. How dare the trumped-up tyke? But behind New Sir's egg head the humming was swelling again. He shut the door with some haste.

Then he pitched into the second year. 'I won't waste my time and yours inquiring into who was making that ridiculous noise. The whole of the second year is in detention throughout break.' The second year drew in sharp breath at the unfairness of this move, and Fergie, Terry and Meena looked sheepish. They hadn't meant it to come to that. Meena asked the question in everybody's mind. 'Does that mean we can't buy no crisps, Sir?'

'Well, of course it does, stupid girl,' snapped the head. 'Nasty greasy objects, anyway, that only serve to make work for the cleaners. Lift up your lids,' he continued, tapping fiercely on a desk. Dazed, the second years heaved up their desk lids. Inside were a great many empty crisp packets and the odd crumpled note. The head picked one out and unravelled it. ' "For those who love," ' he read aloud, ' "for those who wish to love, and for Brian Robson." Ridiculous! I shall find a prefect to supervise you over break and call the staff together to ban the sale of crisps. Never in my life have I encountered such a sloppy, untidy, ill-run school as this.' The second years thought of sunny Monday morning sessions with Rugby Joe when some R.I. always got done after the important business of the week-end had had an airing, and their hearts, which had begun to harden, set solid. They settled into the Amazon basin and stayed there, brooding, till break.

On his way to summon a staff meeting New Sir had two unfortunate encounters. The first was with a large notice board in room one, 'N.U.T. meeting. Break,' it said. 'Cancel this,' ordered New Sir, collaring Mr Mortimer. 'I MYSELF am assembling a staff meeting at that moment in time.' 'Can't be done,' said Mr Mortimer. 'No way,' and half of the staff turned the corner into the bottom hall and joined him in room one.

The second encounter was with a first year boy slipping out into the street. 'And where do you think you're going?' yelled New Sir, clutching him by the shoulder.

The boy looked hurt. 'Just off for the staff cobs, Sir.'

'Staff cobs,' echoed New Sir. 'Whatever do you mean, staff cobs?'

The child fished in his pocket and produced a grubby scrap of paper. He handed it to New Sir. On it was written.

'Mr Tipperton. Two ham salad with onion and salad cream.

Mr Kirkpatrick. Two turkey roll with onion. NO SALAD CREAM.

Mr Mortimer. Four beef salad. Salad cream. Mustard. Pickle. Onion. One cream doughnut – real cream.'

'It's their dinners, Sir,' explained the boy. 'They like to play poker, dinner time.'

'You are never to go for STAFF COBS again, boy, UNDERSTAND?' said New Sir. 'As for poker in the dinner hour, that will STOP FORTHWITH,' and he took the stairs to the staff room two at a time in his eagerness to sort this den of iniquity OUT.

'I am MOST DISSATISFIED,' the headmaster told the half-filled staff room that awaited him, 'with all I have encountered so far. The fifth year boys are unruly louts. We shall have to put the screws on THEM. I have to report considerable movement BEFORE the bell. And I want whoever teaches the fifth year before basketball to escort the boys through the games situation as far as the lobbies.'

Miss Roberts, who taught them that period, reddened. 'But they're fifth years,' she protested. 'We can't go treating them like infants.'

The head held up a protesting hand. 'Pardon me, madam. They are hoodlums and as such must be contained. I want a purge too,' he continued, 'on the second year. Furthermore, the sale of crisps will STOP as indeed will the purchase of STAFF COBS by a member of the first year, and the playing of POKER. Please inform your colleagues. We are *in loco parentis*, after all. Finally, I spied boys entering the building by the door clearly marked "GIRLS" and vice versa. Slackness, slackness at every turn. I shall call School together after dinner to explain correct procedure.' And with a nod the Head swept out of the room.

■

When the head joined the school in the bottom hall after dinner he was a spouting geyser inside. On his return from the dining centre he had discovered a note. 'We greatly regret,' it read, 'the caning of Fergie Fish this morning and wish to draw the headmaster's attention to the strong anti-caning lobby in education in the nineteen eighties.' 'A ban on crisps,' he now bellowed at the assembled children while the staff sat along the wall behind him looking embarrassed. He burbled on. Nobody was taking it in. 'Boys marked boys blah blah girls marked girls blah blah and blah. And FINALLY,' droned the head, 'when I was a Head seven years ago, I had parents phoning in to THANK me for caning their children. Now *those* were parents,' the head frowned horribly over the lectern, 'who really *loved* their offspring. Unlike today's parents who . . .' The head stopped suddenly, cocking his chin as if he smelt smoke.

What he'd sniffed was a hum.

It started, of course, with the second year. But it didn't stop there. Nobody but the second year knew about humming. But they all knew they didn't care for this New Sir. They didn't know that the hum-in had started with Fergie Fish's caning and spread to Terry and Meena and from there to the whole of second year R.I. But they knew New Sir had put a ban on crisps. Nobody had come into the hall with any intention of humming, not even Fergie Fish. But as soon as it had begun, it seemed that it was what everybody had secretly been waiting for:

'We shall over-co-o-ome.'

'STOP THIS AT ONCE,' bellowed the head. But his voice was lost beneath the droning of ten, a hundred, a thousand hives of bees. He held up his hand for silence but the humming broke over the gesture like a Pacific breaker.

The head grew redder and redder. He considered turning to the deputy to stop it. But he knew that if she succeeded where he'd failed he was as good as dead. He chose to stalk from the hall instead, head held high, and flounced up the stairs and straight through Mrs Peters' offer of a cup of coffee with an impatient wave of the hand. She heard the ping of the phone being lifted in the next room. The head was ringing County Hall.

'Macintyre here,' he snapped, when at last he got through to Staffing. 'I find the school where you required me to "hold the fort" quite unworthy of my ministrations. I have rather high blood pressure and do not intend to force it higher still by having dealings with a collection of hoodlums and nincompoops and an insubordinate staff. I trust I make myself clear.' He nodded three times into the phone, then collected his Crombie overcoat from its peg and took himself off home to Mrs Macintyre without so much as a look in Mrs Peters' direction.

'A collection of the worst kind of louts,' he told his wife, who'd taken one look at him and rushed to put on the kettle and get out the chocolate digestives, 'unworthy of my attention.' But he didn't mention the hum.

Back in the school the hall fell silent as soon as the head had left the room. The children shifted uneasily. Whatever had they *done*? Mrs Palmer, the deputy head, got up. 'I suggest you all take yourselves off calmly to first lesson,' she said in an even voice. The school filed out without a sound.

The second year had P.E. first lesson with Mr Mortimer. Fergie Fish was first into the bottom hall. 'What's a N.U.T. meeting, Sir?' he asked cheekily. 'Does it mean all teachers is N U T T Y or somethin'?' And very quietly he started to hum, 'We shall over-co-o-ome.'

Mr Mortimer caught hold of Fergie's wrist and gave him a Chinese burn. 'That wasn't what I meant this morning, Fergie,' he said, 'and you know it. It wasn't what I meant at all.'

Fergie looked up at him. He liked Mr Mortimer and tried hard to feel sorry for what he'd done. He almost got there but he couldn't quite manage it somehow. He opened his eyes as wide as they'd go. 'But, Sir, it *is* Kill-a-Louse Week,' said Fergie.

Spot On!

'And I'm gonna get chucked out of "O" level English.'

Jeanie Parkes looked up from the book she was studying to give Miss Harvey this news.

'Why's that, Jeanie?' Miss Harvey knew only too well what the reason would be – Davenport Secondary's head of English, Mr R. C. Revitt, B.A.(Hons.), J.P. and M.C.P.

Jeanie spoke above the racket of fifth year registration. 'He says my compositions are infantile. He's given me *this*!'

She held up the book – *Model Compositions for Today's Young Person*. Miss Harvey tried not to smile.

'It's a laugh a minute, Miss. It is, honest. Listen to this one. "Science and the Housewife". And *this* – "The Radiogram: Blessing or Curse?"'

Mrs Palmer, the deputy head, stuck her head round the door. 'Excuse me, Miss Harvey.' She was frowning a little at the noise. She cleared her throat loudly and when this brought no visible effect drew a loud blast from the whistle round her neck. 5H stopped talking immediately, one or two shaking their heads as if they had water in their ears.

'It has been brought to my attention, fifth years, that some of the girls are wearing, ahem, *denim trousers* on the way back from the swimming baths. THIS HAS TO

21

STOP. In his absence the headmaster wishes me to draw your parents' attention to the meeting for the "Friends of Davenport", seven thirty in the bottom hall.' She nodded three times and waved a pencil at Miss Harvey. 'Now, Miss Harvey, I wonder if you'd be so good as to dispense these among the "non-exams"? The revised master timetable is on the top. Could you put it on the board for them, please, and check that they have it down correctly? Thank you *so* much.'

Miss Harvey sighed to herself. She hated the first week of term. She collected the timetable blanks and asked Melanie Fish to give them out, boggling at what she read. 'Monday 9.00 a.m. to 10.30 a.m. humanities. Monday 11.00 a.m. to 12.30 p.m. humanities. Monday 2.00 p.m. to 3.45 p.m. humanities.'

'This can't be right, fifth year "non-exam".' She gave a little wince. 'According to this you have humanities *all day* on a Monday.'

'Yeah, 's right, Miss,' confirmed Mick Malone from the back. 'Las' year we had social studies all day Monday. It'll be the same thing.'

'And do you know what "humanities" means?'

Mick shrugged. 'Last year it were 'istory, geography, English. Stuff like that.'

'Then why don't they call it history, geography and English?'

Mick lifted an eyebrow. 'You're the teacher, Miss. Don' ask *me*.'

Miss Harvey returned to the timetable. 'And the first two on a Tuesday, the lads have metalwork and the girls have fabrics. *Fabrics?* Can that be right?'

'Yeah, it is, Miss,' chorused fifth year 'non-exam', and Jaswant Kaur came charging to the front. She shoved a blue denim purse with 'Love' and a wiggly heart embroidered on it under Miss Harvey's nose. 'Look, Miss. Look at what I made in fabrics las' year.'

'Very nice, Jaswant. But isn't there a chance for the *girls* to do metalwork and the *lads* to do fabrics from time to time?'

'Yeah, well, there is, Miss. But *all* the girls wanted to do metalwork and *none* of the lads wanted to do fabrics, so the whole thing got scrapped.'

Jeanie Parkes, studying *Model Compositions for Today's Young Person* from her desk at the front, gave a loud snort. 'Listen to this, Miss. "It was a smiling Friday morning in early September when we began our intrepid trek. Meandering along sun-spilt tracks we at last gained the summit of Crabb's Nob whence we commandeered a panoramic vista of undulating countryside – sparkling appetizer indeed to our week-end of heathland and wind!" I could never write a composition like *that*! The only one in our class who can write a composition like that's Mathew Davidson and he's a flippin' genius. I'll never get "O" level English and me mum'll be that cross!' She looked very down-in-the-mouth.

'But, Jeanie,' said Miss Harvey, abandoning the timetables. 'You're set one for most subjects, aren't you? You should easily be capable of passing your "O" level.'

Jeanie gave Miss Harvey a beetle-browed look. 'Huh! You try telling that to The Rabbit.'

'To Mr Revitt,' said Miss Harvey automatically.

'To Mr Revitt,' echoed Jeanie dutifully. 'You try telling Mr Revitt that.' She shook her head.

'What set books are you doing?'

Jeanie looked blank.

'Your set books. For "O" level literature. You are taking "O" level literature as well, I take it?'

'Oh, no way. Only language. They only read *books*

and that if they're doing C.S.E. T'ain't fair, y'know, Miss. 'S'only the top set don' get to read any books. They've got loads of good paperbacks for the "non-exams".'

Miss Harvey blinked. She was new to the school and it kept giving her shocks.

'Well, surely you must read *something* in class? You can't do,' she glanced nervously at the book Mr Revitt had given to Jeanie, ' "Model Compositions" all of the time.'

'Oh, yeah. There is a book we read in class. We've been on it a year. "Flight of the 'Eron".' Jeanie looked very cheesed off.

'And is it good?'

Jeanie gave Miss Harvey a dark look. 'I wouldn't know. It's written in *Scotch*.'

'Is there *nothing* you like doing in your English lessons, Jeanie?'

Jeanie considered. 'Well, I did write this poem thing once . . .'

'Good. And did you show it to Mr Revitt?'

Jeanie nodded.

'And what did he say?'

'Oh, infantile. He said it was infantile.' Jeanie looked dashed, then perked up. 'I could write a poem for *you*, though, Miss. Now, if you like.'

Miss Harvey nodded, her eyes back on the timetables for the fifth year 'non-exams'. 'Mmmm, Jeanie. That'd be nice.'

■

'What's Jeanie Parkes like at English?' Miss Harvey asked Mr Revitt as they stood together by the enormous staff teapot at break. Miss Harvey reached for it. She needed both hands to lift it. She offered to pour for Mr Revitt who looked sideways at the brown pond in which the teapot stood beside a small heap of grounded tea bags. He waved a well-manicured white hand to indicate his distaste. He stepped from behind the tea bar, taking a key from his pocket, and unlocked a small cupboard bearing a strip of metal with R. C. Revitt punched into it. From this he took his personal jar of Gold Blend. He unwrapped a teaspoon from a paper towel and ladled out an exact level teaspoon of coffee. Then he helped himself to exactly half a teaspoon of sugar from the encrusted pink plastic container, carefully avoiding the centre where sinister brown stains lurked. He decanted every bit of the top of the milk into somebody else's cup and turned to Miss Harvey. 'Yes, Miss Harvey? You were saying?'

'What's Jeanie Parkes like at English?'

Mr Revitt snorted. 'Infantile! Infantile!'

'Will she be taking "O" levels?'

Mr Revitt sniggered, showing stained yellow teeth. 'Not if I can help it, Miss Harvey, so no, she will not.'

'Then she won't have any English qualifications at all, since she won't be taking C.S.E.?'

Mr Revitt was boiling himself a fresh kettleful of water, blocking off the entrance to the tea bar and all access to the staff pot. He snapped off the kettle and made off with his steaming cup. 'Quite right, Miss Harvey. She will not. Hole in one.'

Miss Harvey carried her cup across to her new friend Maureen Muldoon who taught art. 'What's Jeanie Parkes like at art?'

Miss Muldoon grimaced. 'You might say she's an original. But she doesn't apply herself.'

'She will be taking "O" level, though?'

'Oh, sure. She's double entered. If she doesn't get "O" level, she'll get a C.S.E. grade one. She's quite good.'

■

The next morning Miss Harvey was going through the papers from her pigeon-hole. It was like the eternal fount – no sooner had she cleared it of one load of cyclostyled sheets than it filled up with another.

Jeanie arrived to have a word. Miss Harvey didn't ask her what she wanted but read aloud to her from the latest piece of paper. ' "The local group committee of the pilot scheme for the re-orientation of Mode 3 C.S.E. to a proper consideration of community and global needs will meet for a 'buzz' session on Wednesday 30 September at 4.00 p.m." Dear me! I wonder what it means?'

Jeanie shrugged. 'Haven't a clue.'

'Neither have I,' said Miss Harvey. She screwed the paper into a ball and lobbed it into the waste paper basket. 'Yes, Jeanie? What can I do for you?'

Jeanie handed over the poem. 'I don't know why it's turned out funny,' she said dolefully. 'I wrote it about *this*,' and she indicated a spot like a ball-bearing on the side of her chin. Miss Harvey read the poem. She laughed out loud. 'That's good, Jeanie,' she said, handing it back. 'How about entering this?' She thumbed through the stack of papers and handed Jeanie a sheet. Then she turned back to a circular from the deputy head. 'It is hoped that the water shrimps at present dogging the school plumbing system will be exterminated forthwith. Please initial and pass on. P.B.P.'

Jeanie flopped down into her seat in front of Miss Harvey. She was glad Miss Harvey had laughed, of course. She'd meant her poem to be funny. But deep down inside she didn't feel very funny at the moment. The only person who seemed prepared to enter her for 'O' level was Miss Muldoon. And you should hear what her mum had to say about 'O' level art. Then there was the way she was looking these days – her clothes were dreadful, her shoes were awful, her chin was scabby, her forehead was spotty, her fingers were stubby, she'd got no waist. She was . . . well, frankly, she was gross. 'Miss Harvey,' said Jeanie very low. 'Please, Miss Harvey.'

Miss Harvey didn't hear. She'd just found a letter informing her that nothing could be done about a fume extractor for room six. Room six was Miss Harvey's room. It was directly over the darksome cavern known as the metalwork room and it was like living at the maw of Hell – Miss Harvey and her classes were periodically choked by poisonous fumes seeping up through the floorboards. The education department was meant to be battling it out with the engineers for a fume extractor in the arena of County Hall. Miss Harvey imagined memos twirling round memos in an eternal snowstorm along the corridors of power while she and her pupils quietly dropped down dead at their desks.

'Miss Harvey, Miss Harvey, can I speak to you, please?'

Miss Harvey sighed, took off her specs and rubbed her rather sore-looking eyes. 'Speak away, Jeanie. Don't mind me.'

Jeanie ignored this. 'Miss Harvey, I know I made the spot poem sound funny. I meant it to be funny. But I don't, well, feel very funny at the moment if you know what I mean. It's not just my chin and my English that's a mess at the moment. It's all my lessons. And it's me too, Miss Harvey. I'm a mess.' And she hung her head and looked as if she was going to cry.

Miss Harvey told Jeanie to bring her chair round to her desk so that Jeanie could sit next to her. She looked anxiously into her face. 'What do you mean, Jeanie, that you're a mess?'

Jeanie thought about this. What *did* she mean? 'I . . . I *look* such a mess,' she said in the end and glanced meaningfully at her lace-up shoes and over-long skirt.

Miss Harvey suddenly seemed to lose interest. 'Oh, I'll bring you in *Jane Eyre* to read, Jeanie. She wasn't as pretty as a valentine, but at least she could draw! And now if you'll excuse me, I R E A L L Y H A V E T O G E T O N.'

Back in her place Jeanie stared in front of her. Well, that had been a load of use . . . She, Jeanie Parkes, could draw! So what? She didn't want to *draw*. She wanted to be as sexy as Melanie Fish. Melanie Fish was the sexiest girl in the whole school. She'd done this jerky robotics dance once in front of everybody for assembly. She'd worn an emerald green lycra and a black dustbin liner like a mini-dress and strips of leather with spikes round her neck and she'd looked amazing. The whole school'd gone berserk and Mr Revitt had walked out of assembly in protest. It had been great! Jeanie tried to imagine what she'd look like in an emerald green lycra (lumpy) and in a dustbin liner (someone'd throw her on a corporation dustcart) and hurriedly turned her attention to the piece of paper Miss Harvey had given to her.

'Poetry Competition for Schools,' read Jeanie. 'All entries to be judged by a city teacher. Presentation of prizes and poetry reading by Philip Butler.' Even Jeanie had heard of the celebrated local poet Philip Butler. 'Mr Butler will read from his latest collection *A Fillip for the Muse*.'

Jeanie thought she might just enter. She carefully read through 'Ode to a Spot', then wrote it out another fourteen times or so, changing a word here and giving little grins there. Then she frowned. And jogged out to the front again.

By now Miss Harvey had been joined by Ravinder Singh. They were both looking very cheesed off. 'JUST WAIT A MINUTE, JEANIE.' Miss Harvey was no longer sunny side up. After Jeanie had left her with the competition entry sheet Miss Harvey had discovered a form from the Home Office among her post. It required her to fill in the members of her registration group according to nationality. This was based not only on where they themselves were born but on the country of origin of their families. The form dealt in broad sweeps – Africa, Afro-Caribbean, Asian, Americas, U.K., Other European and Others. Ravinder was just telling Miss Harvey, 'Well, me dad comes from Kenya and me mam comes from Fiji, and me grandparents, they come from India.'

'And what does that make you?'

Ravinder gave her a look of deep disgust. 'I'm British, of course.'

Miss Harvey produced something between a grin and a groan. She added another to the Others column and shook her head. It now stood at Others – 28.

Jeanie was getting bored. 'Miss Har-vey!'

Miss Harvey gritted her teeth. 'YES-JEANIE-WHAT-IS-IT-THIS-TIME?'

Jeanie cast a meaningful look in the direction of Ravinder Singh.

Miss Harvey drew in breath. 'O.K., Ravinder, that'll be all. Thank you very much.'

When Ravinder was out of earshot, Jeanie changed her weight from one hip to another. 'I can't enter this poetry competition, Miss.'

Miss Harvey groaned. 'WHYEVERNOT?'

' 'Cos what I wrote ain't poetry. It's funny and daft. "Ode to a Spot", Miss, it ain't a proper poem.'

'Don't you know any published poems that are funny and daft, Jeanie?'

Jeanie thought for a long time. ' "The Jumblies"?' Miss Harvey nodded. Jeanie thought again. ' "The Camel's Hump"?' Miss Harvey nodded again.

'Right, then. Would you call "The Jumblies" a proper poem?'

'Well, ye-es, but . . .'

'And would you call "The Camel's Hump" a proper poem?'

Jeanie twisted her shoes from side to side and inclined her head to one shoulder. 'I *s'pose* it is, yes.'

'THEN SO IS "ODE TO A SPOT". Now, Jeanie, I am very very busy. Will you go and sort your blasted psyche out SOMEWHERE ELSE?'

Jeanie went off chuntering. Nevertheless, she started to copy 'Ode to a Spot' out again, neater this time. She signed her name at the bottom, a cross between William Shakespeare and Queen Elizabeth the First, and filled in the entry form. As soon as the bell went she leapt up and ran to the front to show Miss Harvey her entry.

'Good,' said Miss Harvey, and opened a desk drawer. 'Here's an envelope. Buy a stamp for it after school, Jeanie, and SEND IT OFF.'

∎

Three mornings later Jeanie was in another gloom. She looked so miserable that Miss Harvey had said, 'What's the matter, Jeanie?' before she could think better of it.

'I told Mr Revitt I'd entered that competition.'

'Yes?'

'And he said a friend of his was judging it. A friend of his! I haven't got a chance.'

'Of course you have.' Miss Harvey sounded preoccupied. Her pigeon-hole had been crammed to capacity again that morning.

'And that's not all.'

Miss Harvey looked up. 'No?'

'He's told Mathew Davidson to enter as well.'

'So?'

'Mathew Davidson writes brilliant poems. I showed him some of mine. And he kind of, like, twisted his mouth up and then showed me some of his.'

'And?'

'They're all brilliant, Miss. Proper sort of poems, not like "Ode to a Spot". The one he's entered's called "Palimpsest on a Text of Plato".' She left a space for Miss Harvey to gasp in.

'And what's so good about that?'

Jeanie gaped at her. 'I don't know what it *means*.' She shook her head and descended a few more metres into her gloom. Miss Harvey, eyeing her post, decided to leave her there, from now on, to stew.

∎

Four weeks later Jeanie came to Miss Harvey waving a letter. 'I came *second*, Miss. I came second in that competition.'

'Oh, that's marvellous, Jeanie! Well done! Who came first, do you know?'

'Mathew Davidson did, of course! "Palimpsest on a Text of Plato". I told you it was brilliant.'

'I shall come to the prize-giving. When is it, Jeanie?'

'Next Wednesday. At Gurlington High.'

∎

On the evening of the presentation Jeanie walked to Gurlington High with her mum. All the way she imagined what Philip Butler might look like. He'd be rather on the young side, she reckoned, very pale and thin. He'd have a long soft droopy moustache and wear a black velvet suit.

On the other hand, she had to face it, he might wear filthy frayed jeans and a sweater with holes at the elbows and an earring. Jeanie mentally added a cotton jacket with buttons all over it like a pearly king's, to cover up the elbow holes. Mick Malone had a cotton jacket covered in buttons. It was the most poetic thing on the fifth year base. Jeanie imagined the pearly king saying, 'Yes, Miss Parkes, I was much taken with the community and global significance of "Ode to a Spot" and I thought the word "fester" in the third line showed . . .'

'Pick your feet up, Jeanie, do,' snapped her mother, as Jeanie slithered across the paving stones towards the school in her new red pointed-toed spiky-heeled shoes, wrested from her mother at great personal cost. Her mum had gone a bit like Miss Harvey since her dad left. She couldn't care less what she looked like and tried to brainwash Jeanie to be the same. 'Where's the point,' argued Mrs Parkes, 'in spending hard-earned cash to doll yourself up to please men who don't appreciate the essential *you*?' Jeanie couldn't get her to see that it wasn't the object of the exercise to please *men* at all. She just wanted some trendy clothes and pretty shoes to please her essential *self*.

When they got inside the school there was a terrible hush.

'What time did you say this thing started?' asked Jeanie's mum suspiciously.

A tall thin woman was tapping towards them down the corridor in very high heels. She held up a long finger and said, 'Please would you keep your voice down? Mr Butler is reading,' in an awed whisper.

'Oh, law!' whispered Jeanie. 'What time did it start?'

The woman eyed the red pointed-toed spiky-heeled

shoes with disquiet. 'Seven *thirty*.' Jeanie's mother gave a disgusted click.

'The reading's in the library,' said the woman. 'End of the corridor.'

Jeanie and her mother hurried over the polished boards and Jeanie gently pushed open the swing door. It gave a terrible croak. There were only two rows of people at the far end of the library but two rows of eyes is an awful lot of eyes when they all swivel to look at *you*. Jeanie and her mother cringed their way to the front, lifting their feet high and jerking their necks like ostriches, trying to move without a sound.

Miss Harvey beckoned to them. She'd saved two seats. The one next to Jeanie was occupied by Mathew Davidson who gave her a pitying smile. Jeanie comforted herself by thinking that the Rabbit hadn't come to hear *him* read his poem. She concentrated her scarlet face in the direction of Philip Butler and . . .

Oh, no!

He was old!

He was at least forty with a highly-coloured pug face and wore half-moon specs, cord trousers, a cord jacket, a red kerchief round his neck and . . .

Oh, no!

SUEDE SHOES!

But the poem he was reading was funny! It was about the animals in the zoo and the people who came to look at the animals. It was more about the animals than about the people but at the same time it was more about the people than the animals. Clever! Jeanie snorted and took a quick look at Miss Harvey. She was grinning too. But nobody else was. Her mother and Mathew Davidson had these dead soppy expressions on their faces, like they were thrushes contemplating a bank of violets and about to burst into song. By the end of the poem Jeanie was squirming in her chair with trying not to laugh.

The animal poem was the last in the reading. At the end Jeanie thought Philip Butler looked a bit glum. Perhaps he was sad that nobody'd laughed? She would have been! The tall thin woman who'd clicked in half-way through with a glass of water stood up and said, '*How* interesting! Thank you *so* much, Mr Butler. Mr Butler hasn't told us *exactly* what poetry *is*, of course, but from what he has read to us this evening, I *think* we all *know*. And now it is time to award the prizes for the young people's competition. I have great pleasure in introducing Mr Humphreys, a local teacher, who has very kindly judged this competition for us. Mr Humphreys.'

'Oh, law!' thought Jeanie as a pale precise little man jerked to his feet. He had a black tie with the smallest knot Jeanie had ever seen. It was about the size of a black beetle.

'Errgh-umer-yes-well,' said the precise little man in a very imprecise manner. 'What I must impress upon the entrants before I come to the winning poems is,' he suddenly frowned and glared fiercely at the two rows, 'I DO LIKE MY POEMS NEAT.'

Jeanie perked up a bit. Neat like whiskey's neat?

But no. Neat like neat is neat. 'As you will see,' he continued, brandishing 'Palimpsest on a Text of Plato' and 'Ode to a Spot' by the scruff of their necks, 'both the winning entrants are EXCEEDINGLY NEAT. The poem that came first is also most sophisticated in content and vocabulary,' he leered at Mathew who tried hard to look humble, 'whereas the second prize poem speaks of a condition prevalent among our young people and can perhaps best be described as errgh-err-um quaint.' Jeanie shuddered and fingered a spot.

'Perhaps the fortunate prize-winners would care to approach and grace us with the fruit of their labours?' He had no need to summon Mathew who was already sprinting to the front. He belted out 'Palimpsest on a Text of Plato' in a gusty fashion, pausing to take breaths before every long word. At the end he bowed slightly and said, 'Thank you. Thank you very much!' in a heartfelt manner.

Jeanie slumped deeper into her shoulders. She didn't think her legs could cope. Miss Harvey leaned over and gave her a prod. She shot to the front and gabbled through 'Ode to a Spot' like a contestant in 'Beat the Clock', lost her place on the third line from the bottom, and started the previous two lines over again by mistake. Her eyes grew round as poppies as she realized she was repeating herself and her face took on the expression of one suffering from severe stomach cramps. She dived back to her place at the end, twisting her body from left to right and back again in sheer agony and then collapsed low on her chair like a balloon when someone lets go of the end.

And Mr Butler gave her a wink.

There it was, behind the half-moons, for everyone to see! A great gargantuan wink!

Jeanie decided she would never complain about anything, ever again. Never mind that she wasn't taking any proper 'O' levels. Never mind that her dad had gone off with a flibbertigibbet who dressed fine to please men. Never mind that she had to wear over-long skirts and lace-up shoes to make it up to her mum, and had no waist and a whole constellation of spots. A REAL LIVE POET HAD TIPPED HER THE WINK. A whacky, waggish, worldly, wily, wanton, warm and wonderful wink!

After the tall thin woman had urged the first two rows

to partake of a little liquid refreshment in the entrance hall the beautiful suede shod Mr Butler came up to Mathew and Jeanie. 'Congratulations, both!' he said.

Mathew nodded gravely. 'Thank you, Sir.' He turned to Jeanie. 'Isn't it strange, Jeanie? I thought "Ode to a Spot" was your *worst* poem, actually.' Jeanie looked as if he'd landed her an upper cut and even Mathew felt the need to soften the blow. 'I only meant your worst poem for *you*,' he added kindly. He turned to Mr Butler. 'Jeanie writes some pretty good poems, actually, Sir. When she's not trying to be funny, that is.'

But Mr Butler was eyeing Mathew over the half-moons with a little less than enthusiasm. 'Oh, I should say Jeanie just about *put her finger on it* in her poem, Mathew, and I should know. I can't say I've ever felt the need to pen a palimpsest but I've always been a *dab hand* with a spot.' And he went off cackling towards the liquid refreshment, leaving Jeanie grinning at the latest ball bearing in the glass of a book case, and Mathew to sniff out where they kept the thesauruses in Gurlington High – he was about to launch himself once more upon the muse. 'The poet never rests,' he warned Jeanie, but she wandered off towards the entrance hall where she knew Miss Harvey would have poured her a cup of coffee. Mathew was already in the throes of composition. 'Mouthings on a Monstrous Macula' he took as a working title, and settled down to a little versification in a Jeanie-esque kind of mode.

'And what did Mr Butler have to say to you, Jeanie?' asked Miss Harvey.

Jeanie coughed modestly. 'Well, he doesn't go a bundle over palimpsests, I reckon. He seemed more at home with an ode.' Then she grinned. 'Well, *actually*, Miss Harvey, he thought my poem was pretty well spot on.'

2 Young 2 Go 4 Grils

Mr Timpson came to Davenport Secondary for a term as a student teacher, to help Mr Roonie with lower school geography. He was earnest and nervous, wore jeans, open sandals and no socks, and was very inclined to blush. If Melanie Fish happened to stand next to him in the dinner queue, for example, and greeted him with a friendly, 'Hi, Sir', well, that was enough to send him rosy to the roots of his hair, no problem. Meena Patel and Sharon Marriott of the second year thought he looked cute when he blushed and they were always trying to set him off. But he was getting better at taking deep breaths as the weeks went by, and controlling his blushes.

Meena Patel and Sharon Marriott were called the Siameses by the other second years. This was because they did everything and had everything the same. If they liked a teacher, then they always liked the same one (as in the case of Mr Timpson). When Meena had a fluffy orange pencil case with plastic eyes that winked at you, then Sharon had to have one. And when Sharon had an autograph album (Macdonald tartan – wipeable – with a tasselled pencil) Meena had one too (only hers was red Moroccan leather with AUTOGRAPH ALBUM printed across the front in gold).

They both launched their albums on the same day at

2 Young 2 Go 4 Grils

the same time – the beginning of Mr Timpson's geography lesson. With any luck someone – say, Christopher Crutchley – would write something rude in them and Mr Timpson would ask to see what was being passed around the classroom. Then he'd blush.

The first person to write in Meena's album was Sharon:

> *Memories will fade*
> *Leaves may dry*
> *My friendship with you*
> *Will never die.*

And the first person to write in Sharon's book was Meena:

> *There's big ship's*
> *and little ship's*
> *But the best ship's*
> *Is friendship's.*

Next they passed their books to Caroline Stewart:

> *There's a man lives down our street*
> *He's got no hair but he's got three feet.*

Who passed them to Stephanie Bishop:

> *Teacher, teacher, I declare*
> *Tarzan's lost his underwear.*

Who passed them to Brian Turley:

> *I eat my peas with honey*
> *I've done it all my life*
> *It makes the peas taste funny*
> *But it keeps them on the knife.*

Signed: Brian Turley. Friend of the Earth.

Brian Turley was new to Davenport that term. He was skinny and eager and good at lessons, and, in Christopher Crutchley's eyes at least, too innocent for his own well being. Early on, Christopher had scrawled across Brian Turley's geography book '2 Young 2 Go 4 Grils'.

The next person to have the albums after Brian Turley was Fergie Fish.

Fergie gave careful thought to the claims of each girl on his attention before committing himself to their albums. He scrutinized them across the room. Meena, he decided after a moment or two, was all right. In fact she was ten out of ten, A One Plus, and he couldn't think why he hadn't noticed this before – so she got:

> *Meena bent to pick a rose*
> *She was so sweet and slender*
> *Meena bent to pick a rose*
> *And ping went her suspender.*

Whereas Sharon Marriott had always been slow to appreciate the charms of Fergie Fish:

> *Roses are red*
> *Violets are blue*
> *With a face like yours*
> *You should be in a zoo.*

Fergie then passed the albums to Christopher Crutchley. He had a great deal of time for Chris these days. He was more grown up than Tez and given to remarks like 'I am a man' and 'I know these things' while tapping the side of his nose, and Fergie considered he might well pick up some handy hints from that direction. There were days when Fergie thought that Chris Crutchley was his favourite mate.

On the other hand Chris Crutchley was Mr Timpson's least favourite pupil. This wasn't surprising. He was more or less the least favourite pupil of every teacher in Davenport.

'Chris!' whispered Fergie. 'Chri-is!' His eyes darted to the front with every whisper. (Although inclined to nervousness, Mr Timpson did have his more positive side!)

Christopher didn't hear. He was partially deaf at the best of times and on top of this had just removed his hearing aid. He was deeply engrossed in his geography exercise book. Where Mr Timpson had written 'This is very poor work', Chris had written 'Thank you', and where Mr Timpson had written 'THIS IS REALLY ATROCIOUS', Chris had written 'Thank you very much'.

Fergie watched Mr Timpson turn to the board, did a quick calculation, dived across the gangway, tapped Christopher Crutchley on the shoulder, wiggled his eyebrows in the direction of the albums, dived back into his seat, snatched up a pencil and was scrutinizing the blackboard with knitted-browed concentration – all before Mr Timpson turned round.

Thus prompted, Christopher Crutchley transferred his attention to the autograph albums. He thought for a moment, then scrawled across a blue page in Sharon's:

> *Don't make love on the garden gate*
> *Love may be blind but the neighbours ain't.*

Then he began to scratch the same in Meena's.

'CHERRISTOPHER CERRUTCHLEY!'

Whistling to himself, Christopher carried right on scrawling. He hadn't heard a thing. Nor did he notice Mr Timpson regarding him with irritation and twitching the small microphone all teachers wore round their necks like a mayoral chain when trying to pass on knowledge to Christopher Crutchley.

There was a swift displacement of air – Mr Timpson bearing down on Christopher like the avenging angel and forcibly replacing the hearing aid. His voice crackled and boomed from somewhere directly above Christopher's head. Christopher winced.

'I was just saying, Crutchley, that next week is PLANT A TREE WEEK,' bellowed Mr Timpson. 'This is the most important time of year for TREE PEOPLE. Planting trees is something ECOLOGISTS are interested in. Do you know what ECOLOGY means, Crutchley?'

Christopher didn't. He glared.

Brian Turley beamed up at Mr Timpson. 'I do, Sir. Ecologists are the greens, Sir, I'm a green.' He went on to explain. Mr Timpson looked gratified. If Christopher was generally agreed to be the least desirable pupil in the second year, Brian Turley was fast establishing himself as the most favoured. He was happy to learn whatever teachers chose to teach, with a bias towards any project that involved planting, growing, nurturing and conservation. Biology and geography were his best subjects.

Meanwhile Christopher had remembered his clinic card. Whenever a member of staff recalled the hearing aid Christopher had a back-up system of problem zones requiring urgent attention. He shoved his way between bags and legs to the front. 'Sorry, Sir. Only just remembered, Sir. I'm due at t'clinic twenty past. Me verruca, Sir.'

Mr Timpson scrutinized the clinic card. 'This signature of the headmaster's wouldn't happen to be a forgery, would it, Crutchley?'

Christopher looked outraged and vigorously shook his head. 'I swear on me mother's Bible, Sir.'

'I'll send it along to the headmaster all the same, just to make sure.'

Christopher snatched it off him, muttering something, and ploughed his way back to his desk.

'And don't kick Brian Turley like that.'

'I didn't kick 'im, Sir! I jus' poked 'im with me foot.'

Back at his desk Christopher brooded. He'd get that know-all Turley! He soothed his injured pride by going through his excuse notes. These all followed the same format but the variations were endless. 'Christopher must not do woodwork/baskitball/athleticks/musick as he has a soar thum/week rists/strined tendun/perfrated ear drum.' Plus a note diagnosing a rare but galloping variety of athlete's foot to get him off showers. None of them'd get him off geography, though – not now Mr Timpson had blown his clinic card. He'd get that Timpo as well!

Fergie had seized on the diversion of the clinic card to return the albums to Meena and Sharon. They were disappointed at first to see them come back. Mr Timpson had neither confiscated them nor blushed, which had been the objects of the exercise.

But when Sharon read what Fergie had written in her book *she* went scarlet – with fury! Meena was blushing too – with pleasure – and grinning. Sharon snatched her friend's album and compared her own Fergie entry with Meena's. Then she accidentally-on-purpose dropped Meena's album on the floor and stuck her foot on it. The result was a scuff mark. Sharon scrawled across it, 'SHAZ WOZ HERE'.

When Meena saw what Sharon had done she went redder still. She seized Sharon's book and wrote across the page in angry orange letters, 'YOU ARE A

CHICKY GIRL'. This didn't seem nearly harsh enough so she turned up another page and wrote, 'YOU ARE A NICETY WITCH'. When the bell went Mr Timpson left the classroom as even complexioned and cool as when he'd come in. It was Sharon and Meena who left with a very high colour.

■

Such a friendship couldn't remain in fragments for long, though. The girls were soon reunited. For one thing, since the day of the autograph albums, Christopher Crutchley and Fergie Fish had started fancying one of them each. Fergie had taken to staring at the crisp white cuffs of Meena's school blouse and the piece of twisted black cotton she wore round one slim wrist and sighing to himself. And Chris had decided that Sharon Marriott who took on the teachers and wore sweat bands to lessons was just the girl for him. But as far as the girls were concerned, one admirer each was one too many. Now if *one* lad had fancied *both* of them, they'd have been able to fuss and swoon over the *same* lad, like at the moment they fussed and swooned over Mr Timpson.

Fergie and Christopher found it hard to accept that those they fancied didn't fancy them, and took it out on Brian Turley. They'd sing in unison whenever they saw him coming:

> *'What's skinny and keen*
> *And ever so GREEN?'*

> *'A Turley!'*

Meanwhile, Christopher hadn't forgotten he'd sworn vengeance on Brian Turley and Mr Timpson – it was just that he hadn't hit on a plan yet. But when he received his half-term grades and compared them with Brian Turley's, dreams of revenge grew sweet. Even Fergie was a bit put out when he compared his grades with the Turley's. He told Mr Timpson so at the beginning of geography. 'Attainment D Effort D−! I'm sorry, Sir, you'll have to go!'

Mr Timpson eyed him grimly. 'It's not that you couldn't do better, as you very well know. Persistent misuse of the head, Fergus, that's your problem.'

Fergie ignored this. 'It's the last lesson before half-term today, y'know, Sir. Can we play murderball?'

Brian Turley frowned. 'Oh, *no*, Sir. I want lessons.'

Fergie turned on him. 'Well, I want murderball so you can shut it.' Fergie looked pleadingly at Mr Timpson.

'That'll do, Fish.'

'Oh, go on, Sir. All the teachers play summat with us before a holiday.' He omitted to say this was only at the end of full term and was usually fizz buzz. ' 'S'nothing to it, Sir, honest. You just, like, shove all the desks together 'cept for four, for goals, and borrow a cricket ball from Mr Mortimer and . . .'

'I said that'll do.'

As it turned out the lesson was interrupted anyway. Meena and Sharon groaned when it happened. They'd discovered it was Mr Timpson's birthday and wanted to bring him out in a record-breaking blush. They'd found just the card for the job too. They'd been a bit miserable even before the interruption. It was half-term already – only a few more weeks and Mr Timpson'd lope, blushing, out of their lives for ever, and who were they going to fuss and swoon over when Mr Timpson left? And now it looked as if they were going to be done out of their Mount Vesuvius of a half-term blush.

It was the head who interrupted them, delivering a visitor. The arrival of the headmaster alone, fresh back to school and minus his appendix, would have proved enough to send Mr Timpson a light magenta. Meena and Sharon recognized this and cheered up.

'We have a visitor this morning,' gulped Mr Timpson when the head had left. He was growing rosier every second. 'This is . . .'

But the visitor held up his hand. 'No need to tell them, Mr . . . They all know who *I* am. I'm something of a *celebrity* in this locality, mmm, children, am I not?' He beamed down upon the second years who stared blankly back. Meena threw her eyebrows up at Sharon who gave an expressive shrug.

Christopher Crutchley was one of the few who did know who he was – Monty Pendlebury, the local M.P. He knew because his dad was for ever inviting him to table a motion on behalf of the Crutchleys.

'Put your hands up, children, those who know who I am.' Mr Pendlebury moved majestically down one of the aisles so that those who couldn't quite make their minds up could get an all-round view. Mr Timpson, not thinking straight, followed him.

Christopher Crutchley glimpsed his opportunity. He leaned across to Brian Turley. 'Do you know who that is?'

Brian shook his head, looking worried. Christopher whispered in his ear. Brian thanked Christopher warmly and stuck up his hand.

Mr Monty Pendlebury swung suddenly on his heel, nearly sending Mr Timpson flying. He strutted to the front. Most of the children by now were sticking their hands half up, then lowering them again if the celebrity happened to look in their direction. Mr Timpson, sensing that the honour of the school was at stake, inclined his head slightly in the direction of Brian Turley. He didn't wish to influence the member of parliament's choice, of course. But at least from that quarter due seriousness and accuracy could be guaranteed.

Luckily Mr Pendlebury took the hint. He laid a friendly hand on Brian's thin hair. 'Well, little man, who is it you have standing in front of you this morning?'

Brian smiled up in delight. 'The nit man, Sir!'

Both Mr Timpson *and* Mr Pendlebury turned a very deep ruby. And Mr Timpson continued to glow forth like a peony at dusk long after the famous visitor had taken his disgusted leave. Meena reported that she'd taken a peep at his sandals. Even his big toes had blushed!

Christopher didn't get to hear what the M.P. had said to Brian Turley. He'd been modifying his hearing aid lately so that it cut out at his bidding. Unfortunately, nowadays, it sometimes did it of its own accord.

The outcome wasn't quite what Christopher had expected either. When Brian Turley discovered the extent of his error he proved himself a far more fiery blusher than Mr Timpson'd ever been. Meena and Sharon beheld him with fascination and enthusiasm. No question now who would be their pet when Mr Timpson left. '2 Young 2 Go for Grils' was now 'hot favourite' and a half!

When Mr Timpson and Brian Turley had cooled down a bit, Sharon and Meena wished their former love many happy returns of the day and presented him with his card. It was a pink card inside a pink envelope. On the front it said, 'Hoping this finds you "in the pink" on your birthday' and it showed a shock-headed blonde winking at him through a window. You opened the window when you opened the card.

And as soon as Mr Timpson looked inside he was 'in the pink' all over again! The blonde was winking at him from her bath tub. She was sitting bolt upright, not entirely covered in soap bubbles, and pink as a newly peeled prawn!

Goliath and Dave

In the fifth year at Davenport Secondary there were two basketball stars – Gaz 'Goliath' Gillespie and Dave 'The Pouf' Petrovic. They were as different in physique as a mammothburger and a rather limp gherkin. Gaz Gillespie was the mammothburger and Dave Petrovic was the gherkin.

Goliath Gillespie had the head of a Munster and the body of Michael Jackson with his thriller suit on. Only his shoulders weren't padding; they were solid flesh and bone! He came to the school in the fifth year. Rumour had it he'd been expelled from his last school for arson, larceny and G B H. Dave Petrovic was inclined to fan this rumour. It was Goliath Gillespie who first called Petrovic 'The Pouf'.

In no time at all, Goliath Gillespie ruled the school. He had the teachers where he wanted them, and Melanie Fish for his girl.

Melanie Fish was a Raver. That is to say, she was a cheer-leader for Roylston's premier basketball team, the Roylston Raiders. This made Melanie a Raiders' Raver and meant she hobnobbed with the stars. She'd discoed with Danny 'Demon' Tiverton, smooched with Sonny 'Smiles' Sylvester, jived with 'Jack-in-a-Box' James Navarre, leapt around with Lennie 'Legs' Le Blanc and even kissed Kirk 'The King' Craven. But it was 'Goliath'

Gillespie of Davenport Secondary who held the key to Melanie's heart.

Dave Petrovic was dead put out about this. He was dead put out about Goliath Gillespie altogether.

On the morning of the final of the Ransome Trophy cup competition Melanie Fish could hardly contain herself, she was so excited. The coach that would take her and the other Ravers to the Royal Albert Hall for the match would arrive at school to pick her up at three o'clock. Her kit was folded ready in her bag and carefully stowed away behind the book cupboard on the fifth year base – her emerald and gold pom poms, emerald leotard and mini with its gold flares, gold headband, choker and horse's tail for the half-time routine.

Goliath, Dave and the other Raiders' fans would be coming down on the supporters' coach after school. If only the Raiders could win! It was hardly likely, since they were up against the top-of-the-league champions, the Jenningham Giants, and the Raiders were new to the first division this season. But then it had been hardly likely that the Raiders would be in the final, defeating teams much higher in the league than they were, on the way.

Miss Harvey took one look at Melanie's flushed face at the beginning of English and knew she'd get no proper work out of her that morning – she was too psyched up. So she sent her to do library help with Dave Petrovic. She thought that library help plus Dave Petrovic might prove a soothing influence.

The result was that Dave slaved away doing library help and Melanie practised her chants:

> '*Rai-ders are*
> *Number One.*

DON' YOU FORGET IT!

We are
SuperiAR!
What we are's
ACE!'

she informed Dave, twitching her weight from hip to
hip, flicking pretend pom poms in the air in time to an
imaginary disco beat. She flipped her head back and
jerked forward with her body, then turned and poked a
finger at him.

'We are
A su-per team.
DON' YOU FORGET IT!'

She turned a cartwheel across the library floor and
ended up in the splits at Dave's feet.

Dave, carrying on replacing books, carefully ignored
her. She was obsessed with basketball these days. She'd
even got her basketball T-shirt on for school – 'I'm taking
a TIME-OUT' tattooed across her bosom. It was Dave's
opinion that Melanie Fish spent too much time in the
company of six foot seven inch freaks with muscles like
melons and over-sized craniums. This meant that blokes
of a responsible sort of size, say a well-proportioned five
feet nine inches with a skull to match, no longer got a
look-in. And now there was Gaz 'The Gargoyle' Gillespie.

'Hey, Dave, what do you think to Goliath Gillespie
then?'

Dave restricted his opinion to his wombat-impaled-
on-a-rusty-nail face.

But Melanie wouldn't give up. 'He's dead good-
lookin', though, ain' he?'

Dave considered this. 'If you're into steamy neander-thals with wool on their shoulder blades.'

Melanie pouted. 'What if I am? The trouble with you, Petrovic, is you're just a knock-kneed, twin-toed, rat-faced, stunted, hairless intellectual snob.'

Dave was stung. He fingered his 'No nukes' badge. 'Hey, I play basketball too, y'know. There's room in the game for the little guys. Look at Alton Byrd.'

'Yeah, but you're not Alton Byrd. You've got no power. Not like Goliath, fr'instance.'

It was Dave's turn to pout. 'You mean he's not a subtle, sneaky, cerebral basketball player like me.'

'You're not sneaky. You're just plain weaky.'

'Come to training when the dinner bell goes if you believe that. See for yourself.'

'I might just do that.'

'You just do that.'

They glared.

The bell rang and Melanie charged off to look for Jeanie Parkes. She'd fallen out with Jasmine and Sangita last week. Jeanie was pretty weird, of course, but she was better than no one, and besides, Jeanie thought Melanie was It. She wasn't alone in this, naturally. Most kids in the school thought so – most men teachers too.

Melanie and Jeanie were on their way to the bottom hall for the practice when Melanie let out a shriek. 'Hya, Randy!' Coming into school by a side door was Randy Ventura, the Raiders' American coach! Randy grinned and put his arm round her. 'Hi, Melanie! Are y'arl ready for the best hussle of the season?'

Melanie gave him a friendly punch. 'You bet! What are *you* doing here, anyway?'

Randy gave her a squeeze. 'Wanted to take my mind off tonight's match so I've come round to do a quick basketball clinic. Paul Mortimer invited me in. He teaches basketball around here, don' he?' Melanie nodded. Randy let her go and waggled a finger at her. 'Now this next here's confidential, honey. Your Paul Mortimer thinks there's talent in his squad that might make the juniors next season so I'm here to scout. But that's a secret, mind. So keep quiet about it, hey?' And he tapped the side of his nose.

Melanie nodded, her eyes gleaming with excitement. That had to mean Goliath – Goliath Gillespie in the Raiders' junior squad! Mr Mortimer turned the corner at that moment and came up to Randy with his hand out-stretched. 'Coffee before we start?' Randy nodded. The two of them walked off together. 'You feelin' O.K.?'

Randy shook his head. 'Awful! Jus' diabolical!'

'But it's great you made the Royal Albert Hall, hey?'

Randy nodded. 'It's unreal.' They turned the corner.

Melanie plucked Jeanie's sleeve. 'C'mon, Jeanie.' She had to let Goliath know about the scouting. This was the chance of a lifetime! She dragged a protesting Jeanie off in the direction of the lads' lobbies. On the way she caught hold of a first year lad and shoved him along in front of her. 'Go in the lobbies and get Goliath Gillespie out quick. You know which one he is, don't you?' The kid nodded, eyes popping. Everyone in the school knew Goliath Gillespie!

Goliath came out almost immediately, pulling his vest over his head. Melanie whispered everything she knew. 'Great!' said Goliath as soon as she passed on the news.

'I'm comin' to watch you so you'd bedder get picked.'

'No problem.' He grinned and dodged back into the lobbies.

'You little greaser!' said Jeanie when he'd gone. ' 'E told you not to tell.' But Melanie didn't care. She couldn't wait for Goliath to shoot like a great hunk of moon rock into the orbit of the stars.

Back in the lobbies the first thing Goliath did was scout around for Petrovic's kit. The Pouf was the only serious contender for a place in the team so first he'd fix that div. It wasn't hard to know which bag was Petrovic's. It was dead smart, navy and gold, real poufy. Goliath pulled a face. He'd give that creep a shock. He unzipped the bag, took out Petrovic's shorts, vest, socks and boots and re-zipped it. The Pouf'd think he'd forgotten to put his kit in and go haring off home. By the time he got back the session'd be over. Goliath bundled the kit under his arm and stole out of the lobbies, looking right and left, but no one was in sight. He'd hide it among Melanie's Ravers stuff and tell her about it after.

When he'd done that he charged off to the bottom hall.

Five minutes later Dave came racing down from the library cursing Melanie. He shouldn't have let her go off like that – he should have made her wait and help him finish. Now he'd be late and Mortimer'd kick up a fuss. He made for his sports bag and stopped short. It looked strangely empty. Don't say he'd forgotten to put his kit in. But no, he distinctly remembered shoving in his boots. He snatched at the zip. Just as he'd thought! Was this some idiot's idea of a joke? He rushed round the changing room trying to find where his kit was hidden. No luck! Well, when in the jungle . . . He looked frantically around to see whose kit *he* could nick.

All he could find, though, was a scruffy T-shirt hanging on a radiator and a pair of shorts in a corner with the elastic gone. They were enormous anyway and wrapped around him about ten times like a sari and came down to his knees. Still, they'd have to do. He pulled his belt out of his trousers and trussed himself up. No boots, of course. Well, he'd have to do it in bare feet. Just wait till he got the wimp who'd done this!

Dave chugged off in the direction of the bottom hall. There was a rumble as of underground trains as he approached and the floorboards were vibrating. Dave got himself a basketball from the cupboard outside the door and went in. Great! Mortimer hadn't arrived yet. He saw Gillespie start when he saw him and stare. Dave was certain as their eyes met that it was Gillespie who'd taken his kit. He was going to say something but Gillespie made off to do a lay-up, pounding down the hall to the basket, and Mortimer walked in with Randy Ventura!

Goliath saw Ventura come in, out of the corner of his eye. Instead of going for a lay-up he bounced the ball showily a couple of times, then twisted in the air, converting the lay-up to a backwards dunk. He imagined Marv Haley, the Channel Four commentator, saying, 'Oh, my! A backwards dunk! This is really show time!' and rammed the ball home with all the force of his twelve stone.

Unfortunately he missed. He missed the basket altogether, dunked into thin air and collapsed on the floor with a tremendous thwack!

Randy raised his eyebrows and turned his attention to the opposite end of the hall where Dave was taking a shot. His long thin fingers flipped behind his head and flicked forward in a sympathetic arc after the ball, then hung limp in the air like a concert pianist's long after the last note had died away. The ball curved in a perfect trajectory and fell through the hoop clean and neat. It hardly even made the net toss. Randy glanced across at Mr Mortimer who nodded. Mr Mortimer blasted on his whistle. 'A surprise visitor, lads, and on the most important day of his coaching career too! I guess he's come to look at you lot for a bit of light relief. Mr Ventura,' he held out a mocking hand, 'over to you.'

Randy lifted a lazy hand to them. 'Hi, guys!' he called over, chewing. 'How ya doin'?'

The lads turned to each other in delight, punching one another in the chest. Oh, great! Ventura came bouncing the ball across the hall, loafing over, easy, easy.

'O.K., guys. Some first impressions. Shootin' now. You were doin' some things that were junk. Like, too much show boat, too much dribblin'.' He looked at Goliath. 'You now. In attack I think the dribble STINKS. When it comes to shootin', they should BAN THE BOUNCE.'

'Now you.' He aimed a finger at Dave. 'That was a super sweet jump shot.' Dave blushed purple. 'O.K. Gather round the basket, guys.' He turned his back on them when they got close and tipped the ball up from his bum over his head and into the ring. 'It's easy, guys. An easy game.' Dave pulled a face at Mick Malone behind Ventura's back and made a swelled head sign. He was dead impressed! Randy started aiming for the basket then, real easy. Jump, flip with the hands, into the basket. And again. Jump, hand flip, in it goes!

'What d'ya notice, guys?' he called as he jumped, flipped, scored every time. The lads looked at one another, shifty-eyed. Dave put his hand half up.

'Yeah?'

'You landed on both feet, Sir.'

Sir! He hadn't meant to say that. It just came out automatic. Dave blushed again. He sounded like a creep.

'You said it. On both feet. And talkin' of feet.' He gave Dave a dirty look. 'Nice shoes you got there.' Dave turned a shade pucer and looked hard at his toes. 'And wha's *that*, for Chrissake?' he pointed at Goliath's hand. Goliath always wore a stained glove on his right hand. It served no useful purpose, having no fingers and no palm to it and fastening round the wrist with a webbing strap. But it was Goliath's hallmark and the Davenport teachers had long since abandoned any attempt to force him to take it off.

'OFF!' said Randy Ventura. 'If you're gonna play basketball with me around.' Goliath took it off without a sound. Amazing! If Mortimer had spoken to him like that it'd have ended in a punch-up!

'Aw righdee, a word about kit.' Ventura gave Dave another filthy look. 'Basketball's a game where you wear white socks, right? If you look smart, there's a fair chance you'll play smart. O.K. Into defensive position, guys: you gotta SQUAT. Palms UP. Those rumps've gotta be DOWN. Move with your legs underneath you. You're gonna go like a roller coaster to start off with. But you gotta get control.'

Goliath soon felt as if he had iron rods stuck up the backs of his knees. It was all right for the Pouf – he was nearer to the ground to start off with. He soon got fed up and moved across to Melanie like King Kong, scratching under his armpits and making humphing noises. 'Me Tarzan, you Jane.' Melanie was laughing enough as it was – at Petrovic's kit! When Goliath approached playing the gorilla she nearly fell off the bench. 'Take your time,' shouted Ventura and Goliath sobered up. 'Just ten minutes to go now, Randy,' warned Mr Mortimer. Randy nodded. 'And you want me to see a bit of a ball game? O.K., you guys, let's scrimmage. Here we go.'

'Great!' thought Goliath. 'I'll show him now!' Mr Mortimer blew the whistle and lifted one hand. Jeanie smirked at Melanie. 'Throw up time.' Melanie gave Jeanie a nudge. 'Tip off time, you nerk!'

Goliath jumped for the ball for the blues, Mick Malone for the reds, Goliath got his great fingers to it and tapped it to Ravinder Singh who bounded off sideways like a syncopated crab, hand outstretched to ward off the reds' defence. But Dave Petrovic was dancing backwards in front of Ravinder, fingers dangling. He suddenly flicked out a hand like a kitten's paw and stole the ball right from under Ravinder's nose. He saw an opening, spurted and penetrated, not realizing Goliath was right behind him. As Dave rose with the ball, Goliath banged it down again from a great height. It was like a giant's sledge-hammer coming down on a drawing pin. The ball landed with a reverberating boing on Dave's skull. Even Melanie winced. 'That'll teach you, Garden Gnome,' muttered Goliath. 'Get back to your gnomeland, bloody immigrant.' Petrovic staggered.

Meanwhile Goliath had scooped up the ball with what looked like one finger and tossed it down court to Ravinder Singh who torpedoed it to Dinesh Dodhia. Goliath thundered down to take his place under the basket, Dinesh bounced the ball in to him and Goliath rammed it into the net, grasping the rim after this bim bam boom of a dunk! Dave brought the ball up, but Goliath, Dinesh, Ravinder and the other two blues were in a three two zone now, moving like the tide, drawn by the ball. Dave peered between their hairy legs looking for Carl Gregson who was leaping and lunging across the key in readiness. But Goliath moved in and blocked him off. In desperation Dave drove forward and appeared to rise and shoot and Goliath rose with him, powering heavenwards ready to pummel Dave into the ground as before. But Petrovic had faked the shot and now double pumped, soaring up like a harp-twanging cherub in a perfect diagonal and dropping the ball into the basket from somewhere behind Goliath's right ear. Goliath recovered and crunched Dave's toes as he landed, pummelling upwards with his fist. 'Take *that*, Dwarfshire Nipper, and don't try shootin' with the stars.'

Dave yelped and bent double, limping in circles round the key. Mr Mortimer, who'd been looking at his watch and didn't see, blew the whistle. 'That's all we've got time for, lads.' Dave and the others made off – it was nearly time for the bell – but Gillespie held back. He raised his eyebrows at Melanie and tapped an ear. She was near enough to Mortimer and Ventura to hear what they said.

'Well, what's the verdict, Randy?'

Randy Ventura traced a pattern with his toe round a knot in a floor board. 'They're promisin',' he admitted, 'both of 'em, the giant and the little guy. But they're both kinda sloppy, y'know? The giant lacks self-control. Then the small guy's dress don' show the mentality of a pro. I'm sorry, Paul. But this is a competitive business. Let 'em enter the summer trials. Mebbe they'll sharpen their ideas up by then.'

Mortimer nodded, disappointed. 'I can't understand Petrovic. He's usually well turned out.'

Randy shrugged. 'Folks is unreliable. 'S just the way it goes.'

Melanie walked slowly across the hall, dreading telling Goliath. He spat when he heard. 'Well, if that's the way Ventura wants it, 'e can 'ave it. We'll get him, O.K.?' Melanie began to feel sick. She liked Randy. She didn't want anything happening to him. Goliath caught hold of her arm. 'C'mon. Which is Ventura's car? Quick, before 'e comes out.' Melanie stared at Goliath. She could refuse to tell him. But she was scared of what he might do to her if she did. She pointed. 'It's that red one over there.' She watched numbly as Goliath scratched the entire length of it with a knife he flicked out from his glove. The blade flashed in the sunlight as he ran. 'That'll do for now. I'll get Ventura later.'

None of the Ravers could understand why all the way to London Melanie Fish was in such a peculiar mood.

■

By the time the coach was nudging its way round the centre of London Melanie was in a real state. She should've told Randy what had happened instead of going off meekly to registration like that. By the time they left school, everyone was in the bottom hall being rowed by Mr Joseph for wilful damage to a visitor's car. And it was all her fault. If only she hadn't told Goliath why Randy had come into school. She *had* to warn Randy now. Oh, God, what would he say?

The coach had reached the Albert Hall. All the figures on the Albert Memorial seemed to be leaning towards Melanie in accusation. So they'd sit on, thought Melanie, faces white and calm, staring through marble eyes towards the arena where the Raiders seethed and surged and she sat on the side line, on what should have been the most exciting night of her life, scared stiff!

In the changing room she unzipped her bag. Her fingers felt heavy and lumpy. Dully she pulled out her costume and pom-poms. Then she stared in amazement. What was that, stuffed down the side? It looked like, yeah, somebody's *basketball* kit. Even the boots were there. No wonder her bag felt so heavy. Whose kit could it be? It was dead smart! Who wore smart kit?

A picture formed before her eyes. Of Petrovic, but in his scruff. It was *Dave's* kit, she bet! And the only one who knew where she'd hidden her Ravers' stuff was Goliath. He'd nicked Dave's kit and planted it on her! What a sneaky rotten thing to do!

She had no time to think about that now, though. 'C'mon, Melanie,' urged Penny Davies who was in charge of the Ravers and taught them their chants and routines. 'Get changed now, please. I want to have a quick run through.'

As they practised their half-time routine Melanie saw Randy arrive with the Raiders. She wanted to chuck her pom-poms aside and charge over to him there and then. It seemed ages before Penny let them go. Melanie rushed over to Randy and caught him by the sleeve. 'Randy, you know when you came into school today?' An irritated look came over Randy's face. 'Not now, Melanie. I'm mad enough about that already. I wanna keep calm before this match, all right?'

'But you have to know because . . .'

Randy held up a hand, backing off fast. 'Do I heck have to know. You can tell me when this is all over, O.K.?' He made off towards the changing rooms. Melanie stared miserably after him.

In no time at all, it seemed, the Ravers were standing shivering with excitement, waiting to go on. They were playing the theme from *Star Wars* and as the lights came up in the vast hall, the hairs on Melanie's neck rose with them. She couldn't help feeling the old tingle and thrill, however worried she was. She could see right into the arena and stared at the great red marble pillars, the gold roses and garlands and red velvet curtains and, suspended from the black and gold organ, the Channel Four poster, three giant figures leaping, fingers straining, for the ball.

Now she was running forward with the others, whooping and waving and turning cartwheels. The heavy beat pummelled in the background, like blood drumming through a rib cage. And here came the Raiders, bounding in to greet their fans. The cameras lumbered in like camels for close-ups of the stars. Melanie watched the Jenningham squad nervously as they jogged on in their turn – 'Shoulders' Murphy, six feet eight inches of hair and muscle. Paul Packer, Lloyd Fowler and Kenny 'Cool' Collington. It was like staring up Jack's beanstalk when you tried to take in Cool. You half expected leaves to begin to sprout!

'And now for the amazing Cinderella club of the basketball league,' Marv Haley was telling the TV audience. 'They sure have a tough assignment ahead of them this evenin'.' Melanie watched in a kind of daze as the team was introduced. What if she didn't manage to warn Randy at the end of the match? 'And now the one they've all been waiting for – Danny Tiverr-ton!' Melanie's favourite player winked at her and she couldn't even manage a smile. Danny ran out, pressing his fingers to his lips, then firing kisses to his fans, the diamond stud in his left ear flashing shards of light.

The Raiders were leaning towards one another in a circle now, laying their hands in. 'One, two, three defence,' and the ref held up the ball. The ball rose and Danny had his fingers to it but Shoulders Murphy won the tip. He tapped it to Paul Packer who threw a long pass to Cool Collington. Who instantly scored. Melanie sighed. Let the ball reach Cool's icicle fingers and the basket was assured. Next Danny had a chance to score but the ball hit the rim and Cool grabbed the rebound. Cool tossed the ball to Fowler but Lennie suddenly lunged and intercepted. 'Lennie sure is a lurker!' crowed Marv. The turn-over led to a basket. Randy nodded his approval, smoothing his tie, and sat down. Usually he paced and squatted during the match like an animal in pain. But the ball was back down the court and now Lennie fouled Cool in the act of shooting. The ref bounded to the officials' table. 'On the arm.' Lennie's eyes were bulgy and glazed as he lifted his arm in acknowledgement. Cool moved to the free throw line.

After Cool's shots the game really hotted up. Craven scored for the Raiders, moving so fast as he whammed in the shot that he bounced straight into the middle of the Ravers! Melanie and the others scattered, shrieking. Craven hit the barrier and limped back on to court, wiping his face with his vest.

But then the Giants scored five baskets on the run. 'Break-through time,' murmured the American commentator. It was nip and tuck all the way after that, though, and in the dying seconds of the first half the Raiders struck back, scoring two consecutive baskets and bringing the lead down to six!

As Melanie leapt on to the court at half time in her emerald green leotard, left hand on left hip, right hand cupping right ear, she felt so weird she thought she might faint. She went through her routine like a robot, her thoughts not on the amazing score but on how Goliath intended to 'get' Randy.

Danny won the tip off at the beginning of the second half. He tapped the ball to Sonny whose hands were waggling for it. There was a lot of movement under the basket, elbowing and shoving and generally carrying on. Sonny bounced the ball to Danny who jumped backwards in an attempt to free himself for the shot. Packer lurched forward to block him and let fly with a vicious arm. 'He-is-a-mugger,' breathed Marv Haley. Randy Ventura was on his feet, pointing and shouting. The ref blew for the foul and Ventura raised his hands in apology.

Packer lifted his fingers in a scoop and shook them behind the ref's back. Danny on the free throw line was pawing like a horse. Sweat gleamed on his dark neck. He flexed his knees and spun the ball, bounced it and his shoulders rose and fell in a great sigh. He shot the ball. It rolled right round the rim of the basket. And out! Danny stuck his tongue in his cheek and a finger gun to his temple. The crowd laughed. 'Bend yer knees, Danny!' yelled the crowd as he prepared for his second shot. Danny scored. One finger pointed at the basket as the fans bayed their delight.

The Raiders were on an up escalator now. Craven collected a Giants' rebound and Navarre shot from far out and scored a three pointer. He ran backwards to take up a defensive position, shoulders hopeful. 'Only *two* points between the teams we thought were so ill matched!' sang out Marv Haley. But even as he said it a foul was called on Lennie. The Raiders' supporters were outraged. 'Use your eyes, ref!' they roared. 'Watch white nine.' Randy Ventura pranced like Rumpelstiltskin, screaming at the ref. The assistant coach pulled him gently back. He could forfeit the game that way! Cool was at the free throw line. Fergie Fish held up a sign that read MISS IT! But there was no chance of that.

The Raiders were still holding the Giants, though, and the Giants were getting upset. The Raiders were playing gritty defence and re-bounding well. Time and again the crowd yelled 'Good D Good D' and the Ravers chanted relentlessly, 'De-fence! De-fence!' spurring them on.

'Fifty seconds to go and only four points in it! There's time yet, and this crowd lifts the Raiders all the way. They could still turn this ball game right around.' As Marv spoke the Ravers were carrying the fans with a solid 'Rai-ders! Rai-ders!' which turned to a formless screech as Lennie flew through the air and gained the ball. 'He came from out of the sky!' breathed Marv. Lennie drove, scored and drew the foul. 'And this crowd has gone berserk, berserk!'

After Lennie's free shot the Giants were only one point in the lead! The crowd was on its feet. The Giants were really rattled now. They didn't dare risk a long shot and the possibility of losing possession. The ball ricocheted round the Giants' fingers like a pinball. Cool had the ball now and tried to shoot. Lennie sprang and got his fingers to it. Cool picked up the loose ball and bounced to regain control. Lennie shot out his hand and knocked the ball free, Danny was already half-way to the basket, Lennie lobbed the ball to him, the crowd was already counting down, 87654 . . . Danny launched his shot and the ball fell clean through the net as the hooter sounded. RAIDERS, BY ONE!!!!!!!!

The scenes after the match were amazing! Continual snowstorms of torn paper twizzled in the air. Fergie Fish catapulted the Ravers with pellets, Lennie was carried on the shoulders of Danny and Craven to hack down the basketball net, Randy kissed the emerald and green beribboned cup and told Marv Haley that the Raiders' success was entirely due to his gold and green jacket, a present from his wife, and Petrovic decided it was time to let Melanie know that he cared. He'd discovered there was to be a special reception for the teams after the match. Now he found out which room it was to be held in and settled down to wait.

Melanie, meanwhile, was more agitated than ever. Her fingers shook as she changed into the silver jump suit she'd brought for the reception. She was ready before the other girls and hung around waiting for the Raiders and Randy to come out. Then she would grab Randy by the arm and tell him all she knew.

But when he came out of the locker room the press were waiting for him and she couldn't get near. All the way to the reception he was talking to clamouring journalists. As they reached the room where the party was being held Dave stepped from behind a pillar and worked his way into the middle of the crowd. 'Press,' he muttered as he went through the door. He kept his head well down in the hope that he wouldn't be spotted. From behind another pillar out stepped Goliath. 'Press,' he muttered, flashing his bus pass at the bouncer, and attaching himself to the back of the admiring throng. He watched as someone handed Ventura a foaming pint of beer.

Dave, with a besotted look on his face, was taking in how Melanie looked in her silver jump suit. Pretty good! He had to act fast! Before Goliath made his usual take-over bid for her, he had to let her know that she was fancied by a far worthier man! He felt in his pocket for the tube of love hearts he'd bought that morning plus Fergie Fish's catapult that Fergie'd hired out to Dave at a favourable rate. He selected one that said, 'You're sweet', extended Fergie's catapult and aimed.

At that moment Goliath lurched in front of Melanie in the direction of Ventura. He intended to nudge the coach's arm, as if by accident, on his way to the bar and send his beer flying all over his poufy green and gold jacket. That'd do for a start.

The love heart caught Goliath smack in the middle of the forehead. He flung out his arm in surprise, banged the coach's arm and Ventura chucked the whole pint pot right over Goliath! Beer poured down his jeans and all over his trainers. Ventura, high on victory, threw back his head and roared with laughter. Dave shot forward in alarm.

Ventura recognized them both. 'Hya, guys!' he said,

raising one hand. 'What ya doin' here? Come to ask me to change my mind about havin' you on the junior squad?' He put an arm round each of them. 'Well, I tell ya, tonight I am feelin' ALL HEART. Tonight I am feelin' NO PAIN.' He nodded at Goliath. 'You'd bedder get yourself down to practice next Thursday and I'll take another look. So there's no hard feelin', hey, now I've baptized you with m'beer?' He nodded at Petrovic. 'You too, O.K.? There's one place goin' on the junior squad and may the best man win.'

When Ventura moved to the bar to collect another beer Goliath shook out the legs of his denims from the knee and inspected the damage to his trainers. Meanwhile Melanie drew Dave away and whispered. Dave looked interested. 'You don' say!' Melanie nodded. 'And you're goin' to tell Ventura he did it?' Melanie nodded harder.

Goliath was searching the floor for what Petrovic had fired at him. He couldn't believe his eyes when he saw it was a love heart! And when he turned it over and read the message, 'You're sweet', he let out a roar and turned to flatten Petrovic.

But he wasn't there. They'd started up the disco and The Pouf was boogying! With Melanie Fish!

And when Fergie peered in a few minutes later, looking for his catapult, he couldn't help grinning! Melanie and Dave were moving smoothly up and down the floor. In fact, it looked like Dave Petrovic had got his sister in a full court press!

The Davenport Kipper

Saturday morning. The letter-box clattered. Fergie Fish's mother looked up from *Surviving the Teen-age Years: A Parents' Guide*. Fergie kept *his* eyes firmly on his copy of *Basketball Monthly*. Melanie slept blissfully on upstairs. Mrs Fish sighed and went through into the hall.

'*Another* letter, Fergie,' said his mother when she returned, tossing the envelope on to the table. 'That's the seventh in a fortnight.' She looked at him curiously. 'Whoever are they from?'

Fergie grunted. He could hardly tell her that he didn't have a clue! He pretended to be deep into the latest league clash between the Orpington Ogres and the Roylston Raiders. His mother shrugged, remembering Rule Number One of *Surviving the Teen-age Years* – 'Their secrets must be theirs and theirs alone'. Tactfully she took herself off upstairs.

As soon as she was out of the room Fergie groped for the letter. He stared numbly at the envelope. As usual his name in wobbly red letters stared back at him. Slowly he turned the envelope over. Yes, there they were in the centre of the flap – the initials T.D.K. and the outline of a kipper! Fergie's fingers felt like chewed strings. He tried to stick his thumb into the top of the envelope. It slithered to the floor. Fergie bent to pick it up. He noticed that his left toe was twitching and a big blob of bacon fat was stuck to the table leg like a sleek white slug. The clock on the sideboard thrummed. The pattern of twirling ferns on the carpet wiggled before his eyes. He stood up, shaking, and went through into the kitchen. He jerked open the cutlery drawer. It came out in a rush, scattering its contents, gouging his leg and crushing his bare foot. Fergie bent over in pain. His mother came running downstairs.

'Whatever are you playing at, Fergie?' she said, bending to pick up knives, forks and spoons. She said it crossly and ignored the way Fergie was dabbing at his leg with a towel. 'She'd be sorry,' thought Fergie, 'if she knew she was talking to a man whose days are numbered.'

Fergie knelt and helped her with the cutlery, heaving the drawer into the gap. He kept back one knife. A single slit hung between him and his fate. He drove the knife in, jerked to the right, to the left, and peered inside.

It was as it always was – no letter but the neatly cut out fly-leaf of yet another book. He drew out the thick sheet and unfolded it.

'MUD AND MAGGOTS,' read Fergie with a shudder. '*A Coarse Fisherman's Guide*.' And printed underneath the usual mysterious message: 'The Davenport Kipper'. Fergie got to his feet, knees trembling. The Kipper had struck again!

On wobbly legs he climbed the stairs. He ignored his mother when she asked him if he wanted another slice of toast. Safe in his room he leaned against the door for a moment, then breathing deeply crossed the room and opened his desk. He drew from it another six envelopes and spread the contents along the bed: – '*Fillet and Fin*', '*The Friendly Fisher*', '*Hook, Line and Sinker*', '*Aquarium Antics*', '*Herring Trawling in the Mid-Atlantic*', and '*How I kept a Pet Piranha*'. Next he spread out every envelope, each with the fearsome initials T.D.K. Every fly-leaf had the same teasing print out – THE DAVEN-PORT KIPPER. There was something mighty *fishy* going on!

Fergie was shivering. The same thought kept entering his mind and would not go away. There had to be some connection. It couldn't be just a coincidence. IT WAS AT KATERINA WAINWRIGHT'S SÉANCE THAT A KIPPER HAD FIRST SWUM INTO HIS LIFE.

He'd been warned against séances often enough, of course. His mum had warned him, and they'd all been warned at school. No table-tapping. No playing with a glass. You never knew where it might lead . . .

You never knew indeed!

It was no joke! It was bad enough having a surname like Fish without being haunted by a phantom kipper, sending him messages from beyond!

Yet there was nothing ghosty about the messages. The fly-leaves were real. They came from real books, cut out cleanly with a razor blade or something. The messages were on real flesh and blood paper, not on ectoplasm ballooning from an envelope. And they were somehow connected with school – the *Davenport* Kipper! There was nothing ghosty about school. Except for Miss Bickerstaff. She was a bit of a ghoul!

It was all Katerina Wainwright's fault, Fergie decided. Katerina was in Fergie's class. She was half-Greek – and only about a quarter there – with great vacant eyes in a thin pale face. In fact, Katerina was thin and pale all over, except for her hair, which was thin and dark. She slunk and slid around the school like a skinny black cat. Some of the kids called her Witchy Wainwright. When she'd invited Fergie to her house for the séance, Fergie'd said straight out, 'You gotta be jokin', Katerina. No way!'

But Tez Tindale overheard. 'Why not?' said Tez to Fergie. 'It'd be good for a laugh.' He stuck out his arms in front of him after the manner of a ghost, and waggled his fingers in Katerina's blank face. 'Is there anybody the-e-e-erre?'

So in the end, of course, Tez and Fergie had gone round to Katerina's a week last Friday, and there'd been Tez, Fergie, Katerina and Katerina's big sister Maria at the séance. Maria, at least, was O.K. She was rounded where Katerina was all skin and bone, jolly where Katerina was serious, and straightforward where Katerina was kind of sneaky. Maria had dressed up for the séance in her mum's dressing-gown. It was rather a fine dressing-gown, with navy blue quilting round the collar and cuffs, and Maria had made it finer still by sticking paper cut-outs of stars and moons all over it. She'd fastened her long dark hair up in a curtain of yellowing net. When she stood up she looked taller than usual, and not nearly so round. Fergie felt his flesh creep. She was quite witchy and fine. She set up a little table with a shiny slippery top in the front room and scribbled the letters of the alphabet on scraps of paper and the numbers one to ten and the words 'Yes' and 'No', and arranged them in a circle round the table top. Then the four of them took their places. Maria turned off the main light so they sat by the glow of a lamp and the light from the smokeless fuel fire. (Maria and Katerina's mum and dad worked late in their Greek take-away, so they wouldn't be disturbed.)

'Con-cen-trate,' bleated Maria when they'd all sat about a bit in the dim light. 'Bring the spirits in up-on us! En-cour-age them to co-ome!' The door to the front room moved as she said it, and Fergie's stomach jerked. But it was only Katerina's black cat Tiptoes. Tiptoes! What a terrible name for a cat! Still, the cat did come in on its tiptoes, hunching round the door.

Maria set a small wine glass with a thick round base on the table top. 'Fingers on the gla-a-ass!' ordered Maria. 'Clo-o-ose your eyes! Not a sou-ound!' Fergie very much wanted to giggle. He thought he could feel Tez's giggles too, vibrating through the glass.

Then Fergie got an awful shock! The glass was beginning to warm up! His finger was tingling too. This wasn't anybody playing a joke. It was *his* finger, so he ought to know. It was warm at the tip, and throbbing, like when you come in from playing in the snow.

'Is there anybody the-e-erre?' demanded Maria after a moment in a hooty sort of way. 'Is there anybody the-e-erre?'

And ever so slightly, as if in answer, the table rocked, and the glass under Fergie's finger began to move!

It didn't feel as if anybody was pushing it. Or if anybody was, then it was Fergie as much as anybody, and he couldn't help it. The glass was moving slowly but surely in the direction of 'Yes'!

'Goo-oo-ood!' hooted Maria. 'Whooo is your message fo-orr?'

The glass moved rather slowly, then quicker, and shot off in a skid, out of Fergie's control, towards the letter F. Fergie's heart did a flic flac. F for Fergie? Oh, don't say there was a message for him!

The glass began to slither in a kind of arc now, as if it might bend round towards, yes, the letter E. But now it seemed to be meeting up with some sort of block and couldn't continue. It did flit across Fergie's mind that he might be causing the block. But he didn't have time to worry about that now because the glass was sliding off back towards the centre and was drifting, rather uncertain this time, towards the letter R. And here went the glass again, into the centre, then retracing its path. Fergie felt better. FRR ...? What kind of a word was that? And again the glass shifted back to the centre, then out as if drawn by a magnet to the letter R. Fergie grinned in the gloom.

'Needle's got stuck!' came Tez's cheerful voice, and Fergie risked a giggle.

'SSSSSSHHHHHHH!' hissed Maria with a fearful frown. 'You'll RUIN the vibrations. Just concentrate, PLEASE!'

But it made no difference. The glass did seem to be stuck in a groove. Off it went again towards the letter R, then at the last minute it shot off across the table to the letter G. FRRRG ... Oh, no! This was getting too much like 'Fergie' again for comfort! Fergie pressed down hard. The glass jerked a little, and was still.

Maria jumped up and switched the main light on. Everybody sighed and blinked. Fergie concentrated hard upon a picture of a temple against a very blue sky. Had he stopped the glass from working? He wouldn't like to say.

'FRRRG?' queried Maria. 'Don' make sense!' She shrugged. 'FRRRG? FRRRG? Perhaps it was trying to spell out FRRROG?'

Fergie tried to look convinced, failed, and stood up. 'C'mon, Tez. Let's go for some chips.'

But Tez wasn't ready yet. 'FRRRG,' he purred deep in his throat. 'FRRRG. FRRRG,' and Tiptoes came shoving and rubbing round his leg. 'FRRRG. FRRRG,' she throbbed in reply. Maria laughed. Katerina stared into space.

'Frrrg,' went Katerina quietly. 'Frrrg Frrrg

FRRRGIE.' She spoke in a kind of trance. A piece of
coalite fell from the fire and flames flared.

'She's got it!' shouted Tez. 'Katerina's got it! It's a
message for Fergie. C'mon, Ferg! Don' you wanna know
what it is?'

Fergie did not! His heart was thumping and his head
was throbbing. Life was puzzling enough, without receiving messages from beyond! But Tez had snapped off
the light. There was nothing for it but to put a numb
finger back on the glass.

It didn't stay numb for long though! The same tingling
warmth came flooding back. 'Glass, Glass,' sang out
Maria. 'Comple-e-ete your message ple-e-ease. What is
your message for FRRRG?' And as soon as she spoke,
away went the glass, helter skelter, off towards a second
word beginning with F. Fergie's mouth went dry. Was it
going to spell out F-I-S-H? Well, it wouldn't get the
chance! He pressed down as hard as he could. The glass
sheered off and tried to reach the letter I by a roundabout route. Fergie put his thumb down. It dashed off
towards S in a perfect frenzy. Fergie barred the way. It
scooted off in panic towards H. Fergie was in control.
The glass tugged and pulled, but it couldn't get away. It
jiggled and jerked and trembled and tapped, and suddenly
it was still.

'Can't make its mind up,' said Tez in the darkness.
'First it went berserk. Now it's gone mardy.' Fergie let
out a high nervous giggle and relaxed his hold. The glass
wobbled a moment. Then it moved off smoothly on a
different track. In a calm collected manner it began to
write. 'K' it wrote and 'I'. Fergie's finger moved with it.
It seemed to have lost all its strength to resist. 'P' wrote
the glass and 'P-E-R'. 'KIPPER!' whispered Tez in
awe. 'It's done a word, a proper word for you, Fergie. It's
done "KIPPER".' Fergie trembled in the dark.

And now the glass was on the move again. But it didn't slither towards the letters this time; it went for the numbers. The number 4 was the one it chose. Then slowly and steadily it started for the letters once again. 'C' and 'A' and 'T'. And was still.

'KIPPER 4 CAT.' Whatever could it mean?

'Glass! Glass!' urged Maria, half rising. 'More message, PLEASE. Oh, come ON, Oh Glass!'

But that seemed to be it. The glass was stubborn now. It wobbled slightly, then was still and wouldn't budge again, however hard she sang. In the half-dark Tiptoes rubbed and nudged and purred.

Maria put the light on. 'Well,' she said. 'KIPPER 4 CAT! You're gonna get a kipper, cat. "FRRG" couldn't have meant "Fergie" after all.' She looked doubtfully across at Katerina who was bending to scoop up Tiptoes. Katerina handed her to Fergie. Embarrassed, Fergie scratched her neck.

'Yeah, well,' said Tez, getting up and nudging the table, setting the letters fluttering. 'That were a load of use. A message for a cat! C'mon then, Ferg. We gotta be off. Be seein' you, girls.' Maria looked a bit put out, but Katerina's expression never changed. She was fixing an object on the far wall with her usual blank green stare . . .

■

In his bedroom Fergie shuddered as he gathered up the messages. There had obviously been some mix-up. The ghostly kipper hadn't appeared to the cat – it had taken up with Fergie instead – the *Davenport* Kipper. Probably it was lying in wait for him at this very minute, biding its time and sending him spooky messages via the G.P.O! Fergie felt sick and faint and there was a ringing in his ears . . .

Then Fergie realized that the ringing wasn't in his ears

74

at all — someone was leaning on the front door bell. He ran to the window and, oh no, not again! Outside the gate was the post office van!

In a daze Fergie heard the sound of his mother's footsteps clacking in from the garden where she'd been hanging out the washing. Shaking, he counted to ten and heard her high surprised voice and the front door close. 'Fer-gie?' shouted his mother up the stairs. 'Parcel for you this time. Whyever didn't you answer the door?' Fergie didn't reply as he started down the stairs. In the hall his mother lifted the package to her nose. 'Fergie, this parcel SMELLS!'

Well, that didn't surprise Fergie in the slightest. What else could his mother expect? That parcel was long and thin and flat. IT WAS SHAPED LIKE A FISH!

'Aren't you going to open it then?' demanded his mother, beside herself with curiosity this time. Fergie shrugged and started back upstairs. With a supreme effort of will, his mother shrugged too and went back into the kitchen. On the way she comforted herself. It looked the wrong shape for, let's say, dirty books.

Back in his bedroom Fergie tugged at the string. There were two of them when he got the parcel open. They lay side by side in a cellophane shroud, a fat yellow butter flower at their heads. As Fergie shook them free of the wrapping a little hand-written card fell out. 'The Davenport Kipper' it announced in red. Fergie was trembling all over. There was no doubt about it. His fishy fate must be very close at hand. The Kipper was drawing closer by the minute, his arrival heralded by these two fishy emissaries, TWO KIPPERS IN A BAG!

■

Nothing happened over the rest of the weekend. Every time the door bell rang, though, Fergie broke out in a sweat. He half expected when he opened the door to find a life-sized kipper on the step, balanced on a fin. His dreams were full of fish – ghostly shades flicking opaque pearly tails between fingering weed, or grey-white mushy bodies, floating on the surface of the water, like Fergie's goldfish when he overdid the pellets.

In a way, though, Fergie longed for the kipper to show itself now. It was worse than death, this living in constant suspense and dread, knowing that at any moment you might be clapped damply on the shoulder by a large and ghostly fin. Fergie racked his brains, trying to think of ways of forcing the Kipper's flipper – of making the Kipper make himself known.

Then on Monday morning the opportunity came. It came in the form of a poster just inside the main door at Davenport. Fergie had gone to school early, so as to escape the post. He felt he couldn't take another of the Kipper's o-fish-al communiqués this early in the week! 'Fancy Dress Disco,' declared the poster, and there was a picture of Harlequin and Columbine doing a flash dance. 'Friday 12 December, 7 p.m. Top Hall.'

Fergie considered the poster. Yes, he thought he might go. He could do with a bit of light relief – he'd been under a lot of stress lately. What would he go as, though?

Then it came to him! Of course! With a name like his, HE'D GO AS A FISH. A goldfish, maybe . . . That'd be good!

And Fergie had an ulterior motive. If there *was* a ghostly Kipper, a Davenport Kipper, haunting the school, then Fergie-as-a-Fish might tempt it to show itself, and face up to Fergie, fin to fin!

'You goin' to that?' demanded Tez, coming up behind him with Katerina and Maria. Fergie nearly jumped out of his skin. That Kipper! It was ruling his life these days.

'Think I'll go as a Mohican,' said Tez. 'How 'bout you?' But Fergie wouldn't say.

Over the next week Fergie assembled his costume. First he made himself a great fish head out of a shiny orange cushion-cover he found in the attic. He cut out holes for its eyes and stuck on two great circles of black felt around the holes. This gave a startled popping effect. Then he cut out a great round mouth hole and attached two pink flannelette sausages, stuffed with old tights, in a curve, top and bottom, so that they looked like two great puckering fish lips. His mother found an orange curtain that matched the cushion cover and Fergie spent three nights making a fish suit, sketching in hundreds of tiny scales with a magic marker. Fergie's mother was greatly relieved to see him occupied these days on his costume. At least he was acting like a fairly normal human being, and since the parcel there'd been no more peculiar post.

Fergie too was very relieved about that. All the same, it didn't prevent him from feeling uneasy. He had a sense that the Kipper was biding its time, ready to flash forth and grab him when least expected.

The costume was almost complete now. Even Melanie thought it was good. Fergie had made two great orange flippers for his arms. To complete the look he borrowed some goldy-orange cords from his mum and attached two black cardboard tail fins, one to each ankle. When he kept his feet together they stuck out and down, like a tail. They flopped about a bit when he walked but added up to quite a floaty effect.

The night of the Fancy Dress Disco, Fergie stood arranging himself in front of his mother's long mirror. First he pulled on the orange cords and arranged the tail fins so that they spread out correctly. Then he wriggled into the tubular fish costume with its cheeky dorsal fin. He pulled the large orange flippers over his arms and lifted the fish head over his ears. By the time he'd arranged the eye holes so that his own eyes stared out of the middle of the black rimmed holes and got the O of the fish mouth over his own mouth, he looked quite good. He practised opening and shutting his mouth very slowly and wished he had some little helium balloons to float upwards like air bubbles when he mouthed.

In the pleasure of dressing up he quite forgot the fishy fate the evening might hold in store. When his mother stepped back in amazed admiration at her fine fish Fergie suddenly gave her a big hug. He loved her so. Would he ever see her again? Next time she clapped eyes on her son, would he be stretched out flat as a flounder, a harpoon through his heart?

When Fergie arrived at school there was already quite a party atmosphere. Tez was waiting for him at the entrance. He wasn't dressed as a Mohican but wore black boots and a leopard skin drape, with pimply looking muscles made out of egg box sections attached by elastic to his calves and upper arms. Fergie looked puzzled. 'Who *you* s'posed to be?'

'Mr Puniverse,' said Tez proudly, flexing a pimple. 'Any road, it's better'n a *fish*.'

There were some great costumes – babies and fairies, Micky Mice and Madonnas, Noddies and Big Earses, and loads and loads of punks. Dave Petrovic looked really boring, though. Fergie couldn't see why he'd bothered coming at all, dressed like that. He wore a *suit*, just an ordinary suit, and he carried an executive briefcase and a rolled umbrella. The only thing that was funny about his costume was his bowler hat.

Until he turned round! Then Fergie couldn't believe it! The whole of the back of the costume was missing and

round *that* side he was wearing frilly French knickers and
a bra strap, suspenders, a garter and stockings! Fergie
nudged Tez and nodded towards Petrovic and they both
exploded, lolling against the wall. Then Mr Tipperton
teetered by in drag, looking like Kenny Everett when he
wears that blue shiny evening dress, his beard and an
awful lot of boob. Dave and Tez creased over, they were
laughing so much. Tez murmured to Fergie, 'It's all in
the best *po-ssible* taste!'

When they'd paid their 20p into the potty of the baby
on the door, they started up the stairs to the top hall.
Fergie nudged Tez again and pointed to a notice. Usually
it said 'Caretaker on girls' stairs'. The caretaker didn't like
strangers wandering round his school and he always left a
notice saying where he could be found. Someone had
stuck an omission mark on the notice tonight, though,
and added a message of their own – 'Caretaker dead drunk on
girls' stairs'. Tez and Fergie punched one another in
delight. Fergie felt happier than he'd done in ages. When
the world was so joky and funny and daft, how could
phantom kippers be lurking in the darkness, waiting to
do for human beings?

Upstairs in the top hall there was already a writhing
wriggling mass. Fergie peered into it for a fellow fish but
he couldn't see one. He felt a familiar stir of fear. A fish in
the flesh is a lot less scary than a phantom fish flicking
about the corridors in the dark!

The second years were jiggling in a solid block in the
very centre of the floor, not dancing with the opposite
sex like the fifth years did. They gave up jiggling as a
solid block, too, say, every thirty minutes or so, for
reinforcements of orange and crisps, doled out in one of
the classrooms by a parrot and a peanut. (Honest! This kid
had made himself a shell!)

The evening was slipping away fast. Behind the jumping horses at the end of the dimly lit hall some of the older kids tried to get down between the gym mats but the teachers were for ever flashing torches and yanking bodies to their feet. They patrolled the corridors too, in case anyone had crept out for a fag on the sly. Fergie felt reassured by those wavering lights skimming up and down the dark places of the school. No kippers could lurk undetected where so many teachers paced the boards.

Suddenly there was a commotion at one end of the room. Everybody was jumping up and down to find out what was going on. Fergie climbed the wall bars with Tez and there was Maria Wainwright, dressed as a kissogram girl! She looked rather like the back view of Dave Petrovic, only in the round! She wore a black leotard with red bows down the front and a flouncy red mini, black stockings, red suspenders and tall black boots, with a great scarlet bow on top of her head. 'Who's the kissogram for?' yelled the delighted lads, as they pressed round Maria. Some of the first years offered their mouths up for a kiss.

'For Mr Puniverse,' giggled Maria, and Tez clung to the wall bars for dear life, blushing fiercely and jerking his head. But Mr Tipperton plucked him down and offered him up to the kissogram girl while the school laughed and cheered.

'The last dance!' cried out Mrs Hart, who was a great romantic. She was spinning round the hall in a kaftan and thonged sandals, dangling a sprig of mistletoe over unsuspecting heads. The last dance! Fergie didn't know whether to feel regretful or relieved. The Davenport Kipper hadn't put in an appearance, but the suspense would only drag on. It'd nag at him, like the toothache, never quite letting him be. And here came Mrs Hart, a soppy smile on her face, brandishing the mistletoe. Well, she could leave Fergie out of this. He didn't have anyone to dance with, and, anyway, kissing was daft.

Then it happened! What Fergie had half expected all evening came to pass. He felt a hand clamp his shoulder. Fearfully Fergie glanced sideways at the hand. He'd die if it had scales!

But it wasn't so much a hand as a paw! A soft black and white paw with a neat pink claw curling out of each pad. Fergie whipped round and found the paw belonged to a very fine black and white cat, a slim glossy cat, with a bell on a green ribbon round its neck, thick feathery whiskers, a luxuriant shiny tail and beautiful wide green eyes.

It was a queen of cats, in a black velvet mask, bordered with grey lace and with silver sequins at the edges. The cat's legs were encased to the thighs in fine blue suede boots, like a fisherman's waders.

'OOOH, YES!' cooed Mrs Hart. 'The cat *must* dance with the fish!' and she waved the mistletoe over their heads. The cat lifted its fine whiskery face to the goldfish's puckery lips. Fergie felt as if he was swimming dreamily through warm sunlit water as he bent and kissed the cat's pink mouth. 'Who are you, Puss-in-Boots?' murmured Fergie, mesmerized by mistletoe.

The cat made a deft movement with her furry paw and flipped off the cat head complete with starry mask. The face changed to human but the green eyes stayed the same. IT WAS KATERINA WAINWRIGHT!

Only, not the Katerina he had known and misjudged. Not a pale skinny witch with straggly hair and a vacant look, but a Katerina with top-of-the-milk skin and green petals for eyes, sleek as a leek in her lycra and seven-league boots. 'A-MA-ZIN'!' declared Tez as he twizzled past the goldfish with his kissogram girl. 'Ain' Katerina lookin' GREAT?'

'D'ya wanna come round our house tomorrow, Fergie?' coaxed Katerina. 'We could play, like, records, and have a Greek take-away?'

■

'Would you like a drink first, Fergie?' asked Katerina the next evening, shy now she'd got Fergie where she wanted him, after a year and a half! Her long fine hair was coiled in a shiny black snake on the top of her head and she was wearing a skinny bat-winged sweater and LEATHER TROUSERS under her fisherman's boots. 'A ... a coke, please, Katerina,' spluttered Fergie, eyeing the stuffed pike in an illuminated perspex coffin that hung on the opposite wall.

And now a photograph caught his eye. How come he'd not noticed that before? As soon as Katerina left the room, he moved, like one transfixed, over to the telly where it stood. It was a photo of Katerina, taken with her dad. Both were wearing waders and were up to their thighs in river water, holding up dead fishes and grinning like fiends! As if in a trance Fergie slid across to the bookcase.

Yes, there they all were, lined up in a row. *Mud and Maggots*, *Fillet and Fin*, *The Friendly Fisher*, *Aquarium Antics*, *Herring Trawling in the Mid-Atlantic*, *How I Kept a Pet Piranha*, and *Hook, Line and Sinker*! Fergie took a furtive look over his shoulder. He flipped *The Friendly Fisher* from the shelf.

The fly-leaf had been neatly cut out.

A coal fell from the fire and a flame flared. 'FRRRG!' came a sound from his feet, and Tiptoes was there, nudging and rubbing and making demands. 'KIPPER 4 CAT.' 'KIPPER 4 CAT.'

And suddenly Fergie sensed what it meant! The glass hadn't *wanted* to write KIPPER. It had *wanted* to write FISH. Only, Fergie hadn't let it. 'FISH 4 CAT.'

That cat! What if it wasn't Tiptoes? What if the cat was . . . KATerina? And FERGIE was the Fish!

Fergie sighed. Those messages! He'd been reading them the wrong way round all this time. They weren't *from* the Davenport Kipper, after all. They were *for* the Davenport Kipper.

Fergie *was* the Davenport Kipper. And well and truly hooked!

The Bacon and the Rose

The same term that Jeanie Parkes won a prize for her poem 'Ode to a Spot', Miss Harvey handed her another cyclostyled sheet. 'Poetry Workshop,' it read. 'Brinsdale Community Centre. Saturday 6 December. 10 a.m. to 1 p.m. Students over fourteen years welcome.'

'Why's it called a workshop?' asked Jeanie suspiciously. 'Do you have to *make* things or something?' Jeanie's practical skill was nil, and the only workshops she'd heard of were where you nailed and planed and sawed and glued. Oh, and the Drama Workshop she'd once been to in school. That was horrific! She'd spent an entire afternoon pretending to be an espresso coffee; it had been a fifties piece.

'The only thing you have to make is a poem,' said Miss Harvey. 'And you know you're quite capable of that. But if it's like the poetry workshops I've been to, the poems'll come ready made, and all people'll have to do is read them aloud and hope the others'll clap.'

Jeanie was surprised. She couldn't see Miss Harvey writing a poem. Whatever would she write it about? She couldn't believe Miss Harvey'd ever been in love, for instance – not with those specs! Nor could she imagine her writing the 'Oh, hoorah for the first whiff of spring tral di ra' sort of poem you find in women's magazines.

Perhaps she wrote politically aware poems about butter mountains and the retail price index?

Jeanie thought she might just go along. The Brinsdale Community Centre was in a part of town her mother didn't approve of, which was good enough reason in itself.

So the next Saturday morning found Jeanie riding a ninety-three bus and waiting for the driver to tell her where to get off. She was wearing the red pointed-toe shoes, and 'Ode to a Spot' was carefully folded, along with one or two other offerings, in the pocket of her jacket. She'd even bought some special tights for the occasion – sheer black with a pattern of diamonds and stars.

The conductor turned round. 'Here you are.' Someone rang the bell as he said it, and the 'Bus Stopping' sign lit up. Jeanie felt giddy. She hung on to the bar by the door to keep herself upright. The doors opened with an asthmatic wheeze. 'That's the centre.' The woman who'd rung the bell looked curiously at Jeanie. 'Be careful, love. Do you know the area? Even I've been approached.'

Jeanie began to walk towards the centre. It was just like a large version of the double mobile in the playground at school. There was a great asphalt car park in front and a supermarket to one side. A black kid walked towards Jeanie with an enormous cassette radio turned as high as it would go. He stared at her, then turned round and walked backwards, still staring. Was he a poet? She didn't dare ask. Jeanie looked at her watch. Only quarter to ten. She was early. She looked around, taking in the scene. There wasn't much to take in! Just the great parking space flanked by high-rise flats and a few crippled trees surrounded by fences like calipers.

Jeanie headed for the supermarket. From the safety of

the shopping trolleys she watched the poets arrive. First there was rather an old bloke, with eyebrows like Dennis Healey's. He was accompanied by a short woman, dumpy as a tea-cosy, wearing a green hat crammed with cabbage roses. Jeanie pulled a face. It hadn't occurred to her that any of the poets'd be old. They did say they welcomed students, after all.

The next to arrive was a considerable improvement! He had hennaed hair and wore a red boiler suit and duck egg blue boots. The bloke who followed him into the centre was boring by comparison. He was thin and short and wore granny specs, dirty grey cords and a v-necked sweater, like a kid's. Then a couple started across the parking lot. The woman had what looked like a dead sheep round her shoulders over a long dark skirt. She was talking a lot and waving her hands at a foxy-looking bloke with a red beard and gold-rimmed spectacles, wearing very well pressed blue jeans. As the woman came closer Jeanie could see that she had a great many bits hanging off her like the White Queen – beads, and a fringed scarf slung across one bosom, and a shawl-thing drooping from a hip. Finally a hefty-looking bloke roared up on a motor bike in leathers and a crash helmet, all straps and black beetle sheen. When he got off Jeanie could see he had a pillion passenger. Her crash helmet was lemon and from underneath it rippled a mass of pale hair. Jeanie looked at her watch again. Ten past ten. She couldn't leave it any longer. Slowly she followed the black beetle and the princess to the door.

The foyer was entirely filled with Sikhs. They were talking furiously, waving coke cans at one another and nodding violently. Where was she supposed to go? The beetle and the blonde had disappeared. She looked timidly at the notice board but it was filled with posters advertising women's peace vigils and blues and conferences for the Association of Teachers of Ethnic Minorities. Jeanie approached an open door to the left of the entrance. An elderly Sikh with blood-shot eyes was smoking, his feet propped up on the desk. 'Wh-where are the poets, please?' stuttered Jeanie. It sounded mad!

The Sikh removed the cigarette and fixed his eyes on the diamonds and stars. 'Top of the stairs,' he said. 'Straight ahead. There *is* a notice.' Jeanie stumbled out backwards and began to edge and slither towards the gesticulating Sikhs. Sure enough, as she circled one group and bordered another she saw a notice on a small wooden easel. The easel had been folded up against the wall, out of the way. At the top of the stairs Jeanie paused. She could hear the bubble of voices and the occasional scrape of a chair, and someone coughed. She took a deep breath, turned the handle and shoved. The door stuck. She put her shoulder behind it and nearly fell into the room.

The room was already unsteady with smoke. The poets were sitting against a great plate glass window, dark shapes in the fug. Apart from the poets there was nothing in the room except a lot of vandalized plastic chairs. The man with the eyebrows called over, 'Come ye on in.' Jeanie approached. 'And what might you be called?' said the man, waggling the eyebrows.

'Jeanie,' said Jeanie, wriggling.

'Come and sit down by me then, Jeanie,' said the older man, 'and we'll fill each other in on who we all are and what we all do.'

Clean Jeans looked not a little annoyed. '*We* thought we'd begin by formulating what we hope to carry away from this session. State how long we've been practising poets, and when we're feeling a little more, mmm, laid back, maybe read a poem aloud.'

The Black Beetle rocked back in his chair and blew out smoke. 'How about some guy going over to the supermarket for a coffee brew, yeah? I take it there is a kettle in this joint?' He blew more smoke in the general direction of Clean Jeans.

'Oh, quite. Surely,' said Clean Jeans, looking efficient. 'I'll just buzz off and get it from Sukh downstairs.' He buzzed with enthusiasm.

The Black Beetle didn't seem inclined to turn his suggestion into action and be the one actually to go and buy the coffee brew. The Dead Sheep smiled secretly and blew out smoke rings. The Fairy Princess bit her nails. Granny Specs was making changes to a piece of paper he'd fished from his pocket, and hadn't even heard. Hennaed Hair was admiring his reflection in the plate glass window. 'Well,' said the stout woman at last. 'I'll just pop over to the supermarket then.'

'I'll come with you,' said Jeanie eagerly. She didn't want to be left on her own with that lot. They looked like they'd all turned to sphinxes and would issue a complicated riddle every twenty-five years!

'You're still at school, I imagine?' said Green Hat, looking sideways at the diamonds and stars, as they descended the stairs. 'My husband warned me they'd all be louts and layabouts. He wouldn't have allowed me to attend if he hadn't known George would be present to subdue the unruly element.' George, Jeanie took it, was Hearty Brows. 'What are you going to grace the company with, my dear? Though nobody could exactly grace *that* company, in my view. I shall read a little verse inspired while gathering the flowers of the elder last summer.' She nodded at Jeanie. Jeanie nodded absently back. That sounded a descriptive sort of poem. The only one she'd brought that she'd call descriptive was 'Ode on a Pot of Lemon Curd'. And she couldn't imagine she'd be exactly gracing the ears of the Black Beetle with 'Oh, purée of primrose, oh, buttercup brew!'

When they returned with milk, coffee and sugar the hatted one washed a quantity of mugs in a dirty kitchen that smelt of sour milk, with a little help from Clean Jeans – and Jeanie too, of course. The Hatted Lady wrinkled her powdery nose at the rusty-looking tea-spoons, and wiped the cup and saucer she'd found for herself on tissues from her handbag when she caught sight of the community towel.

Then they all sat around sipping coffee and telling one another how long they'd been writing poems. This ranged from three years to twenty-five, or, in the case of Jeanie, about eight weeks. On hearing this, they all smiled and looked pitying. The rest of coffee time was spent listening to Clean Jeans and the Dead Sheep filling one another in on what they'd done over the summer.

'Camping in the Outer Hebrides,' said Clean Jeans. 'A-ma-zing! Compleete-ly unpolluted air for the kids, y'know? Wow!' He leaned across one knee, which was folded in the direction of his left ear, and flicked the ash into the Hatted Lady's saucer. 'How about you, Nancy?'

'Oh, overland to Iran,' said the Dead Sheep, blowing out a smoke ring and draping a fold. 'Fan-tas-tic!'

'Fan-tas-tic!' echoed Clean Jeans dutifully. The Black Beetle looked as if he was going to throw up.

'I spent the summer wrapped up in a blanket,' said Hennaed Hair. He closed his eyes as if in deep pain.

The others looked non-committal. Except for Jeanie, who looked thrilled. 'Why was that?' she asked eagerly. Hennaed Hair looked at her as if a grub had spoken. 'Oh, for the experience,' he said, nodding. 'A primordial back-to-the-womb experience, suggested under various chemically induced states.' He nodded again. 'Also, I feel the cold. I spent the winter sleeping on a radiator.'

The Black Beetle cleared his throat and said, 'Ain' it time we read a token poem apiece, yeah?' Everybody shrank about a metre into their shoulder blades and looked incapable of reading anything, but the Hatted Lady recovered first and said she'd set the ball rolling. Jeanie watched the Dead Sheep lower her face to her finger tips. The elderflower gatherer turned out to be pregnant and there was a lot about the hands that gleaned the elderflowers changing little nappies and that kind of thing. Jeanie stowed away 'gleaned' for future reference, but decided the poem didn't sound much like real babies to her. Jeanie had seen her older sister Sharon shake the baby Shawn as if she'd like to swot cobwebs with him, and Dennis changed the nappies in their house. But she did give a thought to how much her Aunt Pauline, who was into cookery clips, would like the elderflowers.

The one called George then read a poem about the wind. It was full of 'Blow, blow', and 'Oh, no! Oh, no!' and made Jeanie feel quite low. She thought of Hennaed Hair who felt the cold, and peered through her lashes to see how he was taking it. His eyes were tight shut and he looked in despair.

There was a pause and the Hatted Lady said that since they'd seemed to find the elderflowers something of a tonic in a depressing age perhaps they'd care for another, about the onset of spring. But the Dead Sheep stopped tunnelling into her eyeballs and said not now, thank you very much, and she'd read a poem instead, which she did, and it was *filthy*, Jeanie would never have believed it.

At the end the Hatted One said very loudly, 'More coffee anyone? How about half and half?' But everybody ignored her and the poems came torrenting out after that.

The Bacon and the Rose

The one Jeanie found most unusual was Hennaed Hair's.
It ended up with:

> *'Oh, there's too many of me tonight*
> *And the lamp-posts are getting longer.'*

'Brilliant!' said Jeanie warmly, though the eyes of the
others had glazed. Then they all insisted it was Jeanie's
turn. She was so flustered that she was well on with, 'Oh,
purée of primrose, oh, buttercup brew!' before she re-
collected that 'Ode to a Spot' had at least had a vestige of
critical acclaim. At the end they all smiled politely and
said they wished they'd written poems half as good when
they'd only been writing for eight weeks.

Then the Black Beetle read one that seemed to have its
inspiration in higher mathematics and Jeanie wished she
hadn't come. The Fairy Princess bit her nails and said she
didn't write poetry actually. And everybody seemed to
have forgotten about the little thin one (whose specs, on
closer scrutiny, were held together by bright pink elastoplast). He even seemed to have forgotten about himself.
So Clean Jeans cleared his throat and said, 'Thank you all
for coming' and 'It's been fun' and 'Perhaps we can all
get together again some time?' But it didn't sound as if he
meant it and Jeanie had the feeling he had staged the
whole thing simply in order to get together with the
Dead Sheep.

Jeanie left the room side by side with Elastoplast Specs.
He said, 'I liked your poem, Jeanie. Here.' He rooted
around in his pocket and pulled out a scrap of paper
which he handed to her. 'I'd like to see your other poems
some time if you'd let me. I live quite near.' He smiled at
her and ran ahead down the stairs. Jeanie looked at the
piece of paper. 'Peter Downes', it said, and an address.
She put it in her pocket, pleased.

'Hey!' She heard running steps behind her and it was Hennaed Hair. 'Would you like to come for a cup of coffee in town some time?' He indicated the folder. 'And I could show you some more of my work?'

Jeanie couldn't believe it! Two real poets wanting to see more of her, Jeanie Parkes! And Hennaed Hair was so fanciable! Wait till the girls at school heard about this!

'When?'

'How about now?'

Jeanie looked at her watch and calculated. She'd promised her mum she'd be back, to help her with the Friendship and Service Guild stall at the church bazaar. She remembered the way her mum had sat up late, making fluffy blue rabbits and Orvilles in nappies. 'I can't today,' she said wistfully.

'Tomorrow then.'

Jeanie's heart sank further. 'I can't. Not on a Sunday.'

'One morning next week?'

Jeanie squirmed. 'Can't. Got to go to school.'

Hennaed Hair looked rather taken aback. 'Well . . . next Saturday morning?'

Jeanie nodded eagerly. 'Oh, yes!'

'O.K. then. Turkey Café. Ten o'clock.'

'Great!' she said, and saw her bus coming round the corner. 'I've got to go now.' She started to run. Then turned. And Hennaed Hair blew her a kiss!

■

On Saturday Jeanie was ready to go to the Turkey Café at quarter past nine. She'd looked longingly, over the past week, at every dead sheep coat she'd seen in a shop window, but she hadn't a hope of affording one in the next twenty-five years. Still, she'd been through her mother's drawers and discovered an old tippet with a fox's head complete with teeth, various scarves and a shawl, and these she pinned about her person. She put her school coat on top of the lot so her mother wouldn't see it and make her take it all off again. The night before, she'd gathered all her poems into a folder with a Harlequin on the front shedding a large tear.

She decided to walk into town because the clock didn't seem to be moving. Even so, she was outside the Turkey Café at quarter to ten. She went in, ordered a cup of coffee and read through every poem she'd written three times over. Compared with the lamp-posts getting longer they seemed infantile in the extreme. She sat and watched people coming in and out until half past ten, when she was on to her third cup of coffee. She'd just decided that Hennaed Hair wasn't going to show up when the door crashed open and he crashed in.

He looked around, saw her and dashed over. From behind his back he produced a long thin cellophane packet and handed it to her. Through the cellophane she saw a single long-stemmed rose.

A single *red* long-stemmed rose! She couldn't think of anybody at school who'd ever been given a single red long-stemmed rose, not even Melanie Fish. Jeanie kept staring at it. She didn't know what to say.

'What'll you have?' he said, hooking out a chair with his toe and reaching for the menu. 'Oh, by the way, you'll have to pay for this, I'm afraid. I've run out of money.' He pointed to the long-stemmed rose. 'Poetry doesn't pay.'

'You mean you've actually had poems *published*?'

But he was looking at the menu and he didn't hear Jeanie's question.

Jeanie couldn't believe her luck. Here she was with a real live poet probably starving in a garret somewhere. What a pleasure it was to buy sustenance for such people!

Perhaps she'd become a technological wizard, earn a packet and become a patron of the arts.

She drew out her purse. 'Would you like something to eat as well?'

Hennaed Hair had been rifling through his sheets of poems. He'd clearly found a good one and was reading it with eager attention, beating time as he did so with his hands. He waved her question away as if he couldn't be doing with such mundane matters when cheek by jowl with the muse, then looked up and said, 'Well, maybe just a cheeseburger.'

Jeanie nodded, delighted, and beckoned the waitress, feeling important. 'Two coffees, please, and a cheese-burger. With relishes.' She rolled her tongue with pleasure round the last word.

When the waitress had gone Hennaed Hair didn't say anything for a long time and his eyes went glazed. Jeanie shuffled a bit. His eyes re-focused and he shook himself. 'My mind's in Ancient Greece today.'

Jeanie smiled enthusiastically but inside she felt more inadequate than ever. She'd never met anyone who drifted off to Ancient Greece without warning. She didn't know what to say and Hennaed Hair was looking bored. Then he perked up. 'I take it you'd like to see some of my poems?'

Jeanie swallowed and nodded. What if she couldn't understand one of them?

'Here's one I wrote after the poetry reading last Saturday. I couldn't sleep,' he said, blasting her with his eyes, 'for thinking of you.'

Jeanie wriggled on her chair. A poem about her? Inspired by her? Even Melanie Fish in her dustbin liner hadn't had a poem written about her!

Jeanie read the poem. It was beautiful and brought

tears to her eyes. It called her 'my sweet nurse' and cast her in the role of Florence Nightingale, and Hennaed Hair in the role of a fighting hero with terrible wounds. In the poem Florence Nightingale looked more like the Fairy Princess than Jeanie, in fact, with long gold hair and soft white hands. Jeanie thought of her own hair, which was of the purest mouse. But then poets are like that – they see beauty and truth in things that are not beautiful, like mousy hair and stubby hands.

'It's so *good*,' she said, and blushed. It seemed the wrong thing to say, when it was all about her.

Hennaed Hair nodded. He leaned forward and spoke in a whisper. 'I couldn't sleep last night because I heard this piece of music in my head. I thought to myself: "Who wrote that?" and I realized it must have been me. It came whole, you know. An inspiration. Only trouble is,' he sighed, 'I can't write a note of music.'

Jeanie fell back in her chair, as disappointed as he was. 'Couldn't you find someone who can, and sort of hum it, bit by bit?'

The poet shook his head. 'It's gone now,' he said, 'beyond recall.'

When he'd finished his cheeseburger (which he did at great speed) he asked Jeanie if he could have another. 'Of course!' said Jeanie, feeling for her purse. 'Haven't you eaten for a while?'

'Not for twelve hours or so,' said Hennaed Hair gloomily. 'Mum's away.'

Jeanie blinked. '*Mum's* away!' That didn't sound like John Keats, pining for Fanny and spitting up blood. 'Where do you and your,' she swallowed, 'mother live?' Surely mum couldn't be sharing his garret!

'Franningham Mansions,' said Hennaed Hair, naming the most exclusive block of flats in town. 'Want to come back there now?' And he looked at Jeanie as if he could eat *her* up, toothy tippet and all!

Jeanie felt herself blushing. 'Oh, *no*,' she said and added in a rather chilly manner, 'I'm afraid I have some shopping to do.'

Hennaed Hair looked sly. 'I'll come with you then.'

So they walked round the supermarket together. Hennaed Hair produced another poem and very kindly read it to Jeanie as she snatched things off shelves and flung them in a trolley while her brain jibbed and squeaked. It was difficult concentrating on what her mum'd need for a week's vegetarian pie, macaroni cheese and nut cutlets when Hennaed Hair kept blocking the gangway and holding an arm up to stop her because he'd reached an important bit, like Moses parting the sea.

At last Jeanie reached the checkout. 'Wait a bit, though,' she said, and ran back to the refrigerated counter. She fished a packet of bacon out. When she'd paid she said firmly to Hennaed Hair, 'I've got to be going now. But it was *very* nice meeting you. Here you are, a present,' and she handed him the bacon, 'in exchange for the rose.'

For the next few weeks Jeanie struggled with a poem. It was about the rose. She wrote the poem in a sad mood because she'd never dare see Hennaed Hair again. And he was so gorgeous. It was a downright shame.

Jeanie tried to say all this in the poem. She even brought in Florence Nightingale, not to mention the full piece orchestra and the elongating lamp-posts. But the poem didn't work.

Finally she thought she might go and see Elastoplast Specs about it. She still had the scrap of paper with his address. She looked it up in a street guide and it was near the community centre. She felt quite excited at the thought of seeing him again. She had this feeling he'd be pleased to see her too. He couldn't have many girls in his life. Once more on a Saturday morning Jeanie caught a ninety-three bus.

She soon found Heathcoat Road. It was a street converted into flats and bed-sits. The houses rose to three storeys with gables and scalloped roofs like the gingerbread house in *Hansel and Gretel*. Some had patterns of navy blue bricks among the red, and many of the doorways were decorated with carved stone flowers and scrolls. The glass in the door of number seventy-three was frosted, then patterned with urns and flowers, pretty, like old lace. But the letter-box gaped black and the paint was peeling. When Jeanie pressed the bell there was a tinny ring. Nobody came. She rang and rang. No one.

Builders doing up a house across the road looked at Jeanie and laughed. 'They'll not be oop,' one shouted.

'Honest?' Jeanie shouted back. 'Won't they honestly?'

The man laughed. 'I don't know.'

Jeanie began to write a note. She wanted Elastoplast Specs to know she'd called and to think it was a pity he'd missed her. But it sounded banal.

'Writing your memoirs?' shouted the builder. Jeanie looked up and laughed.

'Are you looking for me?' A man in a beret had come out of the entry.

'Oh! No. I was looking for . . .' she poked in her pocket for the paper. 'Peter Downes.'

The man looked at her curiously. 'What do you want to see heem for?'

'About some poems,' said Jeanie grandly. 'He does live here, doesn't he?'

But the man shook his head. ' 'E used to leeve here, not any more. Owed too much rent.' Jeanie's face fell. ' 'E leeves at number eighty-five since last Tuesday,' said the man triumphantly. 'Allow me to show.' He led the way to a house that looked even more run down than the first. No old lace here. Just navy blue glass that gave nothing away. He indicated the bell with a flourish. 'But you'll 'ave to reeng 'ard,' he said as he turned away ' 'E'll be writing poe-tree.'

Jeanie didn't like his sarcastic tone. She gritted her teeth and pressed long on the bell. Almost immediately there was a movement in the passage, and a man in a none too clean vest and braces came to the door.

'Is Peter Downes at home?' It sounded daft as usual, as if she was someone from Jane Austen calling to leave Peter her card.

'Yeah,' said the man, 'but you'll have to wait,' and he disappeared into the back.

Peter appeared in a very old dressing-gown tied round with string. He blinked at her for a moment, then recognized her and held out his hand. 'You've brought some poems. Please, do come in.'

It wasn't very smart in the hall. 'Come into the kitchen.' He looked at Jeanie for a moment. 'It's rather sordid, I'm afraid.'

It *was* sordid. Jeanie hadn't seen anything like it. It gave her quite a shock.

On the table were a lot of dirty mugs and plates, a packet of sugar, a bottle of Domecq sherry (empty) and a mouse trap. There was a stained old sink, old brown curtains in tatters and a grimy window overlooking a yard full of old mattresses. Nothing else.

'Would you like some coffee?'

Taking in the scene Jeanie wasn't too sure. She gulped. 'Yes, please.'

'It's filthy coffee, I'm afraid,' said Peter, pulling a wry

face. He picked up a rather used-looking spoon and raked around in a very small pot.

'What's wrong with it?' asked Jeanie with forced cheerfulness. 'It's Nescafé. Very nice.'

'It's not Nescafé, though. That's just a blind.' Jeanie looked startled. What if she was carried off for the white slave trade in a drug-induced haze?

Peter noticed Jeanie's face and grinned. 'It's cheap and nasty coffee in a Nescafé jar.' He took the mugs to the sink. Jeanie heard the splash of water. She craned her neck. That amount of water – cold – couldn't have got the grime off those mugs in a thousand years. He turned, waving the mugs vaguely in the air to dry them. 'I'll have mine black,' said Jeanie hurriedly. 'And no sugar.' She eyed the kettle suspiciously. It was furry on the *outside*. When Peter handed her the mug she sniffed tentatively. It smelt like coffee. She took a sip. It tasted of what Peter had said: filthy coffee. Ah, well. There was a horrible pause.

'Expecting mice?' asked Jeanie desperately, nudging her head towards the trap.

'Oh, that's been there for ages,' said Peter, blinking at it vaguely. His spectacles hadn't been fixed. 'Can't afford cheese, so I keep hoping the mice'll leap on out of a sense of duty.'

He couldn't afford *cheese*? What did he eat then? Jeanie looked tentatively round and saw a small tin plate with the remains of what looked like cat food and a small crust of bread. Jeanie's stomach lurched. 'You should get a cat,' she said, watching him closely.

'Yes,' said Peter, looking her steadily in the eyes. 'I should, shouldn't I? I'm very fond of cats.' He didn't look at all well. His skin was pocked as pebble-dash. And was he thin!

'Do you want to come through,' said Peter gesticulating, 'to where it's warmer?' Jeanie wasn't sure that she wanted to move at all. At least in the kitchen there was nothing to sit on. Through where it was warmer you never knew what might be sharing your chair!

Peter led the way into what turned out to be his bedroom. Jeanie gulped and hung on to the door knob for a moment. She hadn't refused luxurious seduction in Franningham Mansions only to fight her way, screaming, from a Heathcoat Road squat!

What struck Jeanie, though, was the warmth after the dank chill of the kitchen. 'It's not so bad,' she thought. 'In fact, it's quite nice.' There was a small double-bar electric fire directed towards the door so that the heat welcomed her as she walked in. Over by the window – the long tatty beige curtains were half drawn – was a music stand and a small table with an old-fashioned typewriter on it, a clarinet, an anglepoise lamp and a black swivel chair. And a single sheet of paper – covered with minuscule writing and a great many fierce black blanks. 'Sit down,' said Peter, indicating what Jeanie had carefully kept her eyes from till now – a half-made double bed. She sat down abruptly, as if he had pushed her. Still, he seemed more interested in the contents of her folder than the contents of her clothes! He was eyeing it greedily. 'I'd like to read what you brought,' he pointed to the Harlequin file, 'if I may.' He paced the floor reading and occasionally grinning. At the end he nodded. 'Yes,' he said. 'I like them. Specially "Ode to a Spot".'

Jeanie felt encouraged. 'I couldn't get the rose poem quite right.'

'How did it come to get written?'

Jeanie enjoyed telling the tale. She told it, bacon and all. But she didn't say who had given her the rose.

'Let me have another look at it.'

Jeanie handed him the poem and looked sideways, embarrassed.

And saw something that made her turn hot and cold! There at the bottom of the bed, half slipping down the side, was something she'd not noticed before – a cheap white nylon nightie with cherry-coloured ribbons down the front.

Immediately Jeanie wanted to be off. She felt nothing but disgust. These poets! They were just the same as the lads at school. Oh, they offered you roses and coffee. But all they cared about was sex. She reached out for her poem, saying, 'I have to be going now, Peter. I've got some shopping to do.'

Peter handed her the poem back immediately, but he looked very surprised. Jeanie was already at the bedroom door. He didn't try to persuade her to stay. She heard him switch off the electric fire as he followed her out. He saw her to the front door. 'Bye,' she said abruptly and charged off down the street. She didn't want him calling after her, inviting her to visit him again.

'Hey!' Despite herself, Jeanie turned round. He wasn't chasing after her. 'Jeanie, I've been thinking – you didn't bring the bacon into the poem. You only had the rose.' And he lifted his hand in farewell.

Jeanie lifted hers back. She nodded too, and lifted the folder in acknowledgement. Yes, he was right. That was why the poem hadn't worked. She'd been leaving half of it out! She swung on her way, grinning to herself. A poem was forming in her mind. It might be even funnier than 'Ode to a Spot'.

She was half-way to town before she realized that she

hadn't seen any of Peter's poems. She wondered if they were any good. The cherry-ribboned nightie wearer must think so! You'd have to love Peter for his mind! Fancy living with him in that slum! Jeanie thought of the fanciable and brilliant Hennaed Hair and pulled a regretful face. Pity he'd been a half-crazed sex-fiend mouldering in Franningham Mansions instead of that tender undiscovered talent, hungering in a garret somewhere . . .

Yella Custard

On Friday afternoons the fifth year helped in the community. Melanie Fish was in a working party that was clearing the canal of bike wheels and rusty washing machines, and Dave Petrovic helped out at Davenport Infants' with free expression and sand and water play. Two weeks before Christmas he was doing a bit of face-painting with the six-year-olds.

'Are you coming to have your face painted then?'

A thin little boy with freckles and a pale face who was playing all by himself in the Wendy house shook his head till his dull hair flopped up and down.

' 'E won't do anything,' sneered Spiderman, alias Gary Howard. ' 'E's dead scared of every bloomin' thing. Ain't you, Custard?'

The thin boy turned away.

'What's his real name?' hissed Dave.

'Paul Cuthbert. But we call 'im Custard 'cos 'e's yella.'

Sunita Gohil was tugging at Dave's sleeve. 'Dave,' she whispered. 'Will you make me into a white face clown?'

Dave set about whitening Sunita's brown face. He drew black diamonds round her eyes and stuck a red plastic ball on the end of her nose. 'Do you want to be a happy clown or a sad?'

'A sad.'

Dave did Sunita a big red mouth turning down and

drew a large black tear on one cheek. Sunita squeaked in delight and ran to look at herself in the mirror.

'What do you want to be, Rosie? Spiderman or a clown?'

'Spider*woman*.' Rosie turned her face up to Dave. 'And I want a *blue* face.' Dave covered Rosie's face and began to veil in the blue with a thick black web.

All the time he did it he was thinking about Custard.

When Dave had finished drawing on Rosie's web he told the infants the news.

'Not next week but the week after that you're going to the big school. The teachers are doing a pantomime. You're going to see *Sleeping Beauty*.'

The girls jumped up and down and opened their mouths at one another in delight. The boys pulled down their eyelids and tripped one another up. All except Custard. He sat still and his face didn't change.

'And you're all going to sing a song when the Sleeping Beauty wakes up.' Dave picked up his guitar. 'Listen first. Wel-come back, Wel-come back.' He played three simple notes. 'Now it's your turn.'

'Wel-come back. Wel-come back,' sang the infants, their eyes going distant and their fingers creeping like spiders for something to play with. Custard's eyes were distant already and he didn't sing. His hands hung heavy as fish.

'What's the matter with that kid Paul Cuthbert?' Dave asked Mrs Midgley, the infant teacher, at afternoon break.

'Nothing, I don't think, is there?' replied Mrs Midgley. 'You'd never know he's there!' There were twenty-nine mixed infants in Mrs Midgley's class and twenty of them made the noise of two hundred. At least Paul Cuthbert was quiet!

'Too quiet,' thought Dave. He shrugged. 'That's just it. I'm not sure he *is* all there.' He grinned. 'Unlike some.'

'Who does Paul Cuthbert go home with?' he shouted to Gary in the yard at the end of break. Gary stopped being a fire engine just long enough to pull a face. 'Nobody.' He started the blue light flashing again. 'Dah der, dah der, dah der.'

'You mean he walks home on his own?'

'His *mam* comes for him every day,' said Gary scornfully, '*and* she brings him to school as well. Custard's mam looks like a *gran*,' and he took the handbrake off.

'Where does Cu- Paul live?' shouted Dave, grabbing Gary before he could engage first gear.

'Newbold Street,' said Gary, pulling his shoulder back to get away.

That wasn't far from where Dave himself lived. Perhaps he could speak to Mrs Cuthbert when she came to collect Paul at three and suggest that on Fridays he could take Paul home from school to save her the bother?

At five to three Dave was in the cloakroom helping the infants to put their coats on but keeping an eye out for Paul to see he didn't escape. Paul pulled his coat on as if it were made of iron, it seemed such an effort. He fastened one button, into the wrong button hole, and then seemed to run out of the will to do more. He straggled towards the door, and crossed the yard in a slow zig-zag.

Over by the gates was a group of mums, many with pushchairs, chatting and laughing. They looked young and cheerful in their quilted coats and jeans, flowered jackets and patterned skirts.

All except one. She stood apart from the rest, watching through dull worried eyes with a cat's cradle of creases beneath them. Paul was very like her, Dave thought, walking up to her, suddenly nervous. 'Mrs Cuthbert?' Paul shrank even further into the collar of his coat. 'I wonder if I could help you by bringing Paul home next Friday? I'm working in the school at the moment, with Paul's class, and as I live quite near you, I thought . . .'

But Paul's mother was looking at Dave with horror. 'Oh, no. I couldn't allow that kind of thing. I don't know you and you're far too young.'

'I'm sixteen,' said Dave, feeling annoyed. 'I'd be careful with him, honest.'

'No, and that's final,' said the woman, beginning to look angry. 'Paul wouldn't like it either, would you, Paul?' And Paul shook his head till his hair flopped.

'I . . . I just thought it'd save you a journey, that's all.'

'Yes, well, I don't shirk *my* responsibilities,' said Mrs Cuthbert fiercely, and she took Paul's hand and hurried him away.

The next Friday the infants were drawing pictures. 'Anything you like,' said Mrs Midgley, and Dave wandered round to see what they were drawing. Gary was doing a tank, spiky with guns, Sunita, a house with four windows and a door in the middle and a tree like a cloud, and Rosie, Superwoman rescuing Superman from an alien web. Paul wasn't doing anything except stare out of the window.

'What are you going to draw, Paul?' asked Dave.

'I don't know,' Paul spoke so low that Dave could hardly hear what he said.

'Shall I tell you what to draw?'

'If you like.' He didn't look at him.

'How about . . .?' Dave searched in his mind for something he could draw. 'How about drawing your dad?'

Paul gave a sort of moan. Dave looked at him alarmed. Paul had put his head down on his arms and was crying.

Dave took a guilty look round. Luckily Mrs Midgley was out of the room.

Suddenly Paul snatched up a felt tip. Quickly he drew a simple shape. Dave shivered. It looked like a large black dustbin! Paul flung his face back on to his arms and started crying again. Dave hesitated, then put his arm round him. Paul went rigid, then slightly turned his head towards Dave.

Dave brought *his* face down on to the table next to Paul's. 'Is your dad . . . dead?'

Paul's breath came out in a jerk. His head heaved in a nod. Dave said, 'Like mine. My dad's dead too.'

Paul's face shifted a little.

'*I'll* draw for you if you like. I'll draw Sleeping Beauty waking up. We shall see her next week.'

When Dave had finished Paul's picture he played carols for the infants to sing: 'Away in a Manger' and 'While Shepherds Watched' and 'We Three Kings'. Gary Howard stuck his hand up. 'Dave, Dave, can we have the one about the fat man?'

'The one about the *fat* man?' Dave put his palm to his head. Was Gary getting mixed up with Father Christmas?

'Yeah!' Gary looked at Dave in disgust. '*You* know. Round John Virgin.'

∎

On the last Friday of term the Davenport infants made their way, in twos, down the main road to the secondary school. Sunita Gohil joined herself to Mrs Midgley and Paul Cuthbert sidled up to Dave.

The infants and their teachers had places of honour right at the front. The Davenport Christmas panto was a traditional event. The parts were all taken by members of staff, except for one – the principal girl. This was always one of the fifth year. Sometimes they made a joke of it and had one of the lads in drag. But this year there was no doubt who'd be principal girl. Melanie Fish was a natural. Too natural, in the eyes of the deputy head!

When all the children were sitting down, 'Killer' Kesterton, the senior master, came out on to the front of the stage and held up his hand for quiet. 'First I want to welcome all the children from Davenport Infants who have come to see the panto this afternoon. Now I want you all to enjoy yourselves so cheer the goodies, boo the baddies, but I don't want any ridiculous *whistling*, thank you very much!'

The sound of light bird-song rose from the centre of the hall. Mr Kesterton peered.

'Was that you, Fish?'

Fergie looked outraged. 'No, Sir!'

'I'm delighted to hear it. Now if you're all ready, you're about to see the staff as you've never seen them before.' And he left the stage.

He was replaced by a man dressed as a butler with a great red nose.

Fergie nudged Tez Tindale. 'Mr Tipperton. He drinks enough!'

'Welcome to the city of Daven*sport*ia in the land of Semolina. I have to tell you that I am responsible for all the GIRLS in the palace.'

On the back row Jeanie Parkes drew in breath and glanced down at her new 'Women are angry' badge.

'WHAAAAA-HEY!' bayed the first and second year lads.

'And the first to visit us on this winter afternoon is the French maid, BIBI!'

A woman of about fifty wearing a bright red wig, black stockings and a tiny black waitress apron came in, all coy behind a huge orange feather duster. She came over shyer still when she pretended to see the crowd for the first time, tittering and hiding her face. Fergie craned his neck to see.

'Who's that? Who is it?'

Tez scrutinized Bibi. 'I reckon it's Mrs 'Art.'

'Mrs Ooh? Oh, yeah, the one that teaches cook'ry. Yeah, could be, I suppose.' Fergie giggled. 'Should be called Mrs *Tart*.'

Bibi turned round with her back to the school at that moment and bent over to dust the corner of the chair, showing a lot of bright blue French knicker edged with shocking pink lace. 'Cor-err!' groaned Fergie and pretended to hide his eyes.

'O O O O H!' squealed Bibi. 'I must get on with my cleaning. Here comes the K E E E N G!'

A very small round man came on to the stage, wearing yellow tights, red satin knickerbockers and a fine blue velvet cloak edged in white cotton wool with black felt tip arrows all along. His face was hidden behind a copy of *The Sun*.

Tez gave a shriek of recognition. 'It's Wally!'

'How d'ya know?'

'S'got to be Mr Wallace, ain' it? That small and that fat?'

'Oh, yeah. Yeah, you're right.'

'What ees you doin' 'ere, Keeng of Semolina?' demanded Bibi, giving him a playful swipe with the feather duster. 'I 'ave my dusteeng to do, and 'ere ees you, keep getteeeng in my way.' She knocked lovingly up against him.

'Oh, it's the christening party for my dear little daughter, the Princess Aurora,' cried the king, making a grab at Bibi's feather duster, 'and the queen has invited lots and lots of squealy squawly *babies*. I've come in 'ere to read my newspaper,' he flashed page three at the rocking school, 'and get a little peace. OH, NO!' he squealed, glancing off the stage. 'Here come those dratted babies NOW. Let me out of here!'

Again the school craned to see. It wasn't difficult this time. Here came Mr Mortimer! He may have been capped for Great Britain many times for basketball, but today he had a pink *bonnet* tied round his huge bearded face and was dressed in a great white nappy like a giant Gandhi, white woolly socks and enormous pink bootees with pink bobbles. Around his neck hung a grotesque pink dummy.

He was followed by another baby, a smaller one this time, running with its back to the audience and carrying a huge plastic potty.

'Who's that? Who's that?'

'It's Greedy. I reckon it's Greedy.'

Mr Reed turned to face the audience, yowling, and drew the arm holding the big plastic potty right back, about to throw the contents all over the audience.

Fergie gasped.

The baby took aim and tossed. The school drew itself up like a wave and Paul clutched Dave. Tiny bits of paper fluttered over the infants in the front row. Paul glanced up at Dave with a tiny smile.

Miss Muldoon, the art teacher, came on next, dressed as Little Boy Blue. She was tall, with auburn curls, and wore blue shorts with braces. She came in hand-in-hand with Killer Kesterton in a red frock and white apron, carrying a crook – Little Bo Peep! The first years yowled with laughter. Bo Peep and Little Boy Blue skipped around the first few rows, giving out sweets.

'Not just the infants!' yelled Fergie.

'Chuck some back 'ere!'

Dave watched Paul stare at his sweet in its yellow wrapping. He slowly undid it, giving Dave an anxious look. Dave grinned at him. 'Go on! It's O.K.'

The queen now glided on to the scene. Amazing! It looked like the deputy head. 'I think all these babies require some milk,' she declared loftily. 'Send for the Right Royal Cow.'

The school hooted and rocked. A pantomime cow danced on to the stage waving a hoof. Little Bo Peep skipped up to milk its great plastic udders and squirted the infants in the front row. Paul shied away and laughed out loud!

But Little Bo Peep suddenly began to cry. 'What's the matter?' demanded Little Boy Blue.

'Well, Morten Harket was invited to this christening party and he hasn't turned up.' From behind the cardboard throne up popped a puppet of Morten Harket with swirled back hair, wearing a leather jacket with the sleeves pushed up and a dog collar round one wrist. 'Here I am, Bo Peep, and here are all my clones.' And six Morten Harkets pranced on to the stage, all wearing leather jackets with strips of leather wound round their lower arms. They looked amazingly similar except that one of the Morten Harkets was black.

'*That's* Mr Wright.'

Fergie punched Tez. 'You don't say!'

'The guest we *don't* want at this party is the wicked witch,' explained the queen. 'So if anyone sees her, let us know.'

The Morten Harkets stopped writhing and divided into two groups and behind them was:

'You daft bastards, the wicked witch!'

Fergie put a hand over Tez's mouth. 'You shouldn't say that word.'

Tez tried to bite Fergie's palm. The result was slimy and Fergie took his hand away. 'I was only acting. Teachers can't tell you off when you're acting.'

The wicked witch cast her spell. The queen had hysterics. The black Morten Harker detached himself and came over to her. 'What's your problem, lady?'

She told him that her daughter would die if she pricked her finger. Dave felt Paul stiffen.

'She won't die,' said Morten Harket. 'I can work magic. She'll go to sleep for a hundred years.'

The school cheered and sixteen teachers walked solemnly across the stage, wearing placards – one, two, three up to sixteen years! 'All the spinning wheels in the kingdom were burnt,' explained the king. 'One day the Princess Aurora went exploring in the old tower.'

On came the Princess Aurora in a long crinkly blonde wig. 'Melanie Fish!' roared the first and second year boys. The wicked witch appeared again, yanking on a spinning wheel. For all their warning boos and yells Princess Aurora would insist on having a go and fell down in a dead swoon on a convenient couch. 'That's my girl-friend,' Dave whispered to Paul in pride. 'She'll wake up soon.'

'Now,' said the queen. 'We need some nice *sensible* trees. C'mon, wave your arms, everybody, and let's have some gentle trees swaying in the breeze.'

Fergie swayed as if blasted by a force ten gale. The queen eyed him sourly. 'I said a tree, Fish. No need to take on the job of the whole forest.' Mr Mortimer's baby, brought in by Mrs Mortimer for the pantomime, gave a screech and waved a plump arm. She had on a woolly green dress and looked like a little round shrub.

Miss Harvey was a stripling that didn't want to grow where she was planted. She stamped her foot. The queen lifted a warning finger. 'Don't you stamp your roots at *me*.'

There was a commotion from among the trees. Creeping between their waving branches came Mr Timpson, the student teacher, carrying a purple balloon on the end of a stick. Rugby Joe, dressed as a peasant, appeared and greeted him. 'Whither are you going, Sire?'

Mr Timpson tapped him briskly on the shoulder and blushed. 'Take your hat off when you speak to *me*, Serf.' The headmaster escorted the prince through the forest and at last they spied the Princess Aurora twitching slightly on her couch. 'AHA!' cried the prince, and the blush deepened. 'Just what I've been waiting for all term.' Dave looked a little uneasy. The prince turned to the school. 'What do you think I should do?' His face was fiery!

'KISS 'ER!' yelled the first and second year lads. 'KISS 'ER. KISS 'ER. GO ON!'

The prince looked coy. 'Shall I? Shall I kiss her, do you think?'

'YEAH! YEAH! WHEY-HEY!'

The prince peered into the audience. 'Have I your permission, Petrovic?'

It was Dave's turn to go scarlet as the school guffawed and Princess Aurora panted, trying not to laugh. The prince put his hand to his ear. 'I can't quite hear you, Petrovic. SHALL I KISS HER?'

'YE-E-E-ES!' roared the school on Dave's behalf. Paul clapped his hands over his ears.

'All right then. If you say so.'

He bent slowly down towards the blonde wig. Up swung Princess Aurora. 'UGH, not *you*,' she said, pulling a face. 'I want someone young and *handsome* to kiss me. I couldn't fancy you.' But she went dead red as she said it.

Mr Joseph elbowed the prince out of the way. 'How about me? I have a very nice little pad in the forest. Psychedelic, with flashing lights.'

The princess looked as if she hadn't a clue what he was on about and shuddered. 'Oh, no! You're only a serf and you're *really* old. I want someone *young* to wake me up.' She peered out and scanned the lines of the school, then fell backwards in a dead faint.

'PE-TRO-VIC! PE-TRO-VIC! PE-TRO-VIC!' blared the school. Paul didn't know they were shouting for Dave. He leaned against him. 'She will wake up, won't she? She won't really . . . die?'

Dave was too flustered to think straight. 'Of course not.' He glimpsed a way out of his embarrassment. 'If you go up there, she'll wake up. Just go up there and she'll smile at you. Go on.' He gave Paul a little shove. And to his amazement Paul started up on to the stage!

Of course, the school went crazy! He looked so small, staggering up the steps to be greeted by Mr Joseph, who put a hand on his head. 'How about this one? Is this one young enough for you?'

Aurora opened one eye. She grinned from ear to ear. 'Oh, he'll do very nicely, thank you.' The eye shut again.

Mr Joseph nudged Paul. 'You have to kiss her now. Go on. Give her a quick peck.'

A look of horror and panic spread over Paul's face. Dave felt very uncomfortable.

But the infants saved the day. 'Go on, Custard! Go on! Go on! Kiss 'er. Go on!' And Custard started to blush. Very fast he brushed Princess Aurora on the cheek. She woke immediately and took hold of his hand. Together they came to the front of the stage. The whole school roared at the sight of a prince who was half the princess's size.

Then Custard started to smile. The smile spread and Custard started to clown. He lifted the Princess Aurora's hand to his lips. The school went crazy again. Dave reached for his guitar. He played the first notes of the infants' song. 'Wel-come back. Wel-come back.'

■

Mrs Cuthbert was waiting for Paul after the pantomime. She watched in astonishment as he charged over to her, brandishing the prince's purple balloon. They crossed the road, Paul with his face up to his mother, chattering away.

'See ya, Paul,' yelled Gary Howard. 'I'll call for you tomorrow mornin', O.K.?'

Dave watched as Paul nodded and grinned at Gary, and waved his balloon.

Eye! Eye!

Dave Petrovic hated the first day of term. The corridors were crassly over-polished. The staff were grotesquely over-keen. Instead of the sane, time-honoured way by which one human being greets another, 'Mrng ... brrr ... brrr,' they were leaping about going, '*I'll* do Magna Carta, and *you* can do manorial records.' 'Great! And what after that?' 'The Paston letters? The Black Death? It comes round to what in the end? The Tooders? The Stooerts? Government records?'

Dave gave a low groan.

Things were no better on the fifth year base. Dave's nostrils were assaulted by a strong aroma of pine forest and his eyes by the sight of Miss Harvey's backside as she leant over a desk applying a J-cloth and Jif to the more licentious comments on the sweet mystery of life.

Dave retreated rapidly to the corridor and pretended deep interest in the selection of paintings for the new term. They were as predictable as ever. 'Sunflowers', a Michelangelo cartoon, a clothed Gauguin ... Dave worked his way down them like a robot till he reached the bulletin board and 'Fifth Year Duties', where he groaned again. Not only library help but first year library supervision as well.

On Friday afternoons the first years worked on projects of their own. This was supposed to help them get to know the library and to find out more about subjects they were keen on. All the fifth years who'd ever done library supervision had been reduced to quivering blobs within two weeks.

Jasmine Samuel came up behind him and read the duty list over his shoulder. 'Mmm-mmm, man! Situation looks dread!'

On his way to first year library supervision Dave rehearsed his approach. 'I'm Petrovic. You fear me,' or, raising his right hand as he walked down the corridor, 'See this? Deadly!' Jasmine Samuel, turning the corner at that moment, grinned at him. 'Gwan, Dave. Give it 'em hot and strong.'

'Hey!' There was the sound of running feet behind him and a very small girl pranced up. She looked as if she couldn't be more than third year juniors, never mind first year secondary. 'You're Dave, aren't you? You're gonna do our library supervision, aren't you?' She settled into her stride beside him and said with touching simplicity, 'I'll just keep you company on the way.' She gave him a sunshine smile.

Dave softened. She was such a sweet little thing with those dark curls and great dark eyes behind National Health specs. The way her long socks wrinkled round her stick-like legs quite touched his heart.

'What's your name?'

'Kerry Dixon,' she said, smiling up at him. 'I know you're Dave *Petrovic* and,' she drew in breath as if in deep awe, 'that you're a *prefect*.'

Dave smiled. 'How are you liking the school, Kerry?'

'Great! The lessons are really good and me and my friend Mandy we've got this, like, club for doing things out of school like join the Guides, go up down-escalators, climb derelict buildings and go out on our bikes. Joining the Guides is the best thing we've done so far,' she gave Dave another ravishing smile, 'and climbing derelict buildings is the worst.'

'I don't think you should be going anywhere *near* derelict buildings,' said Dave anxiously, 'let alone climbing them.'

'Oh, we're all right,' said Kerry, thrusting out her stomach. 'We're tough.'

The rest of the first year seemed nearly as O.K. as Kerry. Three small boys came up behind Kerry and Dave in the corridor but they kept their distance and Dave could hear them saying, 'It is. It isn't. It *is*. It *isn't*. It IS,' and cheering softly when he turned into the library. And the ones who were already there stood up when he came in. They all giggled a bit at first but they settled to assembling their books for their projects in a fairly business-like fashion.

Kerry edged up to Dave. 'We're doin' The Eye in biology,' she said, 'and it really int'rests me, The Eye, Dave.' And she headed off to the human biology section with all the enthusiasm of the A1 student. For the rest of the lesson she bent assiduously over a book and copied things out.

The only disturbance was from a bright-eyed youth who arrived twenty minutes late and announced, 'Sorry I'm late but I had to take the dog to be circumcised.' But the rest of the first year were so hard at it that they seemed oblivious (though Kerry gave a bit of a snort).

Dave looked at him sternly to see if he was joking. He stared innocently back. 'What's your name?'

Kerry looked up from The Eye. 'He's Basharat, Dave. And this one's Swipe-A-Ferret,' she indicated the boy to the left of her, 'and this one's Biff-a-Badger.' She giggled.

Basharat swung his briefcase briefly about her head but soon settled down opposite to her. It was then that Dave noticed that Kerry was entirely surrounded by boys.

At the end of the session, when the first years had left, Dave made his way round the library straightening tables, pushing in chairs and picking up scraps of paper that had been dropped. He found a pink bit that was all screwed up and unravelled it.

▪ The Eye ▪

Today we did the eye in biology. Each group was given an eye and a scalpel. The eye itself was black and had pink round it. When we cut it open we could feel the retina and the pupil. The retina was very slimy and slippy and soft.

As soon as I had the eye in my hand I had this feeling like I wanted to put it down. So I threw it at Michael Earnshaw and it dropped on the floor. Gary Purvis came by and trod on it. When I had picked it off Gary's trainer, I put most of the eye in Mandy Leadbetter's pencil case when she wasn't looking. When we had finished dissecting the rest of the eye I looked at another group's finished eye. It looked in good condition. Ours didn't even resemble an eye. It was a bit embarrassing trying to explain to Mrs Roberts why we didn't have all the eye.

Mandy Leadbetter hasn't found the eye in her pencil case yet!!!!!!!!!!!

Dave's stomach churned. Little savages! He bet it was that vagabond Basharat. Dog to be circumcised indeed! Dave recalled Kerry's interest in the eye. He grinned affectionately. She had such neat little fingers. He bet she was ace with a scalpel!

On the way down from the library Dave met Jasmine. 'How did you get on with those bangers?'

'Oh, peachy. Un piece de cake.' He thought of Kerry's bright face. 'In fact, they're really dead sweet.'

Jasmine looked pitying. 'A word of advice, boy.'

'What?'

'Do not wear ear-muffs in the land of the rattlesnake.'

'*What?*'

'Don' let 'em fool you, Dave, with their big-yeyes and dem inn-o-cence. All kids is crooks. Jus' take it from I, man.'

Dave ignored this. 'You a Rasta, Jasmine?'

'Stop chattin' nonsense. I man is no Rasta.'

'You ain' no expert on eleven-year-olds either. So don't come me that.'

Jasmine shook her head. '*Wot* a stupid picny! Jus' wait and see, Dave. You'll learn!'

■

At break the next day Kerry arrived unexpectedly on the fifth year base, looking for Dave. The other fifth years stared in amazement at the black-haired, black-eyed sprite who came dancing across the floor. 'Sorry-to-disturb-you, Dave. But Joseph wants this lady taken across to the double mobile. She's givin' a talk to the first year girls.' Dave shrugged, nodded and followed her out. The prefects had to do this 'host duty' if required, showing visitors round the school.

When well clear of the base he beamed down at Kerry, glad of her company again.

'What's she going to talk to the first years about, Kerry? Do you know?'

Kerry looked at him through coal-black eyes. 'Dinosaurs.'

'*Dinosaurs?*'

She nodded and darted off, giving him a winsome grin.

After Dave had shown the visitor to the double mobile he had a free period which he spent doing library help. He stared gloomily at the great stack of books topped off with a piece of paper that said 'Q U E R I E S' that awaited him on the librarian's table. He opened the first and found an elaborate note.

'This book does not have a loan card. You are welcome if you feel so inclined to make out a temporary card. Otherwise take this book to the resources office with an explanatory note ('card missing' will suffice).'

Dave sighed. The head of geography, Mr Roonie, was in charge of the library. Mr Roonie was famous for his pin-striped suits, velvet bow ties, green baize waistcoats and, when he forgot to take them off, his bicycle clips, and his systems were as elaborate as his clothes. He had an abiding fondness for notes. Mr Roonie had even been known to leave notes in empty boxes that said, 'Empty box'.

Dave turned to the next note. 'Although there is no evidence of a loan's having been made, *The Joy of Sex* has vanished from the shelves. Could it have been put back in the wrong place?'

Dave cheered up considerably and sprinted for the stacks. He'd never have suspected that Davenport library would give shelf room to *The Joy of Sex*.

His enthusiasm soon dwindled. There was nothing remotely resembling it anywhere to be seen. He ran his eyes idly along the titles in the fiction section. In flower shops they have notices, 'Say it with flowers.' Well, you could always say anything you wanted to say with books. For example, thought Dave, he could send Melanie Fish a copy of Evelyn Waugh's *The Loved One* in a plain brown paper wrapping. Then follow it up with, say, A. A. Milne's *Now We Are Six* with a discreet '*Teen*' added to the spine, and Kingsley Amis's *I Want It Now*. Then *she'd* put a notice on the bulletin board that'd say 'WHO KEEPS SENDING ME BOOKS?' and *he'd* send her John Le Carré's *The Honourable School Boy* and . . .

Dave was aware of a furtive movement behind the stacks. He darted round and there was a bright-eyed first year enveloped in an enormous anorak carrying an outsize briefcase and looking very shifty. He recognized he-of-the-canine-circumcision, Basharat!

Dave's mind flew immediately to Mr Roonie's 'Memo for Librarians'. 'Keep a wary eye out for students wearing voluminous coats with large pockets. On no account should school bags be allowed behind the barrier. ALL LIBRARIANS SHOULD REJOICE THAT BOOK LOSS HAS BEEN MORE THAN HALVED.'

Dave put on his very fiercest look. 'What are *you* doing here?'

The small boy cowered. 'Lookin' for a book on dinosaurs.'

'Well, you shouldn't be behind the barrier with an outsize bag and voluminous pockets, so SCRAM!'

Basharat scuttled.

Dave scanned the shelves where he'd been lurking, confident of falling upon *The Joy of Sex*. He was disappointed.

■

Dave went straight from library help to join Jeanie Parkes overseeing the first years through the lobbies before dinner. Life for the responsible is one long Duty.

Jeanie greeted him with, 'Seen Jasmine Samuel this morning? She's got a scarf-turban on her head.'

Dave looked sour. 'She'll be for it. You can't wear hats unless you're a Rasta.'

Jeanie rolled her face up in the roller towel. 'This ain' a hat. It's sort of, well, a scarf-turban.'

'Well, she shouldn't be wearin' it. She told me personally she ain' a Rasta.' Dave kicked a locker. 'Know what, Jeanie? She said yesterday that all kids are crooks. And she meant little kids like the first years as well.'

Jeanie looked thoughtfully at Dave. 'She's got a point, though. Kids nowadays, they're *born* knowing. They don' pin the tail on the donkey like we used to, y'know, Dave. It's *at least* pin the tail on the Quangle Wangle Quee.'

There was a noise across the playground like the Hallelujah Chorus – the first year girls being let out. Dave smiled fondly. 'That'll be the first year girls. They've had this woman to give them a special talk this morning.'

Jeanie nodded. 'Yes, I know. On sex education.'

Dave stared. '*I* was told they were having a talk on dinosaurs.'

Jeanie shook her head. '*Definitely* sex education.'

■

The next time it was first year library supervision Kerry said, 'What would you do a project on, Dave? If you had to do one, I mean.'

Dave thought. 'Well, I'm keen on basketball. And my hi-fi system and,' he blushed, 'I'd *quite* like to draft out a new way of organizing the library and resources area.' He realized this was true. He was slowly developing his own 'system'. God, at this rate he'd end up as some sort of nutter like Loonie Roonie who got caught in roller blinds and at whose touch whole music stands collapsed!

Kerry nodded and settled to her research along with the rest of the first years. Dave settled down to a bit of revision – he had his mock 'O' levels next week.

All was quiet in the room. The library windows were open and the Venetian blinds clicked gently against the window panes in the light breeze. The fair-haired Mandy who, Dave was learning, did everything Kerry did, was engrossed in a full colour diagram of The Eye complete with blood vessels. She felt deep into her pink pencil case with 'Side Walk Surfing' on the front in glitter, for her red felt tip.

And felt something in the bottom that was soft and slippery and slimy and jelly-like . . . what could it be? It felt to Mandy like an ancient grape. She cautiously lifted it out and examined it and

'UUUUUUUUUUUUUUUUUUUUUUAAA-AAAAAAAAAAAAAAAAAAAGGGGGGGGG-GGGGGHHHHHHHHHHHHHHHH!!!!!!!!!!'

'Whatever is the matter?' Dave made rapidly for Mandy who was having hysterics.

'There's . . . there's 'n . . . there's an E Y E in my pencil case!'

Kerry was quick off the mark to comfort her hysterical friend. 'Shhhhhhh, shhhhhhhhh, shhhhhhhh, shhhhhhhh,' she said soothingly and when her sobs had subsided somewhat, 'Let's have a look, Mandy.' She exclaimed in disgust and held the eye up for Dave's inspection. After a week among pencil shavings and the black dust that accumulates in the bottom of pencil cases the eye was not in too good a shape. But it was unmistakably an eye, or three quarters of one, nevertheless. Dave's stomach slid sideways.

'WHO PUT THAT EYE IN MANDY LEADBETTER'S PENCIL CASE?'

Dave looked round the first years. Not a flicker. Though Dave got the distinct impression that Basharat shifted. Dave whipped round on him.

'It wasn't you by any chance, was it, Basharat?'

Basharat's horrified denial *sounded* genuine. But Dave wasn't convinced for one moment. Still, he couldn't carry the matter further without some kind of proof.

The bell rang and the first years filed out, somewhat agitated after Mandy's blood-curdling shriek. Dave noticed that Basharat went out protesting his innocence to a fiery-looking Kerry. At the door she turned for a last few words with Dave. 'You got mock "O" levels, ain' you, Dave? So we won't have you next week?' She ran a quick eye over his school equipment, strewn out over the librarian's table, as if taking a last fond inventory of all that he owned. 'Good luck!' She hovered by his table as if loath to take her final leave.

'Thanks, Kerry.' Dave started his usual tour of the library, straightening tables, pushing in chairs, bending to pick up scraps of paper. Underneath Mandy's chair he found a crumpled pink sheet. When he straightened up to unravel it Kerry had gone.

It turned out to be a note! A note for him.

'Dearest, darlingest Dave,
    I'd like to score a three point goal in your basket. Also 'just for the record', I'd come and inspect your woofs and tweeters any time. I also think your resources are terrific!
        Luv-n-hugs from your ardunt admirer
        ???????????????????????
        le x, le x, le x, le x (French kisses)'

Dave blushed. Of all the . . . It had to be – yeah, the milky-curled Mandy! Well, then she DESERVED to get eyes stuffed in her pencil case, the little minx!

It was only when he was on the way home he wondered what had happened to the eye . . .

■

Eye! Eye!

The first day of mock 'O' levels found Dave waiting outside the top hall, reading through Mr Roonie's 'Notes on Examination Regulation'.

1. Every student should have his student membership card *open* on the right hand top corner of his desk. Last year many students were without this essential element in our identification procedure.
2. No crunchy comestibles are to be taken into the examination.
3. At the conclusion of the examination students must not automatically rise on handing in their examination paper but 'stay put' until the member of staff on duty *requests* them to rise . . .

'Right, fifth years, "O" level English literature and "O" level technical drawing.' Miss Harvey flung open the double doors and the fifth year shuffled in, filling in the desks from the back of the hall.

'Some to the front, some to the front,' carolled Miss Harvey impatiently. Dave (Eng. lit.) quickly slotted himself in under the balcony near the back, across from Arif Kasmani (tech. drawing). Arif looked as if he'd already been camping out there for a week. His desk was piled high with calculators, set squares, rulers, geometry sets, tubes of mints, packets of crisps, and was that a Cup-a-Soup? An alarm clock nestled at his feet and on the top of the pile of emergency provisions Arif ostentatiously placed his digital watch.

'Turn over your examination papers,' Miss Harvey consulted the examination clock, *'now.'*

Dave settled to reading his through. Why were examination papers these days so, well, wimpish? 'Kindly enthuse about . . . If you have nothing better to do this morning, please give your esteemed attention to . . .'

Dave had only managed half a page when Arif started on a crunchy comestible. He opened a packet of crisps. Crackle, crackle, crackle. Crunch, crunch, crunch.

Miss Harvey sped down the aisle like a nun on casters and hissed, 'Put-those-away.'

'But-I'm-a-diabetic,' snarled Arif through gritted teeth.

There was a gust of wind on Dave's neck and Mr Roonie swept through the double doors. He'd arrived to see that the Notes on Examination Regulation were fully operational. As he swept past Dave he tapped severely on Dave's membership card which he'd forgotten to display.

Dave shrugged in annoyance and flicked the card open at his photograph and

'UUUUUUUUUUUUAAAAAAAAAAAAA-AAGGGGGGGHHHHH!!!!'

The three-quarter eye, liberally sprinkled with pencil dust and with a green-rimmed pencil shaving for an eye-lash, stared up at him from the middle of his own fore-head!

Miss Harvey bore down upon him like a nun on a power-assisted cloister, while the eyes of the fifth year swivelled round to see who had flipped his lid in their midst.

Dave rapidly recovered his composure. He bent double over his desk as if in acute pain. 'Got-this-chronic-stomach-ache,' he gasped. Miss Harvey signalled to Mr Roonie, who darted at the double to lead Dave off on a conducted tour of the nearest lavatories.

As Dave feigned acute diarrhoea from behind closed doors for Mr Roonie's benefit he racked his brains to think who could be responsible. Try as he would he couldn't dispel the conviction that it was that rogue Basharat . . .

■

The next session of first year library studies did not take place in the library. Mr Roonie was stock-taking and had called in every library book. He had threatened a total boycott of library studies if *every single* book wasn't returned.

There was still not a whisper of *The Joy of Sex*.

The first years were in bubbly mood when Dave went into the classroom to sit with them while they finished off their projects. Dave noticed with disappointment that Kerry wasn't there. Mandy Leadbetter handed him a note from Kerry's mum. 'Kerry is away from school with a bug that seems to be in the area. Yours respectfully, Mrs Dixon.'

'Shut-UP, Basharat,' said Dave, who was in a bad mood because Kerry was absent. 'We don't need to know what the weather's like where you're sitting.' He nodded curtly at the first years to get on with their work and settled to his.

He was aware after about twenty minutes of a slight movement among the class, a movement that approached him, like a wave approaching the shore. He ignored it. There was a flutter and he looked up to see a note had landed on his desk:

> 'To Dave,
> At-the-Front,
> Room 6,
> Davenport Secondary.'

He looked up warily, then opened it. It said, 'Kerry Dixon is in the library in perfect health.'

Dave thought for a long time. Eventually he decided he'd better go and investigate this. He coughed and said, 'I've left something up on the base. Work quietly for five minutes on your own.'

He sprinted across the playground, casting an anxious eye in on Mr Roonie to see that he was safely ensconced in his classroom. He was, and appeared to be drawing a map of Australia from a postage stamp!

Dave sped upstairs and gently tried the library door. It was open. There were no lights on and there was dead silence. He crept down to the barrier behind which lay the books on general loan. He tiptoed into the stacks and peered through a gap in the books into the human biology section.

There on a table with her back to him sat a very small figure in a duffel coat with the hood up.

'Kerry!'

Kerry whirled round on her bottom and glared at him like a malignant leprechaun. She was clutching a book.

'Give me that book.'

Kerry darted her hand into her school bag, scribbled 'Eye, eye, Sir!' on the first page, and slid the book across the table and herself towards the barrier, cackling as she fled.

Dave picked up the book and read the inscription with a disillusioned heart. He shut the book to read its cover. It was, of course, *The Joy of Sex*.

■

The bell went before Dave had a chance to return to the first years. He decided to go to the staff room immediately to announce the prodigal's return. He approached the door that bore a notice, KNOCK AND WAIT. He knocked and waited. At last a rainbow-eyed member of staff (new that term) came to the door. He looked as if he'd been on the bottle for a fortnight.

'Yes?'

'Is Mr Roonie knocking around?'

'Is Mr Roonie KNOCKING AROUND?' He pressed a hand to his temples in mock despair, threw back his head and bellowed, 'ROO-NIE?'

There was a snigger from the tech. drawing master in the corner. 'Seen this? Kasmani's tech. drawing paper. He's written across the top "No time to revise due to illness".'

The new teacher snorted. 'That *should* read "No time to revise due to sex life".'

Mr Roonie came shambling in from the quiet room. He'd got a circular in his hand. 'What's all this rubbish then? You are invited to a careers evening at brrrr. It is hoped that further liaison will be brrrrr. Mr Joseph will speak to staff and parents on gender awareness.' Mr Roonie crumpled the piece of paper and chucked it at the waste paper basket. 'Rot. That's what all that is. A load of rot!'

Dave's heart went out to him. Better this than all that shine and polish, idealism and leaping about.

'Yes? What is it?' Dave handed him *The Joy of Sex*. ''S' been tracked down to a first year girl, Sir. She, at least, seems gender aware!'

Mr Roonie nodded and gave a lop-sided grin. 'How did you get on in your mocks then, Petrovic?'

Dave pulled a face. His results had been dire, particularly the one overseen by the evil eye! Eighteen per cent! 'Oh, so, so. Didn't want to peak too early, Sir.' And they grinned at one another bleakly and nodded in their world-weary way.

Abdul and the Vampires

'1986 or 1406,' scrawled Abdul. 'Written straight after midnight, the first of January, 1986, which is 1406 in my religion. As I sit by the gas fire I see many things which have taken me far away from the world of children. The bitter winds are kept outside by the insulation but I am cold inside. Who cares? No one. I am a loner and shall be ever more.

'Feroz Razak has left school to go to India. Oh, Feroz, you were always a good friend to me, a joyful companion! Whether it was in English, maths or environmental studies. Or whether it was the long discussions we had concerning how to acquire good study habits . . .' Here Abdul broke off and tears rose in his eyes. That wasn't the reason why he missed Feroz so much. He picked up his biro again, scored through the last sentence and wrote, 'Feroz was the only one who didn't kid me about my *****.' Then he turned to the end of the diary and wrote in minute letters teeth.

Abdul reached for his sister's make-up mirror. He was always tormenting himself by looking in the magnifying side. His eye teeth sprang out at him, glittering. He tried to murmur the sentence they'd been taught to say in life skills whenever they felt bad about themselves. 'I am a worthwhile and lovable person.' But all he could see

131

were his teeth flashing at him from the glass. In the end he'd got his mum to write a note to say that he had to go to the clinic about his verruca every week when it was life skills. It had been the most stubborn verruca in the entire history of the clinic.

Remembering how he'd been a failure even at life skills, Abdul felt an overwhelming urge to go downstairs and see if he'd switched the electric kettle off. He *thought* he could remember doing it. But was he remembering last night? Still, even if he hadn't switched it off, it did have a safety device. Still, he might just go and check . . . Abdul groaned, trying to fight off his compulsion. He reached again for his diary. 'Many times have I dreamed of someone who will rescue me from my chronic state. But no one has turned up yet. There is no telling who this great person will be who I shall share my life with. Let us hope she will be a princess who will win the hearts of the family as well as cheer this broken heart of mine, the lost mind, and soothe the hurts that have been inflicted upon me.' As Abdul wrote this he felt a jabbing pain in his right eye tooth. It had been hurting him, on and off, for the past four weeks now.

He reached across and turned on his C.B. set. He had pestered his dad to get him one ever since he thought he might make a new friend over the air-waves (where nobody could see his teeth). But he'd had it for two whole months now and he hadn't dared say anything yet. Still, he could always listen. Perhaps tonight Tez'd be on the air . . .

Tez was Abdul's hero. He was still at school but lessons meant nothing to Tez compared with the trucking life. His dad was a long distance lorry driver and during the holidays he was always off across the country, chatting to other drivers and rubbing eyeballs (meeting

up with them) in cafés up and down motorways. Abdul
had this fantasy that one day he'd rub an eyeball with
Tez and when he saw Abdul's teeth Tez wouldn't even
stare.

'Breaker two one. Breaker two one. This is Truckin'
Tez speakin' . . . Anyone on channel two one who wants
an eyeball? Anybody out there wanting to come in?'

Abdul switched the set off hurriedly. Whenever Tez
said that he got this overwhelming compulsion to say,
'Yeah, yeah. I need you, Truckin' Tez.'

■

During the Christmas holidays the teacher who taught
fifth year 'non-exam' for most of their timetable had a
nervous breakdown, and Miss Harvey had to teach them
for a couple of periods of English a week.

Their ability range was wide, from Sharon Driver who
was hard-pressed to spell 'The dog ran to the man' to
Martin Larter who was capable of spelling 'on-
omatopoeia' but preferred playing pool to doing homework. Then there were Gurinder Karwal and Gurmit
Kaur who looked nineteen but acted six. And Amrik
Singh who was paying the school a courtesy visit between
suspensions.

And Abdul Sheikh.

Abdul had come to Miss Harvey's attention long before
she first encountered fifth year 'non-exam'. You could
hardly miss him, even though he was small and thin and
scared-looking, because he carried all his possessions
strung about his person like a wandering Fort Knox. The
first time he struggled past Miss Harvey he was hung
about with a sports bag, a briefcase, a badminton racket,
a lunch box, a parka, a bicycle pump and a plastic mac.
After this Miss Harvey wouldn't have been surprised if
she'd seen him dangling a mouse trap from one buckle of

his briefcase and, say, an alarm clock from another, after the fashion of the white knight.

Fifth year 'non-exam' were famous for their roistering and rampaging, and they had most of their lessons in a single mobile in the furthest corner of the playground on account of their loud reputation. Miss Harvey could already see them as she legged it past the other classrooms the first time she met them, heads bobbing up and down as if the mobile that housed them was a bouncy castle. She threw a longing look in at one set one who sat meekly, eyes to the front and two by two, as though sailing peaceably across the school day in an outsize Noah's ark.

When Miss Harvey opened the door Martin Larter was smoking and Gurmit Kaur and Gurinder Karwal were fighting a duel with blackboard dusters. Chalk wrapped the assailants in a swirling fog.

'Gurinder Car-Wash!' Swish! Whack!

'Gur-mit the Ker-mit!' Swipe! Clout!

A boy in a turban suddenly levitated from the horizontal at Miss Harvey's feet, supporting his weight on his hands and tapping round in a circle with his toes. He collapsed on his bum and continued spinning, then flipped over and lay flat out on his stomach, panting.

'GET UP AT ONCE!' yelled Miss Harvey. The boy looked staggered when he achieved the vertical, as if it was in the nature of human beings to spin eternally on their rears in an anti-clockwise direction.

'WHAT IS YOUR NAME?' bellowed Miss Harvey. The boy blinked.

Gurinder Karwal leapt across the room and set about Satpal Singh's skull with a sports bag. 'Dick TURBAN, Miss. Get it? Get it?'

'SIT DOWN AND STAY DOWN!' screeched

Miss Harvey, snatching the sports bag from Gurinder who launched himself at a chair and hooked his knees round his desk legs and his arms round the chair back, with a martyred expression.

Miss Harvey ignored the 'Keep out. This means you' sign that was scrawled across the front of the sports bag. Inside was a rancid-looking kit and just one disintegrating exercise book. On the front was a cartoon showing someone with a very small head, very long teeth and horns, surrounded by other horned and toothsome creatures. Underneath were the words 'Abdul and the Vampires'. Miss Harvey turned the exercise book over. On the back it said, 'Better marks for Gurinder Karwal or else . . .'

Miss Harvey handed back the exercise book and sports bag. 'You'll work for the good marks in the lesson Gurinder. Or, if you must, in my room after school every Tuesday.'

Martin Larter winked heavily at Sharon Driver, stubbed out his cigarette and leaned lecherously towards Miss Harvey, placing his palms on her table. 'Is that a promise, Miss?'

Miss Harvey picked up a large dictionary and dropped it, just missing Martin Larter's fingers. 'Ner-vy!' said Miss Harvey. 'Must be the fags.'

She breathed deeply a couple of times. 'Now then. I shall take the register. Janie Binns.'

'Here, Miss.'

'Michael Deacon.'

'Miss.'

'Gurmit Kaur.' Gurmit, her lungs full of chalk dust from the blackboard duster bout, didn't answer but stuck up her hand.

'Gurinder Karwal.' Gurinder unhooked his knees and

elbows and pranced about in the aisle, grinning like something not right and jabbing a forefinger into his sternum.

'SIDDOWN!' screeched Miss Harvey. Her face had gone scarlet and her head was throbbing. 'This is ridiculous,' she thought, gulping fiercely. 'At this rate they'll precipitate apoplexy within the week.'

'Martin Larter.'

'Affirmative.'

Miss Harvey looked up at Martin. He was sitting directly in front of her table and she could see that he was writing the word 'affirmative' in beautiful curving letters on the front of his exercise book. She also noticed with some nervousness his gold signet ring, executive briefcase and the advanced nature of his spelling.

'Theresa Marshall.'

There was a long pause.

'Theresa Marshall.' Miss Harvey scanned the girls – all seven of them. You couldn't miss them because there was currently a craze in the fifth year for the girls to wear everything white – they thronged the corridors like choirs of angels (though their glory diminished somewhat as the day wore on). None of the off-white brigade responded.

Martin Larter looked up from inscribing 'Gomorrah' on his exercise book. 'I should try Terry, Miss.'

'Try Terry?'

'I'd try calling her Terry, Miss. She don't like Theresa.'

Miss Harvey flushed. '*Terry* Marshall then.'

There was a movement among the masculine ranks. Someone lifted an arm to just below half-mast. Miss Harvey peered through the chalk haze. Well, yes, it could be a girl. Her hair was cut as short as a boy's except for the front which hung down in a diamond shape almost to her nose. She was dressed entirely in black.

'Abdul Sheikh.'

A slight scuffling sound came from a heap of objects piled on a desk in front of Theresa. The heap shifted slightly and a small face peered out. Miss Harvey gave him the benefit of the doubt and marked him present. She began to dole out pieces of paper.

'What's this for, Miss?'

'Aw, Mi-iss! Not work!'

'Name on the piece of paper. First I want you to list your favourite TV programmes.' Actually Miss Harvey wanted to find out how many varieties their ability came in. She began to inspect progress, peering over shoulders. Sharon Driver, who'd got as far as 'Bruj' in an attempt to spell 'Bergerac', hastily inked this in and changed it to 'Top of the Poops'.

Miss Harvey had reached Abdul Sheikh. In minute handwriting in the very top right hand corner of the paper he'd written 'Abdul Sheikh'. Nothing else. He peered anxiously at Miss Harvey from the nest he'd made for himself from the sports bag, briefcase, parka, badminton racket and plastic mac. His top lip hovered in a nervous half-smile and Miss Harvey saw that his eye teeth were rather longer, sharper and whiter than is usual and 'Abdul and the Vampires' re-surfaced in her mind. Though anything less like a vampire, with the exception of his mandibles, than Abdul Sheikh, it was difficult to imagine.

'Why haven't you written anything yet, Abdul?' Abdul appeared to ignore the question. Miss Harvey noticed that he was touching the objects that went to make his nest and his lips were moving as if he was counting them. 'I think I've left something in the lobbies, Miss,' he said in a voice that matched his handwriting. 'Can I go and check?'

He looked so stricken that Miss Harvey said, 'I think

you'd better.' He shot off like a greyhound when they spring the door.

'You shouldn't of let him go off like that, Miss,' said Sharon Driver. ''E only goes to see the taps is turned off. 'E's a bit . . .' and she tapped vigorously on the side of her head.

Gurmit Kaur looked up. 'Yeah, you 'ave to watch 'im, Miss. 'E eats cement.'

'He does *what*?'

''E 'ad to go to the 'ead las' year, Miss. For eatin' cement. *And* the plaster out of walls.'

Miss Harvey thought of the sharp white eye teeth and shuddered.

Gurmit turned round. ''E's better'n 'e used to be, though, in' he? Remember when Feroz Razak left? 'E shut 'isself in with about ten desks.'

At that moment Theresa Marshall cried out in pain. 'Aw, Mi-iss!' She had a voice like a cheese grater. Miss Harvey looked across the room, ready to bawl her out, but stopped herself. There was blood running down Theresa's chin! Her mind dashed unfairly to Abdul, then remembered he was out of the room.

'Whatever have you done, Theresa . . . Terry?'

Theresa spread the blood round her chin with a tissue heavily soaked in green felt tip. 'Cut me gob, Miss.'

'Mouth, Miss.'

Theresa stared. 'I'm not Miss. I'm Terry.' She giggled.

Miss Harvey ignored this. 'What did you cut your *mouth* on, Terry?'

'That piece of paper you give us, Miss.'

'However did you manage that?'

'Lickin' the edge of it, Miss.'

Miss Harvey gave her a look. By now she'd reached the front. She knew which ones could spell. That meant she knew which ones could read. She was taking note too of those who couldn't sit still. Next lesson they'd read plays. Anyone who fell into both categories would be given a major role.

Martin Larter looked up from the dictionary and caught Miss Harvey looking at him. Immediately he said, 'What does "sodomy" mean, Miss?'

Miss Harvey looked hurriedly sideways. 'I beg your pardon?'

Martin Larter's eyes narrowed. 'What does "sodality" mean, Miss?'

Miss Harvey had recovered in any case. '*You* have the dictionary, Martin. Not I.'

At that moment Abdul Sheikh crept round the door. He was panting a little, as if he'd whizzed round every tap in the school to see if it was in the off-position, and looked very worn out. He shrank back into his nest and touched each of its materials to see if they were all still present, then began to attack his name with a biro. By the time Miss Harvey had arrived to see if he'd succeeded in writing anything at all, she discovered only a gaping black hole where before it had said Abdul Sheikh. As she looked over his shoulder Abdul got more and more agitated. 'I'm not sure I gave my maths book in to Mr Wallace, Miss. Can I go and check?'

Miss Harvey was ten minutes wiser. 'What? In my English lesson, Abdul? No, you may not!'

The bell rang at that moment, releasing the luckless Abdul. Miss Harvey decided to go to the staff room via the office to look up Abdul's file. It made sad reading. It said in big letters across the front COMPULSIVE CHECKER. Abdul had moved from his junior school straight to the top of the first division. But his years at

Davenport had seen him bump down through the sets, one by one by one.

Back in the staff room she said to Mr Wallace, 'What's Theresa Marshall like?'

Mr Wallace grinned. 'Oh, that one? An *enfant terrible* even in her first year. She threw a jelly at a lad who said it wobbled like a girl.'

■

Tez sometimes came on the air on a Sunday evening when he went with his dad to fill up with Derv, ready for Monday's early start. Abdul had had a bad weekend. His left eye tooth had started hurting and he was just wondering whether he'd turned the taps fully off after having his Sunday night bath when he heard the familiar, 'Breaker two one. This is Truckin' Tez calling. Is there anybody on two one?' A bead of sweat ran down Abdul's backbone and he found himself saying, 'Roger, Truckin' Tez. I copy you.' His reply came out in a wild squeak.

There was a slight pause and then Tez said gruffly, 'Do you have yourself a handle?'

Abdul's pyjama jacket was sticking to his back. He clenched his nails into the back of his hands, willing himself to find inspiration. His reply was squeakier than ever, 'Yeah, this is The Vamp.'

There was another long pause and then, 'Roger, The Vamp. Are you mobile or home base?'

Abdul coughed. 'Home base, Tez.'

'And are you still at kiddy campus, The Vamp? How many candles are you burning?'

Was he still at school? Well, no point in making out he was older than he was. He tried to answer Tez in the manner of the other C.B.ers. The language was all right but his voice was still as high as a girl's. 'I'm burnin' sixteen candles. How 'bout you?' He knew the answer but it'd keep Tez talking.

'Affirmative, The Vamp.'

There was a long pause. Abdul panicked. 'You in a big wheeler, Tez?'

'Yeah, I'm in me dad's fourteen wheeler.'

'And what's your twenty, Tez?'

'Jus' come off the dual carriageway at Heath Lane and heading for the small doughnut where Heath Lane meets Roylston Road. We're gonna fill up with motion-lotion.'

Abdul nodded. The mini roundabout. Yes, he knew where they were. The garage was only about five minutes away from his house. 'An' what'll you be doin' after that, Tez?'

'Oh, go to the chew-n-choke. You know the score.' Abdul nodded enviously. What a life! Travelling all over the country. Eating out in transport cafés.

'What you been doin' this evenin', then, The Vamp?'

Abdul couldn't very well say he'd been thinking of filing down his teeth. 'Oh . . . not that much, Tez. Y'know how it is.'

'Yeah. Well, mebbe you an' me could have an eyeball nex' Sunday in Macdonald's 'cos me dad'll be away then.'

A long silence followed. Tez came on again, sounding impatient. 'Do you read me, you Ding-a-Ling? Got your ear flaps on, or are you mutton Jeff?'

Abdul coughed again. 'Got a touch of the mike fright, Tez.'

'Hey! Don' be like that! You an' me are buddies, right, good buddy? How 'bout this eyeball then?'

Abdul's voice was so high it'd take bats' ears to catch the register. 'I got these rrrrrrrr teeth, Tez.'

'You got *what*, The Vamp?'

Abdul squeaked. 'I got rrrrrrr teeth, Tez.'

Tez was giggling fit to burst. 'We all got TEETH, good buddy.'

Abdul felt as if he was choking. 'My teeth, they're like . . . BIG.'

Tez was laughing more than ever. 'So what, you great turkey? I ain' so beautiful myself. We're mates, good buddy. Got that? I'll catch you again, same channel, same time tomorrow night, O.K.? Ten ten. Let your mike hand slack till I call you back.'

Abdul was grinning. 'Roger D, Tez. I'll catch you again. Take care. Ten ten.'

'Magic numbers on you. Cut out now. You take care. Truckin' Tez leavin' the air.'

∎

The next morning Miss Harvey sensed a change in Abdul Sheikh. He was only carrying his briefcase and this he put straight down on the floor. When she gave the class a punctuation exercise to do he settled down to it right away and didn't start excavating his name as he had done on a previous occasion.

Miss Harvey settled down to her first year marking. With a sigh she picked up 'A Ghostly Tale' number six hundred and forty three. 'This thing had a body like a man but its face was a little diferent. It had one eye in the midle of its forehead and its hair was all green. Its hands met my neck. They strated to squeaze. By this time my wife had fainted. Its fingers pocked into my neck. Blood squitted out. It was revolting.' Miss Harvey shuddered and shifted.

There was a slight disturbance. Theresa Marshall was waving a hand. 'Miss. Please, Miss.'

'Yes?'

'What's a vamp, Miss?'

Teaching fifth year 'non-exam' was giving Miss Harvey a weather eye and a nervous grin. The weather eye was aware of Abdul Sheikh snatching up his school bag, shaking out books and erecting a quick motte and bailey. She tried to concentrate on the matter in hand.

'A vamp? Well, a vamp's a fast woman. You know, Theresa? A flirt.'

It was clear that her answer was not to Theresa's liking. She batted away Miss Harvey's explanation as if it was a mosquito and spat out, 'I'm not Theresa. I'm Tez.'

Now Miss Harvey was aware of a great deal of agitated movement. As soon as Theresa said 'Tez' there was a distinct flurry from Abdul Sheikh. He turned round to stare in horror at Theresa and as he turned, his top lip flew up and his distinctive eye chompers were revealed in all their glory. He looked as wild as a horse when it blasts out its nostrils and rolls its eyes.

Theresa gazed in fascinated horror. Words re-bounded in her head. 'Teeth . . . they're like . . . BIG.' The Vamp . . . could it be short for . . . Vampire? Of course! Well, well, well! Abdul 'Megabite' Sheikh! And there she was thinking The Vamp was a girl! The worst kind of girl too – Melanie Fish-like and wet! Well, thank God for that! She wrote a quick note to Abdul. 'You got *nice* teeth. Smile more. Try it.'

But when Abdul received the note he grew more agitated than ever. He added the briefcase to the pile of exercise books. This was a severe case of overloading and the ramparts collapsed under the strain. Theresa watched sympathetically as Abdul set about his name.

At the end of the lesson she caught up with him as he bolted from the mobile. 'How 'bout you coming in the truck with me and dad one Sunday?' Then when his eyes lit up only to dull again she said, 'Don' worry, Abdul. I ain' *that* much of a girl!'

■

From that day Abdul and Theresa were inseparable. Miss Harvey watched the compulsion to check fade in Abdul, and his nest drop away twig by twig. The other kids didn't take much notice. Abdul had never counted as one of the lads and Theresa had written off the girls. These days Abdul took all his worries to Theresa, even down to detailing every time he got a pang in a tooth. At last she said, 'Shut *up*, Abdul! You're gettin' to be a pain in the jaw.'

Abdul aimed a punch at her, then winced and put his hand to his mouth.

'You should go to the dentist, Abdul.'

'Can't.'

'Why not?'

'Cos they'd laugh.'

Theresa giggled. 'Abdul, dentists are paid not to laugh. When did you go last, anyway?'

Abdul couldn't remember. Not since his eye teeth had accelerated.

Theresa calculated. 'Ab-dul, you can't have been in *eight years.*'

■

It was Jeanie Parkes's idea to present awards at the leaving assembly for the fifth years. 'Mr Joseph won't mind. He can give them out after the usual sorry-to-be-leaving-the-fifth-year stuff.'

The award presentation followed a farewell ode to the school by Mathew Davidson, 'There is much of me that is in this football shirt . . .' (he was leaving his school effects to Davenport as they'd be worth a lot when he became a famous old boy). The school wriggled and the head looked solemn throughout.

He cheered up, though, when it came to the awarding of the prizes. 'Most economical use of resources, Melanie Fish's skirt.' Melanie swivelled to the front in an electric blue mini over a shocking pink lycra to ear-splitting cat calls from the junior school.

'Arif Kasmani wins the school physics prize for Inertia.' The school clapped and jeered.

'Sangita Gohil – the Ayatollah Khomenei prize for Fluff.' Sangita shimmied up in a pea green hat with a veil and ostrich feather, elbow high lace black gloves and a peacock feather boa. The school whistled.

'The memorial chamber pot for eccentric behaviour goes to Dave Petrovic.' Great guffaws.

'The Kepler Award for Mass Movement Studies to the dinner queue.' The school tittered.

'Keith Birchett for the most meaningful contribution to school debate.' Everybody craned their necks. Who *was* Keith Birchett? Oh, *that* one. Nobody could ever remember him saying a thing!

Abdul Sheikh – 'The Boris Karloff Award for Teeth,' intoned the headmaster, and Pete Birkenshawe at the piano broke into a spirited rendering of 'Fangs Ain't What They Used to Be' just as someone started drilling for oil in Abdul's right tooth. He let out a howl that would have put any full-blooded werewolf to shame, and five members of staff leapt simultaneously to their feet and frog-marched him from the room, while the whole school, hair bristling and scalps tingling, swivelled in horrified glee to witness Abdul Sheikh finally throwing a wobbly in their midst. 'Alas, poor Abdul,' murmured Dave Petrovic. 'I knew him a little.'

There was only Theresa Marshall who guessed at the sobering truth: that a trip to the eight-years-spurned dentist could no longer be postponed.

■

Abdul returned triumphantly half-way through Miss Harvey's English lesson to show Theresa his gaps.

'How was it?' she asked tenderly.

'Sho sho. Ah cart eek fut fut arse.'

'Ah! Poor thing!'

'What did he say?' asked Miss Harvey anxiously.

Theresa looked at Miss Harvey in astonishment. 'He can't eat for four hours. Never mind, Abdul,' she added soothingly. 'Straight after English I'll make you a nice jelly.'

Miss Harvey laughed, remembering what Mr Wallace had told her. Theresa looked steadily at her, then turned to Abdul. 'And *tomorrow* night I shall expect you to do me a nice S-T-A-K-E, Abdul. That, or a Vampire Vindaloo.'

Rubber Plant

Varsha Bhatti didn't have a proper friend until Dawn Lockwood came to Davenport half-way through the spring term. Varsha was shy and quiet and the other girls didn't bother with her much. It was Dawn Lockwood's rubber collection that brought her and Varsha together.

Miss Harvey had been talking to the second years about collecting things. When Miss Harvey was a kid she'd collected everything – bus tickets, stamps, train and car numbers, cards out of bubble gum and Ty-Phoo tea packets, old coins, old birds' nests, shells – you name it, Miss Harvey had collected it. She said she wanted the second years to bring into school their most favourite thing that they'd ever collected – the whole collection if they could manage it – to show it to the others and talk about it.

So Tez Tindale brought in his collection of old bottles and talked about how he went looking for them on dumps, Fergie Fish brought in glass marbles, Varsha, her pressed flowers, and Sharon Marriott, live beetles in a jar. But it was Dawn Lockwood's rubber collection that everybody liked best.

Dawn had rubbers of every shape and size. She had a strawberry rubber that smelt of strawberries, a light bulb rubber, a rubber like a lollipop with a bell hanging off it, a football rubber, a woolly sheep rubber and a rubber like a dice. She had spotted rubbers, stripy rubbers, tubby rubbers, slim rubbers, plain rubbers, patterned rubbers, rubbers like playing cards, rubbers with flowers on them, a clown's face that was a rubber at the end of a pencil and a pencil sharpener like an ice-cream cone where the ice-cream was the rubber. She had every kind of rubber you could think of – one hundred and four rubbers in all. She carried them around on an enormous board to which she stuck them with Blu-tack. They were always falling off.

Everybody gathered around after the lesson to admire Dawn Lockwood's one hundred and four rubbers and they stayed on throughout break. Varsha shyly asked Dawn if she could have another look at them at the end of afternoon school and Dawn gave her a funny look and said she could if she liked.

That was how they became friends.

'What's yer name?' Dawn asked Varsha as she fingered the strawberry rubber with a longing look in her eyes. She picked it up off the board.

'Varsha.'

'Varsha what?'

'Varsha Bhatti.'

Dawn grinned. 'I shall call you Batty then.'

Varsha didn't want to be called Batty, but she didn't like to say so. Dawn's grin was fierce! Besides, she knew Dawn called everybody names. For example, she called Miss Harvey Fang Face.

'Your name's Dawn Lockwood, isn't it?'

'No-o!'

Varsha looked surprised. 'But Miss said you were called Dawn Lockwood when she introduced you to the class.'

'So? I *was* called Dawn Lockwood until las' week. But me mam's left me dad, and she don't want me calling meself Lockwood no more. I'm Dawn Stewart now 'cos me mam was called Stewart before she married me dad.'

Varsha nodded, looking upset.

'What's a' matter with you?'

'Well, it's sad.'

'What's sad?'

'Your mam leaving your dad.'

'What's sad about it? 'E knocked 'er around. Any road, he weren't me proper dad.'

'So Mr . . . Stewart. He was your proper dad?'

'Was 'e 'eck! Me proper dad was Pete Deacon. Then me mam left 'im for Kevin Stewart and I wouldn't call meself Stewart *then*. But now I couldn't care less.' She shrugged.

Varsha didn't know what to say. She just stared at the strawberry rubber in her hand. It looked like a little fat heart.

Dawn gave her another funny look. 'You can 'ave that rubber if you like.'

Varsha felt herself blushing. 'Oh, no, I couldn't.' She put it down fast.

''Course you could. 'Ere, take it.' She handed it back to Varsha. 'I've got another one at home. You can 'ave these 'n' all.' She handed her the lollipop with the bell, the playing card and the dice.

Varsha was so pleased she didn't know what to say. She zipped the rubbers into her pencil case as if they were diamonds.

Dawn was shoving the board into a huge bag. Varsha didn't want her to go off just yet.

'What was your last school like?'

Dawn pulled a face. 'Rubbish. A dump. Dead strict. Not like this one. There we was contained.'

'What do you mean, you was contained?'

'They wouldn't let us do 'owt. You couldn't move from your place or leave the classroom. The teachers came to you: you didn't go to them. They said we was contained.'

Varsha nodded. 'It doesn't sound very nice. But they're quite strict here.'

Dawn looked scornful. 'No they ain't! They're soft!'

The other girls in the class couldn't stand Dawn but the lads really went for her. Christopher Crutchley even got round to asking her out. 'Go out with *you*,' sneered Dawn. 'I ain' that desperate!'

Christopher Crutchley, who had recently become the most fancied lad in the second year, looked amazed, then unconvinced. He tore a piece of paper from his geography book. ''Ere's me phone number,' he said, scribbling on it. 'Case you change your mind.'

Dawn laughed. 'I don' travel with phone numbers.' She ripped the paper into little pieces and threw them in Christopher's face.

Varsha thought Dawn was wonderful, the way she dealt with the lads. If any of them laughed at Varsha or pulled her plaits, Dawn'd menace them with a chair as though they were lions.

The teachers didn't like her, though, any more than the girls did. She was always being sent to Mrs Palmer, the deputy head, for being rude. In the end Dawn suggested to the deputy head that she might like her to chop some wood in the yard whenever she was rude. The deputy head took her up on this suggestion. Wood chopping seemed to be the only thing that kept Dawn quiet. Very soon Dawn didn't bother going to lessons because she always got sent out anyway. 'Deputy 'ead wants me,' she'd tell the teacher at the beginning of the lesson, 'to go and chop some wood.' The only lesson

Dawn went to was English with Miss Harvey. Though she was always late for that.

She'd come in grinning. 'Sorry I'm late, Miss. 'Ad to see the deputy 'ead.'

'That sounds grave.'

'It were a social call, Miss. She wanted me to chop some wood.'

Varsha didn't believe Dawn *was* chopping wood half the time. She suspected she went off into town.

Sometimes it worried Varsha that Dawn was her best friend. She knew what her mum and dad'd say if they knew. 'A lazy no-good person. Stay away.' But Varsha didn't think she could. It was interesting, having a friend like Dawn.

She couldn't make Dawn's family out at all. She'd been to her house once or twice when her mam was out and they seemed quite rich. They had a video, a stereo, squeaky leather furniture, mushroom-shaped lamps with stainless steel stands, a shaggy carpet and a cocktail bar with stools in one corner of the living room. Yet Dawn hadn't got a winter coat.

She always said she didn't need a coat. But she shivered like anything when she and Varsha were waiting at the bus stop after school. Miss Harvey walked by one afternoon when Dawn was crouching, hugging herself and going brrrrrrrrrrhhhhhhhhhh. She stopped.

'Don't you need a coat, Dawn?'

'Brrrrrrrrrrrhhhhhhh. No, I'm hot, Miss.'

'Are you sure?'

'Brrrrrrrrrhhhhhhhh. 'Course I'm sure, Miss. Brrrrrrrrrrhhhhhhhhh.'

But she was still shivering after five minutes in the warm bus. That was the night she told Varsha that she was dead fed up with her mam.

'How come?'

'Well, she's always gettin' new stuff. Y'know, clothes an' that. And she doesn't give me 'owt.'

'Don't you ever get new things?'

'If I do, I get 'em meself.' She gave Varsha her funny look. '*When* I get the money, that is. *When!*'

'What's she got?'

'Oh, a jump-suit. Them shoes that tie with laces round your legs. All stuff like that.' Dawn looked fierce. 'Know what? Bet I could fight anyone on this bus!'

Varsha didn't doubt it. Her only fear was that some day she might try!'

It was true Dawn never had any money of her own. Not long after this she broke her arm.

'What happened to you, Dawn?' asked Miss Muldoon, 2M's house tutor.

'Fell out of a tree, Miss,' said Dawn cheerfully. 'Can't give nothing to class charity this week, Miss. I *did* 'ave 5p. But it's got stuck up me pot.'

It was hard sometimes being Dawn's friend because she was always telling lies. She told Miss Harvey that the dustbin men had walked off with her school bag when she left it outside the front door while she went round the back to pick a winter cabbage. Varsha knew it was a lie because Dawn's bag was hanging at that very moment on her peg in the lobbies. Besides, Dawn's house didn't have a proper garden, never mind a winter cabbage. It was just that Dawn hadn't done her English homework and she didn't want Miss Harvey to know.

Dawn peered from under her eyelashes at Miss Harvey to see how she'd taken the lie. She didn't look too convinced. So Dawn turned on the tears.

Miss Harvey eyed her nervously. 'What's the matter now, Dawn?'

'It's me rabbit, Miss. It died last night.'

Varsha was so taken aback that she'd said, 'But she hasn't got a rabbit, Miss!' before she could stop herself.

Dawn glared at her. 'Me budgie then.'

After Miss Harvey had finished with her, Dawn came up to Varsha and twisted her arm up her back till the tears came. 'Swear you won't ever grass on me again, right?' Wincing, Varsha swore she never would again.

Meanwhile, the rubber collection grew. Dawn now had a rainbow rubber, a camera rubber, a Miss Piggy rubber and one like an electronic game. So she passed some of her old ones on to Varsha. 'I've got two of them already.'

'Where do you get all your rubber collection from?'

'All over the place. Me mam gives 'em me mostly. For little presents and that.' Varsha was just going to say that she'd thought Dawn's mam never gave her anything when she remembered the arm twist and stopped.

Dawn's rubber collection was famous by now. Miss Harvey even asked Dawn if she'd give the first years a private viewing the next evening after school. Dawn said she might. After school that day she said to Varsha, 'Comin' up town?'

'What do you want to go for?'

'Oh, I dunno. This and that. 'Ave a look round.'

Varsha went. The shop where Dawn wanted to look round was a toy shop. It hadn't been opened long. The stuff there was great, really different. But very expensive. Varsha hadn't dared go in before. 'Well, *I* don' wanna go in jus' yet,' said Dawn when Varsha told her. 'S'too empty. We'll come back in a bit.'

Varsha stared at her. Usually you left going into shops because they were too *full*, not too empty. But she'd learned to keep her mouth shut now where Dawn was

concerned. They went for a milk shake and by the time
they got back there were quite a few people in the shop.

Varsha thought it was wonderful. She wandered round
and round, looking at the toys and novelties. Her
favourites were a mobile shaped like a seagull, a Pooh
bear that snapped out of a honey-pot when you jerked a
stick, a three-storey dolls' house and a tea-pot with legs.
She liked the joke basket too – mustard sweets and blue
mouth sweets, pencils made of rubber that bent when
you tried to write with them, cushions that made a rude
noise when you sat on them and 5ops with suction
pads to stick them to the floor. There was a basket with
all different kinds of rubbers in too. Varsha had looked at
these when she'd first come in and now she made up her
mind that she was going to buy one and build a rubber
collection of her own. It'd never be a quarter as good as
Dawn's, of course. But she'd got Dawn's rejects to make
a beginning and at least she could have a go.

She was at the far end of the shop when she made this
decision and in a part that was up a little step. As she
turned round she had a good view of the shop. She saw
Dawn glance quickly round her – she was over by the
rubber basket – and shovel about ten rubbers into her
bag!

Varsha didn't know what to do. She blushed with fear.
Dawn had now turned away from the rubbers basket and
was looking at the jokes. What ought she to do? Tell
Dawn she'd seen her and make her put the rubbers back?
Fat chance of that – she hadn't a hope! Tell the shopkeeper? She went hot and cold at the thought. Besides,
she'd sworn to Dawn that she'd never grass on her again.
In her confusion she walked over to the rubbers and
began fingering them, trying to decide what to do, then
looked up in horror to see that the shopkeeper had moved

sideways away from her customers to get a better view of what was going on in her shop. She was staring straight at Varsha with a very suspicious look on her face. Varsha guessed what she might be thinking, and fled!

Outside the shop she thought fast, then rushed round the corner off the main road, up one street and down another and into a maze of side streets. She ran on and on. She knew that when Dawn realized she'd left the shop she'd come charging after her, and she couldn't face her at the moment. She needed time to think. She ran all the way home. She told her mum she didn't want any tea, she didn't feel too good, and went up to her bedroom and cried.

Dawn would be bound to guess that she'd seen her nick the rubbers, wouldn't she, running off like that? And what had the shopkeeper thought? *She* hadn't seen Dawn take the rubbers because she'd been serving then and the queue had blocked her view of the rubber basket. But if she could tell afterwards that some of the rubbers were missing, she'd be bound to suspect that Varsha herself . . . But she didn't dare even *think* about that.

Oh, why had she panicked and run off like that? What was she going to *do*? She wished she dared tell her mum and dad about it all, but she knew she never would dare. What would they say if they knew her best friend was a thief?

That night she couldn't get to sleep. Her forehead felt hot and she kept turning this way and that, trying to find a cool spot. She told her mum the next morning that she didn't feel very well and she didn't think she'd better go to school. But her mum took her temperature and declared that it was normal – she'd have to go.

When Dawn came into the classroom – late – for registration she stopped for a moment as she went past

Varsha's desk. 'Jus' remember, Batty, you swore you'd never grass on me again. Right?'

Varsha didn't look at her. She kept her head right down so Dawn couldn't see she was crying.

That day seemed to drag on and on. The other kids wanted to know why Varsha and Dawn weren't speaking and they kept pestering. And for the first time in ages Varsha went home all by herself.

But there was a worse shock to come the next day. After Rugby Joe had stopped telling them at the end of assembly that some fool had pulled the calor gas screw off in the mobiles and they could all have been blown to bits, he said, 'I want years one, two and three girls to remain behind for a few minutes now, please, as I have something very serious to say to them. Right, the rest of you, you may stand.'

When the others had filed out of the hall, the head left his tall reading desk and came round to face the lower school. 'I'm afraid we may have criminals in the making in this company,' he said sternly. 'Some items were stolen from a local toy shop the evening before last and the owner has good reason to suspect someone from this school may have been responsible. She saw a girl in our school uniform acting rather strangely. If you know anything about this, will you come up and have a word with me about it?' Rugby Joe took a step forward and frowned. 'Right NOW.'

Varsha felt as if any minute she'd go up in flames. Nobody moved. Further down the second year line Dawn Stewart sat on like stone.

The head waited for a moment or two. Then he said, 'In that case, I'm afraid I'm going to have to ask you all to do something rather unpleasant. The owner of the shop has come into school this morning and I want you to walk out past her now in case she can spot the young woman she'd like to question further. I don't want to have to ask you to do this and it's still not too late for anyone who knows more about what happened in a town toy shop the night before last to speak to me in confidence about it.' He paused. Varsha shut her eyes tight and willed Dawn to own up but, of course, nobody moved. 'Now stand,' said the head.

Shaking, Varsha looked across to the main door out of the hall. Sure enough, there was the toy shop owner, with . . . oh, no! A policeman!

The lower school girls filed past the head and the other adults, very subdued. Even though they hadn't nicked from the toy shop, some had taken things from other shops in their time, and even the innocent ones felt as if they were guilty even though they weren't.

Dawn was ahead of Varsha but Varsha knew the shopkeeper wouldn't recognize her. She'd had her back to the woman, after all, when she'd taken the rubbers, and anyway the queue in the shop had blocked the woman's view. Besides, what Dawn wore for school wasn't uniform in the way that Varsha's was. Varsha even had the proper coloured mac!

She felt almost calm, now she knew what trouble she'd be in. 'All I can do,' she thought, 'is to tell the truth. Say it wasn't me. Say I know who did do it but I can't tell because I promised I wouldn't. They've *got* to believe me.' But she knew they didn't have to believe her at all.

Although her feet felt almost too heavy to pick up as she shuffled closer and closer to the shop owner, she held her head high and breathed deeply, determined not to cry. She was near there now. She tried to walk steadily towards the woman but everything was spinning. As if through a mist she heard the shop owner say, 'Yes, I'd like to have a word with this one if I may.'

The head looked in surprised horror at Varsha. 'Oh, now, Mrs Greene. I think you must be mistaken.' He waved the other children quickly on. Miss Harvey, who was filing out with the second year because she taught 2G English first lesson, stopped.

'Oh, I don't think I am,' said the woman with a shuddering laugh. 'I think the sergeant should look in her bag and see what he finds there. I very much fear that this is the one.'

The head spoke kindly to Varsha. 'I'm sorry we have to do this, Varsha, but it's only to clear your name. You have nothing to fear if you didn't take the rubbers. I think we'd better go upstairs to my office.' They all, including Miss Harvey, made their way upstairs. Kids on their way to first lesson turned round when they went past them, to stare. When they reached the head's office Varsha found she couldn't say anything at all.

She was already crying when the policeman took her pencil case out of her bag, unzipped it and tipped the contents on to Mr Joseph's desk. Biros, pencils, a protractor and a plastic ruler fell out – and one, two, three, four, five, six, seven, eight, nine, ten rubbers. The woman pointed in triumph to the strawberry, the lollipop, the dice and all the rest. 'What did I tell you? I have all these in stock.'

All Varsha could do now was to take a deep breath, look straight at the head and say, 'I didn't do it, Sir. I *was* in the shop but it was . . . somebody else. I can't tell you who.'

The head looked sadly at her. 'All right. But just tell us where you got all these rubbers from then, Varsha.' Varsha stared back and slowly she shook her head. A tear dripped off the end of her nose.

Then she heard Miss Harvey. 'Since it's *rubbers* that are the problem, Mr Joseph, I believe there *is* someone else we ought to have a word with. Excuse me.' She left the hall and came back a few moments later with a scowling Dawn, carrying her big bag. She didn't look at Varsha.

'Show Mr Joseph your rubber collection, Dawn,' demanded Miss Harvey.

Sullenly Dawn pulled out her board. When she saw how many rubbers emerged from the bag the shop owner looked rather taken aback.

'Where did you get all these rubbers from, Dawn?' asked Mr Joseph, staring in horrified disbelief.

'Me mam, most of 'em,' said Dawn crisply, staring straight in front of her and never blushing for a second. 'Phone 'er and ask 'er if you like. The number's 612413. She's at 'ome. Go on. Phone 'er if you don' believe me.' For the first time Dawn looked scornfully across at Varsha, 'Oh, and Varsha Bhatti. She give me a few an' all.'

The head reached for the phone, his eyes on Varsha who'd cried out in protest. She heard the phone ring at the other end and a voice say sharply, 'Yes?'

'This is Mr Joseph, Davenport Secondary. I'm afraid to disturb you, Mrs Lock . . . Stewart, but I'm afraid there's been a bit of trouble at school, and I wondered if you could clear up one point. You know Dawn has a very fine rubber collection?' There was a moment's pause, then Varsha heard Dawn's mum snap, 'Yes.'

'Well, I wonder if you could tell me where Dawn got all her rubbers from?' There was another pause, then Mrs Stewart said, 'I give 'er 'em, of course.'

'Thank you, Mrs Stewart,' said Mr Joseph, looking grave. 'That's all I wanted to know.'

When he put the phone down he said, 'I think I ought

to have a word with your parents too now, Varsha. What is their number, please?'

Then Varsha really panicked. She couldn't bear her parents knowing she was involved in all this. It'd just about kill her mum. Her eyes flew to Dawn's rubber collection, looking for something, anything, a clue, that would put the head off phoning. And she saw a rubber that she hadn't seen before. It was a rubber plant pot with little plastic flowers growing out of it.

She pointed at it. 'How much did that cost, Dawn?'

Dawn shrugged. ' 'Ow should I know? You 'eard what me mam said. She bought me the rubbers.'

'Where did she buy that rubber plant?'

There was only one place in town that sold novelty rubbers, as Dawn very well knew. Instead of shrugging and saying, ' 'Ow should I know?' again, which she could've if she'd slowed down and thought, she jerked her head towards Mrs Greene, ' 'Er shop, I s'pose.'

Varsha didn't know why she was carrying on asking questions. She was getting nowhere fast.

'*When* did she buy it for you?'

'I dunno. Sometime las' week.'

This time it was Mrs Greene's head that jerked. '*That's* a lie. They only came into the shop the day before yesterday. It's a new line.'

Dawn turned on Varsha. 'Grass! Grass! You're just a little grass!'

■

It was all around the school in no time that Dawn was for it. Varsha didn't start the rumours. She hadn't spoken to Dawn since she'd called her a grass and given herself away.

Miss Harvey saw to it that some of the other kids from the second year called for Varsha every day and she went home with them in the afternoon too. Slowly she was making new friends.

And Dawn no longer chopped wood. She was in every lesson for as long as the teachers could stand it before off-loading her on the deputy head. The teacher who got the most cheek from her nowadays was Miss Harvey.

One day at the end of school Varsha was behind Miss Harvey in the corridor when she heard her shout, 'And you can stop scratching the paintwork with that coin, Dawn Stewart.'

Dawn turned on her. 'I *ain'* Dawn Stewart no more, so there. Me mam got married last Satday and me name's Dawn Heathcoat now. *And* we're movin' to Derby 'cos me new dad's setting up on 'is own, so I'm through with this dump for good.' And she went off laughing down the corridor without a backward look.

■

Varsha gave her own small rubber collection away the day Dawn left. Mrs Greene, the shop owner, had let her keep the rubbers Dawn had given her, by way of an apology. She'd thrown in the rubber plant as well, 'for your detective work'. Whenever Varsha had wanted to rub something out she'd groped around in her pencil case for her favourite strawberry rubber. But the one her fingers had always seemed to close on was the rubber plant.

Pantomime Horse

Helena Kirby-Monckton came to Davenport Secondary from a pricey private school where they taught her how to make *sole julienne*, *crème brulée* and *thé au citron*, but not how to spell fish and chips, ice cream and a pot of tea.

Pete Birkenshawe, arriving ten minutes late for Miss Harvey's English lesson, drew in breath when he saw her. Her grey eyes watched him as he removed his rucksack and bobble hat and struggled out of his cagoule.

Miss Harvey's brown eyes watched Pete Birkenshawe. '*Why* is it necessary, Peter, to appear in my lessons as if you have just descended the north face of the Eiger? It is a playground you have to cross, and not an Arctic steppe. And why are you ten minutes late?' Pete blinked, removed his glasses and breathed heavily on them. 'Well, Miss, I just went along to the post office at break and there was this great long queue that stretched out even to the crack of doom.' He grinned winningly at Miss Harvey.

'Yes, well, it would do, wouldn't it?' snapped back Miss Harvey, 'seeing as it's pension day.'

Helena Kirby-Monckton, having taken stock of Peter Birkenshawe's cag, bobble hat and 'Cat lovers against the bomb' badge, returned to the essay that would indicate whether she was 'O' level material with a sneer. Pete Birkenshawe caught sight of the sneer. He squinted savagely at the essay title Miss Harvey had put on the board. 'What themes are developed in Act Two of *Macbeth*?' He stabbed at his file paper with his compasses. 'Say it with flowers,' he scrawled across his Arden edition. 'Send her a triffid.' Then he addressed himself vehemently to the task in hand.

'The themes developed in act two of *Macbeth* are cruelty (physical), torment (mental), stabbings and THE FAILURE OF LOVE. It isn't fair, as Duncan does not deserve to die. It is not his fault that Macbeth is tempted by his black and deep desires. Towards the end of the act important themes are greed, blood, murder and THE BETRAYAL OF LOVE (specially on Macbeth's part).' He looked up from his work and glowered at Helena Kirby-Monckton's back.

When the bell went Miss Harvey approached Helena with an encouraging smile. The smile grew rather thin as she scanned Helena's endeavours. She handed the sheet back and said, 'I don't think "O" level is going to be quite the best use of your time with us, Helena. I'll see Mr Revitt about some individual help.' Helena looked dashed but Pete perked up now he knew she was thick. 'Can I see what you put?' he asked casually when Miss Harvey had gone out of the room. Helena handed over her essay, too low to resist.

Peter didn't learn much from her essay on 'Myslef'.

∎Myslef∎

My name is Helena Kirby-Monckton and my favrit hoby is cookray. I like to cook cordon blue and use the sliver and crine darbay and arrang the flars.
When I leave school I shall strat wrok on busyness lunges it will be a good job with a good celery.

Pete looked impressed if mystified.

'What's cordon blue and crine darbay?'

Helena Kirby-Monckton looked sniffily at him. 'Cordon blue's French cookray and Crine Darbay's Crine Darbay.'

Pete nodded. 'Yes, but what *is* crine darbay?'

'Crine Darbay? Well, it's china. Pottray? You know?'

Pete didn't. He'd take it step by step.

'What's crine?'

'Crine? Well, like Her Majstay. She wears a crine.'

Pete got it. 'Oh, Crown *Der*by.' She was gathering up her things so he said quickly, 'Where do you live, Helena?'

'Cinterswell.'

It had a familiar ring.

'Come again.'

'*Cin*terswell.'

Pete recalled Crine Darbay and applied it like a code breaker. 'Oh, Counterswell.' He nodded. 'Very nice.' Counterswell was one of the poshest suburbs on the other side of town.

Helena was looking at him as if he was moronic. 'Yes, Cinterswell. It's what I said.'

Pete registered his rating on the morons scale and smiled enigmatically. 'Do you like music, Helena?'

Helena looked down her left cheek at him. 'Only the clarssics.'

Pete banished Siouxsie and the Banshees at a stroke. 'Oh, same *har*. Only the clarssics for me.'

Arif Kasmani, the richest lad in the fifth year, stuck his head round the door. 'Coming, Helena?' Pete watched her simper and blush. He scrutinized their progress across the playground. He couldn't believe it. Not that creep! He wasn't even literate. (He was in the science fifth.)

In the showers after games he tackled Arif about her. 'How come you know that new girl, then, Kasmani?'

Arif sprayed his dark armpits with 'Stud' and smiled a smug smile. 'We live next door to them in Carlton Grange Road, Birkenshawe, ectualleah. My dad recommended Davenport to her dad when she wasn't making too much headwayeah academicalleah at the Roylston Academeah.'

Pete nodded in gloom. He didn't like the idea of the two of them discussing his cagoule over a stirrup cup in millionaires' row.

That night he spent from five to six in town reading record sleeves. He caught up with Helena Kirby-Monckton next day at dinner time as she was crossing the playground.

'Helenah.' She paused and turned round. 'You know we were talking about,' he drew in breath slightly, 'clarssical music yesterday?'

Helena nodded. Pete nodded in time with her. 'Well, I just want to tell you. My favourite composer's Bellyotz.'

Helena looked uncomfortable. '*Who?*'

Pete shifted impatiently. It was such a strain, not speaking the same language. 'You know, Bellyotz?' He made it rhyme with jellytots. 'I think his Fantastic Symphony's . . .' he waggled his hands in the air, at a loss for suitably elevated expression, 'fantastic.'

He caught sight of the music master lolloping in the direction of junior choir and decided to invoke his support. 'Sir, Mr Tarlton, Sir. You know that Fantastic Symphony by Bellyotz? Well, don't you think it's just . . .'

'By *whom*?'

'By Bellyotz, Sir. I just think it's altogether a . . .'

'Are you extracting the urine by any chance, Birken-shawe?'

Pete hoped that this wasn't a catch question on Bellyotz.

'Beg pardon, Sir?'

'Are you taking the p . . .?'

Pete caught his drift and issued a rapid disclaimer. 'Oh no, Sir. 'Course not, Sir. Just remembered, Sir. Helping out with assembly, Sir.' And he caught hold of Helena's hand in his agitation to draw her Cinterswell ears out of range of the grosseries of Mr Tarlton. She gave an outraged yelp, whipped her hand back and stuck it under her armpit, frowning heavily.

'Before you go, Birkenshawe.' Mr Tarlton clamped a restraining hand on Pete's shoulder. 'I'm counting on your cooperation for the Sponsored Trot.'

'The sponsored *what*?' Pete had a momentary vision of sponsors lining up outside the bog door, cheering lustily, while he heaved and strained on the lavatory pan.

'Jeanie Parkes is organizing a Sponsored Trot. Half to go to the Royal Hospital, half to the school timpani section. She's hired a pantomime horse from the local theatre. She thought you were a natural for the hind legs.'

'Gee, t'anks.'

Helena was grinning like crazy. 'I'll sponsor you. It'll be worth it, to see you as a horse's behind.' She caught sight of Melanie Fish and Jeanie Parkes coming through the school gate. Melanie had shaved the back of her head and spiked her front hair out with gel. Also she'd spent the past fourteen days after school under an ultraviolet lamp. The effect was golden. Even Pete Birkenshawe, five years over-exposed to the charms of Melanie Fish, looked impressed. Helena sensed his shift of interest, and in spite of the bobble hat, felt piqued. Pete was . . . well, she had to admit he was kind of cute. She stopped Melanie to quiz her on where she'd had her hair done, leaving Pete to the tender mercies of Tarlton the Sarcastic. Luckily Miss Harvey stalked into the playground, on her way to the shops. Mr Tarlton hailed her. 'Whither away, Anne?'

Anne! Christ!

Miss Harvey's pace slackened. 'Just withdrawing my good will.'

'Ah, good willus interruptus. Jolly good show.' Mr Tarlton was eyeing Miss Harvey appreciatively, even in spite of the specs. Well, there was no accounting for tastes! Pete left them to it and galloped off to East block to capture his second encounter with Helena Kirby-Monckton in immortal verse:

▪Poem Written in E4▪

It was noon!
It was far beyond noon!
It was love!
It was far beyond love!

That night Arif Kasmani was also hymning the praises of Helena Kirby-Monckton, in diary and song. He had to make his praises rather on the cryptic side, though, in case his father sneaked into the room, as he had a habit of doing, and read them. His dad had a clear development plan laid down for Arif. It read something like: '16 to 28 years: accumulate enough paper qualifications to decorate the hall, stairs and (double) landing of 'The Privets', Carlton Grange Road. 28 years: a discreet interest may be fostered, if properly chaperoned,

with a Muslim girl of Dr Aniz Kasmani (B.Sc. Ph.D.
F.G.S.)'s choice.'

Arif reached a little tentatively for his diary across
which was written in large letters WHOEVER
READS THIS DIARY WILL BE DAMNED
ALTERNATELY with the ALTERNATELY
crossed out and ETERNALLY written in its place.

Inside he wrote: 'Picked a micklemus daisy for
OXOXOX and my OXOXOX brushed her
OXOXOX.'

At this point a door opened in the hall and Arif heard
his father's heavy tread on the stairs. He banged the diary
shut, shoved it under his duvet, opened his biology text
book at random and began hastily to copy the contents of
'The Colon' on to a stray piece of paper.

The footsteps passed his room. Arif heaved a sigh of
relief and recovered the diary. Time for a piece of verse
inspired by his beloved. He reached for *An Anthology of
Major Poets* to furnish a working model and began:

▪TO OXOXOXOX▪

*Come OXOXOX with me and be my OXOXOX
And we will all the OXOXOXS prove.*

As he wrote his brow furrowed. That Pete Birkenshawe fellow could prove a bit of a problem. The fellow
had no breeding, of course (and no cash), but he was
proving unaccountably fascinating to the fair Helena. Arif
got the distinct impression that she found him, Arif,
rather on the *rotund* side, whereas he'd always considered
himself pleasantly plump. Well, there was nothing else
for it – a strict reducing plan was urgently called for. A
mood of deep melancholia descended upon him at the

thought and he remembered the low white house by a
lake that his family had once owned in Malawi. It was
just the right setting for a poem of doleful contemplation.
He set his features into a baleful cast and began.

■Under the Paw-Paw Tree■

Under the paw-paw tree,
I sit and think of thee.
The waves break on the shore
Bearing micro-organisms and essential nutrients . . .

Here Arif was forced to break off, as he could think
of nothing to rhyme with nutrients (except
shoe-tree-ents).

■

The next day Pete Birkenshawe and Dave Petrovic came
across Arif Kasmani working out in the gym. The sweat
was torrenting off him. 'You can over-do this kind of
thing, you know, mate,' said Pete, who found it enough
of an effort in the normal run of things to raise a banana
from the horizontal.

'No . . . gain . . . without . . . pain,' grunted Arif from
underneath a dumb-bell.

'This man knows no pressure,' Pete winked at Dave.
Dave lobbed a basketball at Arif's stomach. 'It's long . . .
it's high . . . it's in for three points.'

The swing doors at the far end of the gym banged
open and Jeanie Parkes stood there, blowing down a
buckled exercise book by way of a trumpet, 'Da der da
der der da da' on a rising scale. Helena appeared in the
doorway, looking rosy. In place of her blonde shoulder-
length page-boy, her hair was now close clipped apart
from three pointed tufts, one springing mid-skull and

one from just behind each ear. The whole concoction was dyed a deep canary yellow.

Arif released a howl and dropped the dumb-bell. Pete, in spite of the evidence of the bobble hat, appreciated a bit of style. 'Wi-cked, Helena. You look fantastic!'

Helena's colour deepened. 'Well, I *was* Miss Brownie Camp, 1979.'

Pete linked an arm through hers. 'I should think so! First Brownie Camp, then the world, hey, Jeanie?'

Jeanie nodded, bent double with the giggles. This Helena Kirby-Monckton was quite a phenomenon, once you'd worked out what she was on about. She'd already invited Jeanie to take tea in Carlton Grange Road, and Jeanie was looking forward to furthering her research.

Helena looked punch drunk and high as a kite. Her grin was broad enough to split her face. Davenport was proving a *million* times better than the Roylston Academy. 'And Jeaneah's been suggesting ways I could do out my room. It's all, like, forget-me-nots and white lace at the moment.' Helena dismissed such frippery with a wave of the hand. 'But Jeaneah said I could do it all black with, like, black net acrorss the ceiling?'

Pete nodded enthusiastically. 'Why don't you grow some bacteria? I had this seven-up can for six months and it went all like hairy and slimy on the bottom.' Pete pressed home his advantage by leading her firmly from the gym before Arif could retrieve the breath blasted out of him by the descent of the dumb-bell.

∎

That afternoon Pete and Helena put the seal on their new-found love down behind the bike sheds. And when Helena promised to make Pete a macramé bobble hat in fabrics, Pete's joy knew no bounds. She was no brain, of course. But he'd known that already. For example, when he'd said, 'I hear Andropov's dead,' she'd said, 'Who's Andrew Poff?' But that was a minor detail. That night he wrote poem after poem, some inspired by the natural world:

> *The mountains scrape the sky. My love is in her tower.*
> *The tree-tops toss and sway. My love is in her bower.*
> *The waves break on the shore. My love is in the shower.*

Others taking the form of a celebration, in rhyming couplets, of a love that knew no boundaries of geography and class.

■Peterkin to Eleanor. A Pastoral■

> *Whenever I say 'Eleanor' I Helena do mean.*
>   *She's very upper-classed, you know. She is a little queen.*
> *And Pete is rather plebby, from the Fletcher's Green Estate.*
>   *He would he lived in Counterswell. It would be really great.*
> *He would he was in Paris, of which the poets croon.*
>   *He would they was in Paris, upon their honeymoon.*

But the next day Helena didn't turn up. Nor the next. Nor the next. Nor the one after that. And so on for a fortnight. Pete took to pounding the streets of Carlton Grange Road, gazing anxiously up at the bedrooms of 'High Hedges'. But there was no sighting, not even a light. He thought of asking Arif Kasmani if he knew what was wrong with her. But pride prevented him. And all Jeanie did was mock. 'What's up with you, Pete? Got a touch of the cordon blues?' On the fourteenth night, nearly out of his mind with grief and frustration, he wrote two lines of deep spiritual recoil:

This fleshly gross affair that keeps me up so late
It is my swift intent to unilaterally terminate.

At last he plucked up courage to ask the teacher in charge of his tutor group, Miss Roberts, if she knew why Helena Kirby-Monckton was away. Miss Roberts, who wasn't in the habit of taking constitutionals behind the bike sheds, had not previously guessed at the painful progress of Peter's passion, but she now sensed hysteria behind his casual tone and sussed the reason why Peter had been looking particularly moribund for the past week or so.

'Of course. She's contracted glandular fever. She won't be back for at least a month.' In fact, it wasn't *Helena* who'd contracted *glandular fever* but *Mrs Kirby-Monckton* who had contracted *a severe fright* on beholding her canary-tufted daughter, and Helena wouldn't be back at all. But Miss Roberts wasn't to know that.

'Glandular *fever*?' Pete shuddered. He imagined his lily-white love turned a hectic rose, pearls of perspiration beading the brow beneath the tufts, and he paled.

Miss Roberts looked amused. 'Yes, the kissing disease, you know.'

'The *kissing* disease?'

'It's passed on by oral contact. No chance of your falling a victim, though, Peter. A rigorous revision programme's the best antidote I know.'

Only now did Pete register the full implication of Miss Roberts's words. At least a month! That meant he'd have to do his 'O' levels without divine inspiration. In fact, all he'd got to look forward to was the Sponsored Trot.

Unless . . . he fished out his list of sponsors. He grinned, banged his fist against the paper and set off with a whoop in search of Jeanie Parkes.

■

Those out walking their King Charles's spaniels along the leafy boulevards of Counterswell on Saturday morning were a little astonished to encounter a pantomime horse solemnly clop-clopping along the pavement. However, they were too well bred to stare, though they did tug rather sharply at Marcus and Candy, Nelson and Lucy when they stopped for an exploratory sniff.

'You sure Ma Kirby-Monckton'll grant access?' mumbled the hind legs to Jeanie Parkes as she delicately side-stepped Marcus's early morning offering to the sidewalks of Counterswell which lay gently steaming in the autumn sunshine.

'Sure,' said Jeanie with confidence. 'She thinks I'm quaint.' Pete didn't entirely dispute this, but all the same he was relieved that Jeanie Parkes's skull was snugly encased in the head of the pantomime horse. She'd lately shaved all her hair off and dyed the stubble orange.

She veered abruptly to the left. 'We're going up the drive now.' After what seemed like a ten-mile hack she said, 'I'm going to press the door bell now.'

Deeply entombed though he was in fur fabric, Pete heard the door bell tinkling 'Home Sweet Home'. He shuddered.

'May God!' trilled a female voice when the door opened. Mrs Kirby-Monckton's.

'It's all right, Mrs Kirby-Monckton,' said Jeanie, reassuring if muffled. 'It's me, Jeanie Parkes. I've come for Helena's sponsor money. How is she?'

'Oh, mach better, thenk you, Jeanieah. She's sunbathing on the back lawn, ectualleah. I'm not sure you

should see her, though, realleah. Though she's not in-
fectious any longeah, I don't suppose.'

'Oh, it's all right, Mrs Kirby-Monckton. I'm not going
to *kiss* her or anytheahing.'

'Whort's thet?'

'I'm not going to *tar* her or anytheahing, Mrs Kirby-
Monckton. I'll just collect the sponsor moneah and I'll be
away in a jiffeah, I mean in a tick.'

'O.Kayeah. I'll just unlork the garage daw and let you
througheah. Oh, you *naughteah*!'

Pete thought it must be Jeanie who was the naughteah,
but at that moment something molten iron clamped his
left calf and he let out a shriek. Luckily the pain was so
intense that the shriek was high-pitched.

'Oh, you naughteah dawg, Lucyeah! Who's in there,
Jeanieah?'

'Oh, just someone from our clarss,' said Jeanie with
heavy innuendo and then in case Mrs Kirby-Monckton
insisted on a positive vetting, 'Ay have a King Charles's
spaniel too, Mrs Kirby-Monckton.'

'Oh, reallyeah? And wort's her name?'

'It's a he. The Ayatollah Khomenei.'

'Oh, *Jeanieh*! And wort's wrong with Rex?'

■

The next bit didn't take long. The telephone warbled as
soon as the pantomime horse was inside the enclave and
Mrs Kirby-Monckton was soon trilling, 'Oh, hullo,
Posyeah. How was Agadiah?' Helena squealed with
delight when she peered deep into the underbelly of the
horse and found Pete nestling there, and it was the work
of seconds for Jeanie to disembark and to persuade Helena
to clamber into the front legs and enclose her blond-and-
canary-curls in the horse's head. (Her mother had insisted
on a perm as soon as she clapped eyes on the tufts.)

'Byee, Mrs Kirby-Monckton,' called Jeanie into the house, and the pantomime horse waved a jaunty hoof through the front door before clop-clopping off down the drive to a soft shoe shuffle. Meanwhile, Jeanie wriggled through a hole in one of the high hedges and caught a bus back to town.

Under a spreading chestnut tree in Counterswell Park, the pantomime horse looked more like a camel as Helena clambered out of the horse's front legs only to clamber back in again the other way round, head and feet pointing inwards while she exchanged hot kisses with Pete Birkenshawe deep within the furry pile, safe from prying Counterswell eyes.

'Whatever *happens*,' murmured Pete from the bowels of the pantomime pelt, 'I mean, say they send you to Switzerland to finish you off or something, you wouldn't give up our three-week-old meaningful relationship just like that, would you?' And Helena swore on the horse's velcro fastenings that bound them that she certainly would not!

The horse's head lolled, disembodied, in the municipal grass, and when Mrs Kirby-Monckton's Lucyeah came sniffing round them in ecstasy, Mrs Kirby-Monckton called her sharply back, thinking, 'That Jeanieah! Someone from our clarss indeed!' while Lucy's tail caught the horse's eyelid, and it dropped in a loaded wink!

Skegness, or Bust!

'Miss, Miss, tell 'em, Miss. Tell the lads, Miss. Tell 'em the *girls* are having the back seat.'

'Oh, I can't do that, Melanie. You'll just have to see you get there first.'

'Right, you lot. Are you ready? The coach is at the traffic lights, I can see it.'

'Create a diversion, Mel, so as the boys won't notice. Do a striptease or summat.'

'You kiddin'? What do you think I am?'

'Go on, Mel. You'll think of something. You'd bedder!'

'Hey, Dave, ain't that a squirrel up on that branch? It's just run up the trunk. Look, over there. In that tree at the side of the school there. It *is* a squirrel, ain' it, Ravinder?'

'Where? I can't see one. You need specs or something, Melanie. You're seeing things. There's nothing there.'

'There *is*. There *is*. Look, it's moving now. You must be looking at the wrong branch. You can see it, can't you, Yunus? You've got good eyesight.'

'Mel, Mel, come on. We've saved you a place.'

'Hey, look, damn it. The girls have got the back seat. We've been done. There weren't no squirrel, were there, Melanie? You were having us on.'

But Melanie had gone, and was even now skipping

down the bus to join the others who were rolling around on the back seat in a state of helpless laughter. Purnima Patel had been watching Melanie's performance with envy. No one would ever ask *her* to distract the boys. They all thought of her as a creep. Nice enough, but no good for a laugh. Well, today she'd show them. Today she was going to be one of the gang. With determination she squeezed herself on to the back seat along with the others.

The lads leapt cursing on to the bus and rushed to the back. They tried to drag the girls to their feet, but they shouted for Sir who had just climbed on and was talking to the driver. He yelled at the lads to lay off it. The girls settled back into their places, smiling triumphantly.

Purnima, squashed in the middle, turned round and knelt on the seat, staring at the traffic going along the main road. By doing this she seized for herself a moment of peace away from the others. That boy Yunus! Her hand still burned from where he'd caught hold of it, trying to pull her to her feet. She'd seen him around school a lot recently. Whenever she was on prefect duty in the bottom hall he always seemed to be walking through. She'd had to tell him off because he was only in the third year and the third years were supposed to be out on the yard. But the other girls had told her to lay off him. They'd taken a fancy to him, she could tell. But they were prefects, weren't they? They couldn't favour one lad above the rest. Well, she wasn't going to, anyway.

She turned round again and sat facing forwards. He was sitting just in front of them laughing with Dave Petrovic. Trust him to be sitting with the fifth years. What a cheek! Yet he didn't look cheeky. He had a nice face – and, she had to admit, was very good-looking. And he dressed trendy for an Indian boy. Today he was wearing jeans with a scarlet webbing belt, the end hanging casually down instead of being tucked in at the back, and a golden yellow shirt, big and floppy.

Purnima clicked her tongue at herself. Fancy wasting all that thought on a third year! And a cheeky one at that! She shoved him to the back of her mind and concentrated on enjoying herself. It wasn't often that you had the opportunity to go off on a pleasure trip like this. She took a quick look round the coach. There were more Indian kids than white ones. Well, it wasn't difficult to know why. It was projects week at school and Mr Tipperton's project had been social games. They'd been playing chess and bridge and scrabble and table tennis all week and the Skegness trip was the highlight of the project. Not a serious day of study – the only social game that they might be playing was football or going on the pinball machines – but it was the day that everyone had been looking forward to. To meet the cost Mr Tipperton had had to fill the coach with fifth years who'd finished their exams. This was one of the reasons why there were so many Indians. They still liked to go back into school – even though they could have been free now – to play cricket and table-tennis and chat to the teachers. So they were around to hear that Mr Tipperton needed people to make up the numbers for his Skegness day.

But the main reason for this trip being so popular with the Indian kids, thought Purnima with a thrill, was that it was a day out, away from the sneaky eyes of parents – and with members of the opposite sex in the party!

There was another delighted burst of laughter. Purnima jumped. Melanie and Sangita were bending over a huge sheet of paper. Melanie was drawing and Sangita wrote something at the bottom.

'Here, Jasmine,' said Sangita, bending across Purnima

to reach Jasmine Samuel. 'You've got the Sellotape, haven't you? Stick this up for us, will you?'

Purnima caught a glimpse of the notice as it was passed to Jasmine. It said, 'Skegness, or Bust' and a huge bosom filled the sheet. Purnima couldn't help smiling. What would their mothers say if they could see what their daughters were capable of drawing? Sangita was scrawling again. With a giggle she handed the finished product to Purnima who passed it to Jasmine. It read, 'I think you're great, but then I've always had bad taste.' She gurgled and displayed it on the back window for the travelling salesman in the flashy car behind to read.

Purnima's heart swelled with the fun of it all. What the heck, she was going to enjoy herself. For five years she'd struggled and slogged and studied for school and for her parents. Now with her 'O' levels behind her – and a place at the sixth-form college for next year – she was going to live a little. After all, it would soon be 'A' levels and college and work, work, work. She was young – time to have some fun before it was too late and life became more serious than ever.

She looked around the bus at the kids she'd been working with every day for the last five years. Over the last year they'd changed little by little. Now that the pressure of exams was over, the change seemed to be complete. Even Abdul Sheikh, who'd always been such a little boy, had had his hair punked and grown up all of a sudden. And Ravinder had acquired gold-rimmed specs and a grown-up air. And as for Dinesh Dodhia, well, what a transformation! He'd even started making suggestive remarks!

She could hear him now talking about Jatinder Singh. 'Now that one's too innocent. It's not good for him. Do you know what he said to Melanie Fish when we were waiting outside school? He asked her what book she was reading and she said it was called *Boy Meets Girl* and asked him if he wanted to borrow it after. And you know what? He shook his head until it looked as if it was coming off and said, "I only like science fiction." ' Dinesh and Ravinder went off into fits of laughter and Purnima grinned to herself.

Just like Jatinder! She pictured the way he shuffled along the road, head bent with embarrassment in case he met anyone. But he was bright! There was no doubt about that. Bright, yet backward. Poor old Jatinder! It suddenly struck Purnima that the same could be said about her. Well, today they'd see a difference!

There was a sudden roar of approval from Sangita, Melanie and Jasmine. The salesman had just condescended to wave and blow a kiss as he accelerated and overtook the coach. At that moment it lurched to the side – time for a coffee break. Purnima, stirring her coffee, sighed to herself. The other girls had just ignored the way she was squashed in the middle of them. They hadn't been unfriendly. They had simply failed to notice she was there . . .

They reached Skegness not long after the coffee stop. Everyone piled out, shrieking and laughing. Sir paused long enough to say that they had to meet on the beach in front of the pleasure ground at half past two for a game of football and then charged off with Miss Muldoon towards the nearest pub. Purnima stood uncertain for a moment, but she wasn't left out for long. 'C'mon, Purnima,' yelled Sangita. 'We're going to the pleasure beach first. Coming?'

She certainly was! She looked out of the corner of her eye to see which lads had joined them. There was Dave Petrovic, of course – and Dinesh and Ravinder and – yes, Yunus too!

They looked round the pleasure beach first, to see what they wanted to go on. Some of the younger kids tagged along. A quiet little boy called Satish came racing up to her to show her what he'd won – a razor blade on a chain. He was as thrilled as anything, but it looked all wrong on him. 'And I'm just like *him* as well,' thought Purnima. She had thought she would enjoy herself, feel part of the gang, as soon as she got to Skegness and caught the holiday spirit. But she was no different. While the others shrieked and laughed, she remained quiet and withdrawn. The kind of girl that the younger ones came up to talk to, but not the ones of her own age. Luckily nobody seemed to notice. But she knew she was out of place and hated herself for it. She longed for the waltzer to stop as soon as she'd got on it, and she shut her eyes when she was supposed to be aiming with a gun at a target. Yunus noticed what she was doing. 'Here,' he said. 'Let me help you.' And he put his arms round her, placing his cheek against hers to take aim. She hit the target and he cheered. She backed away from him as if it was she who had been shot.

It was Melanie who spotted the boating lake. 'Let's go for a row,' she shouted. 'C'mon. Bags the oars.' They raced towards it. Melanie, who had started running as soon as she'd had the idea, got there first and jumped into the boat. Dave hurriedly jumped in after her. Dinesh shouted to Sangita, 'Come in this boat with me, Sang.' Purnima slowed down. Someone was going to get landed with her. Or perhaps Yunus and Ravinder would go in a boat together – and Jasmine and her. She didn't know which would be worse. She didn't like to think that none of the boys would be interested in going in a boat with her – but she knew that's the way it would be.

'C'mon, Purnima,' shouted Yunus. 'You're coming with me.'

He was only being kind. Yes, that's all it was. Fancy a *third* year having to take pity on a fifth year, and a prefect at that. It was pathetic. But nevertheless she was pleased. She caught herself grinning with delight – and quickly adjusted her expression to her usual rather thoughtful, rather mournful look. She remembered Jasmine. How horrible to be chosen last and it could so easily have been her. But she should have known it wouldn't get Jasmine down. 'Looks like it's you 'n' me, boy,' she said, grinning at Ravinder. Purnima decided she could relax and let the holiday begin.

But it was easier thought than done. The others were soon helpless with laughter, soaked through from splashing one another. Melanie rocked their boat so hard that they nearly capsized. 'Time for you to take over the oars, Dave,' she said. 'It's ruinin' me hands. Look at the blisters.' She displayed them, letting go of the oars. Ravinder lunged to catch them before they slid into the water. He managed to get one but the other escaped and he nearly fell in. The boatman yelled at them to stop fooling about and the others collapsed with giggles. But Purnima felt uncomfortable. *Why* couldn't she just relax and not bother, like the others? They did and said whatever came into their heads, and never mind what happened. She seemed to get lost within her head, seeing the world through the eyes of the boatman, the teachers, her parents – where were her *own* eyes? What did she really want to see? Everybody said how responsible she was – but where was the fun or the *sense* of it all?

'What you dreaming about, Purnima?' It was Yunus leaning towards her. 'Do you want to row for a bit? C'mon. You have a go.'

She smiled at him, grateful for the way he was including her, and took the oars. But she thought too much about what she was doing instead of just letting it all flow like Yunus seemed to, and the boat kept going round in circles. Yunus laughed, but not unkindly.

But they were being called in now by the boatman. The day was slipping away fast. They bought some coke and crisps and took their sandwiches down to the beach. Purnima was amazed to see that Dinesh took Sangita's hand as soon as they left the boating lake. As soon as Ravinder noticed he got hold of Jasmine's. The girls looked embarrassed but very pleased. Even when Sir and Miss arrived with the football and they were all walking towards the sea to set up a pitch, the two boys got hold of the girls' hands again, but they made sure they kept behind the adults. When Miss turned round, though, Sangita hissed to Dinesh, 'Miss Muldoon's looking,' and they dropped hands guiltily, but Purnima noticed that Miss only grinned.

The others started playing football straight away. Purnima was determined not to be left out. She took off her high-heeled sandals and played in bare feet. Most of the girls still had their tights on – they couldn't be bothered to take them off. Some of them had already dashed, screaming with laughter, into the sea. When they came out ladders trickled from their toe-nails up their feet.

For a while Purnima appeared to play quite well. She rushed up and down so that it looked as if she was doing something, but she made sure she didn't get anywhere near the ball. Sangita kept tackling the boys, screeching, and Jasmine elbowed her way through all opposition while the lads screamed their approval. Purnima's heart sank. They were good sports. But she'd watched Satish leap bravely for a header. It had been a helpful shot and they'd shouted, 'Good one, Satish,' but Purnima knew it must have hurt him. She'd watched closely as he blinked back the tears, stunned, shook his head a few times, rubbed it, and charged back in again. She shuddered.

'Purnima, here's one for you.' It was Yunus again, neatly dribbling the ball towards her, weaving in circles until he gently kicked the ball straight to Purnima's feet. Without thinking – she was so surprised – she gave the ball a hefty kick and the players cheered. She flushed with pleasure and ran forward without even realizing it. Now she dared to put up just a little effort and managed to knee the ball once and then kick it once again, but then Dinesh kicked her by mistake and she lost her nerve and left the game, wandering towards the water's edge.

It had been cold all day but when they had first arrived it had been bright. Now great grey clouds had blown up and the sea was an answering grey with fierce white flecks at the edges of the waves. Purnima tried not to notice the cigarette and crisp packets and the rather sinister-looking scum that rode there too. She concentrated her eyes out at sea, throwing her head back to enjoy the way the wind tore her hair and stung her cheeks. She loved the sea in this country. Here you felt wild and free, able to do anything, most of all, just able to *be*, to let thoughts and dreams and wishes tear through your head as if blown in by the sharp north east wind. You didn't need to wonder, 'Ought I to be thinking things like this?' or 'What would my mother say if she knew what I was thinking?'

'I wish Yunus had taken hold of my hand when Ravinder and Dinesh held hands with the others.' The pier suddenly loomed in front of her like an angry parent, and she was amazed at what she had thought. Yunus was

a Muslim and she was a Hindu. Her parents didn't approve of Hindu girls talking to Hindu boys in the street,
never mind holding hands with them, never *mind* holding
hands with a Muslim. And Yunus was a third year, and
she was a prefect. She must be crazy! He would never
have dared to hold her hand, even if he'd wanted to. Had
he wanted to . . .?

Oh, he was nice-looking! Such a great grin. She
imagined his long slender fingers stroking the back of her
hand and she shivered.

'Purnima!' Purnima jumped guiltily and turned round.
Out at sea, wading up to his waist, was fat Mark. Also a
third year! How different he was from Yunus! Mark
would never think of Purnima as a girlfriend. He was the
sort who saw girls only as mothers – and always would.
He had chatted away to her on the coach, kneeling on the
seat in front – about his puppy, his fishing, and how he
was going to buy a snorkel and goggles when he got to
Skeggy. He ate all the time, as if in need of a constant
sweetened dummy.

He looked a lonely figure out at sea, wading now
towards her, skin pale beneath the greying, racing
afternoon sky. A blob among the waves, stomach oozing
over his boxer shorts, snorkelled and goggled like some
unlikely sea creature, shivering, quivering towards her.
'Purnima,' he shouted again. 'Will you get me a towel?'

Purnima nodded and looked round the beach for it.
Then she saw that the others were using it to wipe their
sandy feet. She was running over to them when Yunus
came charging towards her. Her stomach lurched in the
direction of her ears. But he was only chasing the ball. It
flew into the sea and he tore in after it, up to his knees in
the water. That shirt and those jeans were new on today!
He'd said so on the coach. 'Yunus, you fool,' she couldn't

help shouting, but he only turned and grinned. 'It's a great game of football,' he said in self-defence.

Purnima felt nothing but scorn for him. What would his parents say when he got home that night with a salt mark on his new jeans? But then, what would her parents say if they knew that she still wanted to hold hands with him, for all he was an idiot? Wanted to, more than anything else in the world. More than good 'O' levels or going to sixth-form college or doing 'A' levels or any of that.

'Purnima!' wailed Mark through chattering teeth. Purnima ran towards the little crowd of girls who were snatching Mark's towel from one another and slapping each other with it. The ends kept trailing in the sand. As Purnima ran up there was a diversion and the towel was forgotten. Further down the beach a streaker (male) was charging into the sea urged on by his cheering mates. The girls were all of a twitter. 'Oh, Purnima, did you see that?' Agitation, agitation. Giggle, giggle.

Purnima tried to keep her eyes on shaking the towel but they seemed to swivel of their own accord. She caught sight of the man's bottom leaping above the waves, white below his narrow brown back, rising out of the water like two pale melons. Smaller melons than she'd imagined. Neat at the bottom of the long curve of his back. Guiltily she looked away. How stupid the men were, shouting and jeering like that! And the girls, screaming and giggling and drawing attention to themselves! Her mind switched back to Yunus running into the sea with all his clothes on. She flung the towel over her arm and made back towards Mark before her mind could travel further and make more guilty pictures.

The towel was soaking! And sandy. Mark pulled a face and went 'Yuk!' when he took it. She couldn't exactly blame him! They started across the sand together. The others had gathered up their parkas and sweatshirts and shoes and were making for the promenade. Purnima watched anxiously as Sangita and Jasmine ran squealing away from Ravinder and Dinesh and Yunus. Yunus caught hold of Sangita before Dinesh did. Purnima could have sworn that his arm went round her shoulders for a moment or two. Tears rushed to her eyes and she mumbled to Mark, 'Got sand in them.' But he hadn't noticed. He was too busy trying to squeeze himself into his shirt, his spherical body still wet. At last he had his shirt on. There were far fewer dry patches than wet ones. The sight of him irritated Purnima. She snapped at him for kicking sand up at her. 'I never!' he said indignantly.

'Ooh, Purnima,' he said when they reached the edge of the beach. (By now Dinesh was holding Sangita's hand again and Yunus was teasing her, flicking at her hair while she and Dinesh batted him away, laughing.) 'Ooh, Purnima, I've forgotten summat. Wait on. Wait there.'

'What've you forgotten, Mark?' asked Purnima, thoroughly fed up with him. (Yunus looked over his shoulder but seeing her walking with Mark he turned away and was now flicking Sangita's hair more than ever.)

'Me pants!' exclaimed Mark in tones of deep grief. 'I'm going back for 'em. Wait for us.' And he waddled off across the sand, a white globule against the grey of the sky. At last he returned, clutching a pair of sodden lilac pants. Purnima couldn't help staring. Luckily he seemed to have no thoughts of actually *changing* into his pants at the moment. He seemed quite happy just waving them round his head like a flag.

At last she managed to get away. But then she caught up with four smaller kids who were intent on tearing one another to pieces by the shirt ends. 'Sati chapatti!' they kept chanting at Satish. He only grinned and charged at them like a miniature bull. He charged so hard that one boy crumpled, winded. Satish rubbed his head.

'There,' said Purnima, exasperated, leaning over the winded boy. 'Will that teach you?' She heard a laugh and turned round to see Yunus watching her. 'You're good with them,' he said. 'The others don't bother. C'mon. It's time we got on the coach.'

She felt herself blushing. They walked across the car park. Her hand seemed to ache from wanting him to take hold of it. He walked rather close to her but he made no move towards her hand. They didn't say anything, and now they were climbing on the coach, still in silence. Purnima felt bitterly disappointed.

But to her surprise there were changes! The girls were no longer on the back seat. They were sitting in the double seats at the back of the coach. And they weren't sitting girls together. Sangita was with Dinesh, and Jasmine with Ravinder, and Melanie with Dave, of course. 'Hurry up, then,' said Yunus, sounding pleased, giving Purnima a push. 'Go opposite Dinesh and Sangita.' Purnima took her seat by the window and he swung himself round, fingers on the rack, and lowered himself beside her. How tall he was for a third year!

The couples didn't have much to say to each other. Sangita and Jasmine kept making faces at each other and jumping up to mouth messages, giggling and embarrassed. Purnima just sat there, beside herself with happiness. But what if their dads were waiting to meet the bus? They were kidding themselves. They couldn't go out together after today, not like the white kids did, as if it was the most natural thing in the world. It wasn't like that, for them.

There was a party spirit, now that the coach had started

up. Miss Muldoon gave out song-sheets and soon they were all singing – 'I'm for ever blowing bubbles' and 'Daisy Daisy'. Purnima didn't know the songs but she soon got the hang of the tunes. Yunus bawled away beside her as they swung round the country lanes. She noticed that Satish was wearing a badge with a dazed-looking little man on it. 'Avoid hangovers. Shtay drunk.' 'How long have you been sitting on these, Jeanie?' somebody asked, waving a squashed looking packet of biscuits. Everybody laughed.

When Miss Muldoon came to the back to collect the song-sheets, the kids broke into 'Build a Bonfire'.

> *'Build a bonfire, build a bonfire*
> *Put the tea-chers on the top.*
> *Put Mr Tipperton in the mi-ddle*
> *And set fire to the flaming lot!'*

Mr Tipperton stood up and shook his fist at them and they all laughed. Then he and Miss Muldoon stood up and sang very loud:

> *'Build a bonfire, build a bonfire,*
> *Put the pu-pils on the top.*
> *Put the fifth year in the mi-ddle,*
> *And set fire to the flaming lot.'*

Purnima felt she couldn't bear to leave it all. She didn't want to go to sixth-form college any more. There'd be no Yunus walking through the bottom hall grinning at all the prefects every morning. Or rather, he'd still be there and she wouldn't – and he'd be grinning at another girl and forgetting about her.

The coach was quietening down now. Some of the kids were playing cards. Purnima saw Dinesh bend towards Sangita and give her a quick kiss. She looked away hurriedly. When she looked back, Dinesh had his arm round her. She shut her eyes in desperation. In the end nothing had really happened. And it could've, if only she'd been different. If she'd been cheeky like Sangita. But because she was the way she was, Yunus'd never dare. Not a Muslim. Not a third year. And they'd soon be home. It would soon all be over.

It didn't matter that he was only a third year. No, it didn't. She knew that the other girls didn't think it did. They'd been giggling about him and commenting on him for weeks now. Purnima kept her eyes shut as her brain raced. She could hear what the boys in front were talking about and it kept getting in the way of her own thoughts. 'And she said if you breathed up a horse's nostrils it'd be your friend for life,' she heard Mark say. 'I tried it on our cat, but it scratched me.'

Always other people's conversations, other people's lives. And today was going to have been so special. And Yunus liked her, she was sure of that. Yes, but unless she showed him she liked him, he'd never know – and it would be too late. It was probably the only chance she'd ever have to show she cared about a boy whom she'd chosen. But it was no good. It couldn't come to anything. She might get into bad trouble at home. It wasn't worth it. And, in any case, she just wouldn't *dare*!

Then an idea formed in Purnima's mind. It made her feel hot just to think about it. But, yes, she was going to do it. Nothing open. Nothing that would make him know definitely that she liked him. But just so that she'd done *something*. So that she wouldn't feel all her life that she'd thrown away a chance.

She still had her eyes closed. And now she sighed lightly, and shifted on her seat as if she was fast asleep. Then slowly, very slowly, she let her head slip down the back of the seat until it came to rest on Yunus's shoulder.

She nearly stopped breathing as it landed. He was talking across the gangway to Ravinder. She felt him jerk slightly as if in surprise. She waited. Then he moved a little as if to make her head more comfortable, and shifted up closer to her.

It wasn't easy, pretending to be asleep all the way back to Roylston. The coach grew noisy again as they were nearing home, and there were loud shrieks that surely would've woken anybody? But Purnima refused to be woken. She lay relaxed, snuggled against Yunus's yellow shirt, smelling the sea and the sweetness of his warm body all the way back home.

But at last there was a great stirring and shuffling that she couldn't block out. A hefty jerk, and the coach came to a stop. What if the dads were already waiting there? But she kept her head firmly down on Yunus's shoulder.

'Purnima,' she heard Yunus say gently. 'Purnima, wake up. We're back.'

She opened her eyes to find herself looking straight into his. She didn't feel shy. He was smiling at her. 'You did have a long sleep,' he whispered to her. 'I hope you enjoyed it as much as I did.' She lifted her head and shook herself, smiling back. 'Oh, I did.'

The dads hadn't arrived. The coach had returned quicker than the teachers had thought. They weren't supposed to be back for another ten minutes. The kids flung themselves off the coach, some shouting their thanks to the driver, others punching one another and bounding about after being cooped up so long.

But Sangita and Dinesh weren't bounding. They were kissing on the pavement while Sir and Miss had their heads down, picking up the last bits of litter into polythene bags. They were taking an awful risk. Sangita's dad could be here any minute.

Yunus turned to Purnima. 'I shall miss you next year. Don't forget us when you're at the sixth form and there are all those new lads around.' He took hold of her hand and lifted it to his cheek and she felt his fingers stroke it, gently, gently . . .

He let it fall just as her father's car was the first to swing round the corner . . .

Uniform

Melanie Fish took a last critical look at herself in the mirror. She was wearing a long pencil skirt, a baggy sugar pink sweatshirt and shocking pink socks and sneakers. Whereas what the school required her to wear was a navy blue skirt, white blouse (or blue and white checked dress for summer) and sensible shoes. When Mr Joseph caught sight of the fifth year these days he was inclined to give up the unequal struggle. Not so the deputy head. Her motto was 'Faint not nor fear'.

Fergie gasped when he saw Melanie. 'You're not going to school dressed like *that*?'

Melanie thoughtfully threaded a sky blue chiffon scarf through her hair and turned her neck this way and that. 'Why not?'

' 'Cos Ma Palmer'll chuck you out, that's why not.'

'I'd like to see her try.'

Fergie shuddered. 'She'll try! You're askin' for it, Mel. Bedder not let mum see you goin' out like that, that's all I can say.'

'Shout out if the road's clear then. Anyway, it's dance first two, and Miss Hibbert couldn't care less what we wear. She likes us to express usselves.'

'She would!' Fergie thought of the new dance teacher with her dark eyes, plaits-'n'-rags, red boiler suit and leg-warmers. Even lads like Mick Malone had started doing dance these days. He could understand why, with Miss Hibbert.

They managed to get out without their mum seeing Melanie. Fergie refused to walk to school with her, though. 'Not with you lookin' like *that*.' So Melanie walked slowly on her own. She'd decided not to bother with registration anyway. It wasn't worth the hassle.

Sangita, Jasmine and Jeanie were waiting for her outside the school gate. They'd decided not to bother with registration either. They'd just go in for dance.

When Mel reached them they looked at each other sideways. Sangita had on a mustard and white tie-dye with mustard tights, short white socks and mustard trainers. Jasmine had copied Madonna and was strung about with crosses and had rags in her hair. And Jeanie, who'd despaired of her mother ever letting her buy any trendy clothes from the shops, had been the rounds of the jumble sales and was wearing a red and black leopardskin mini with a skull and crossbones belt, red tights and the red pointed-toed spiky-heeled shoes. When Mel had taken in what the others had on, she spoke first. 'You look great, Jeanie. Really weird.'

Jeanie nodded but she felt a bit sick. It was what they all wanted to look, of course, really weird. But somehow the others managed to look cute and fanciable at the same time, and *that* made her cross, and yet she hadn't felt at all sure lately that she wanted to look cute, fanciable, weird, or anything at all, and *that* made her even crosser.

The four of them moved off slowly across the yard, then rather quicker towards the dance studio. They peered anxiously round each corner, then scuttled to the next, stopped and peered again. In the distance there was the sound of voices uplifted in song: 'God moves in a mysterious way His won-ders to per-form.' Nobody saw them and they threw themselves down on the studio floor, breathless and laughing. There was the sound of shifting chairs, a swell of voices, a great trampling, then running of feet and the rest of fifth year dance burst into the room followed by a lopsided Miss Hibbert carrying a stereo cassette recorder.

'Allow me, Miss,' said Dave Petrovic, who'd recently taken up dance to keep an eye on Melanie Fish.

'There's a video and camera to come as well, Dave, while you're at it. Go and see Mr Tipperton in resources. And we'll need a television. Go with him, Mick.'

Melanie watched them go, then pulled a face. 'Know what? I reckon I'm goin' off Petrovic.

Jasmine, sensing drama, looked pleased. ''Bout time an' all, Mel. How come?'

'Dunno. 'E's a bit soft.'

'Which man you want then?'

'Dunno. Mebbe Mick.'

Dave came staggering back with the camera, then went off for the video, while Mick trundled the television in.

'What you want with this, Miss, camera?' asked Jasmine, sliding down the wall, legs sticking out on either side of her like a frog. 'We gonna be on telly?' She leapt up off the floor and peered down the viewer. Sangita jumped in front of her and hopped about like a kangaroo, hunching her shoulders and sticking her bottom out.

Jasmine twiddled the lens. 'Me can't see at all. All I man can see is Sangita's backside!'

'Jasmine!' yelled Miss Hibbert. 'Can you afford to pay for that very expensive equipment when you've bust it?'

'No, Miss.'

'No, I didn't think so. So just lay off it.'

'What you gonna do with it, hee?'

'Tape your contemporary dance for the community project. Then you can all see the terrible mistakes you make.'

'Aw, Mi–iss! Not today, Miss. Manjit's away. An' Lexia. An' Loretta. She's away an' all. Let me tell you sometink. Let's do our own Thriller, like Michael Jackson.'

'No, Jasmine. No, no and no.'

Jasmine muttered away. She shoved some chewey into her own mouth behind Miss Hibbert's back, then gave some to Melanie whose mouth was open for it like a baby bird's.

Jeanie nudged her. 'Where's my chewey then?'

'I ain' got any left on me. Well, I *have*. I have some in mine locker. But you can't have it.'

'You're mean.'

Jasmine squared up with her fists. 'That's my problem, not yours.' She put up her hand. 'I can't do this stupidness. I bruck my foot. An' it swell up big. Sight it.'

'How come you reckoned you could do a Thriller, then? C'mon, Jasmine. On your feet.'

Miss Hibbert started the cassette and took up her position behind the camera. The dance was a Good versus Bad dance to the music of Vangelis. Jasmine, Sangita, Melanie and Jeanie were the Goods. Soon they were blasting across the studio hotly pursued by the Bads, making pushing movements with their hands. As they blasted, Melanie looked sideways at Jeanie.

'Jea–nie! You're staggin' on the wrong leg!'

Jeanie glared. 'What do you know about it? Anyway, I wasn't staggin' if you want to know. Look.' She did a leap forward.

'Yeah, O.K. then. A jetée. But you looked like you was staggin'.'

'I did never!'

'You did too. Oh, and you lot. You Bads. Your hands should be stronger. I thought I'd let you know.' She nodded to herself and smirked.

Jeanie had never felt so fed up since her dad left home. Girls who looked like Melanie Fish got away with it all along the line. Not that she wanted to look like Melanie Fish any longer, thank you very much – it was the last thing she wanted! There were other ways of being a girl than Melanie Fish's way, she reckoned. A line for a poem slid into her head – 'Don't join 'em, beat 'em.' Jeanie grinned.

Miss Hibbert had had just about enough of Melanie Fish as well. 'Who's taking this lesson, Melanie? You or me?'

Melanie sniggered. 'You are, I suppose.'

Miss Hibbert swelled. 'Oh, you suppose that, do you? Well, let me tell you, Miss Sup-P O S E, the school's had just about enough of your antics. And you can wipe that stupid smile off your face as well.'

Melanie pointed to Jasmine and Sangita. 'It's that lot, Miss. They keep settin' me off.' She bent over with the giggles and caught sight of herself twenty times over in the studio mirror. An interesting thought flitted through her blue chiffon scarved head. 'Hey, what we gonna wear for this dance, Miss? Us Goods, I mean. I've got this smashing lycra for the Ravers. It's, like, bright white with a gold frill *here*.' She sketched a snaking frill. 'And all like navy blue sequins.' She spoke in tones of deep love.

Miss Hibbert blew up. 'I am sick and tired, Melanie Fish, with this never-ending fixation with what you're putting on your back which quite frankly doesn't interest anybody.'

Melanie looked sideways at Dave and grinned. 'It int'rests 'im.'

Miss Hibbert looked grim. 'Well, apart from a select few.' She looked hard at Dave. 'Some of whom ought to know better.'

'*You* like lookin' nice.'

'I never said I didn't. There's nothing wrong with it. Except when it becomes an obsession.'

'What's one of them?'

'When you can't think of anything else. Like you these days, Melanie. What you're going to wear next. What impression you make when you dance. Just remember Narcissus.'

'What the 'eck's Narcissus?'

'*Who* was Narcissus? He was a handsome young man. He fell in love with his own reflection in a pond. Then he fell in and drowned.'

'*I* don't go round lookin' at myself in ponds.'

Miss Hibbert gave up. 'Oh, never mind. None of you listen to a word I say anyway. JUST LET'S GET ON.'

But Jeanie had listened to what Miss Hibbert had to say. And she was dead right. All Mel *did* care about these days was what she was going to wear tomorrow and the latest weird thing to do with her hair. And the other two were just the same. And even the lads, they were as bad. All *they* cared about was girls who looked tasty in lycras and dustbin liners. Unfair!

'What's the programme for community project then, Miss?' asked Sangita.

Miss Hibbert listed the items on her fingers. 'The contemporary. Your Glenn Miller routine because they like to sing along with the old songs. And a dance drama. I reckon the Ruth Ellis.'

Melanie was delighted. It was she who played Ruth Ellis. Ruth Ellis was the last woman to be hanged in this country. She shot her lover David Blakely (played by Dave Petrovic). But it was another lover, Desmond Cussen (played by Mick Malone) who handed her the gun.

■

The next day after school there was a staff meeting about fifth year dress. The head got wind of it at twenty to nine when he entered the staff room and swept the 'Agenda for Staff Meeting' from its drawing-pin on the wall.

'Sponsored abseil,' 'House tutors – are they of any consequence?' 'Unfair staff contribution to washing up' and, the head's face fell, 'Fifth year dress'. He attempted to rally. 'Well, we certainly have some *colourful* items for discussion. Though what exactly we do about the fifth year and their dress . . .' He went off shaking his head.

At quarter to four battle was engaged. 'Has anyone noticed that we only get this mannequin parade on certain mornings?' inquired the deputy head lightly. She gave Miss Hibbert's leg-warmers an old-fashioned look.

Miss Hibbert tossed her plaits. 'I hope you're not accusing me of encouraging them, Mrs Palmer? I actively discourage them, if you want to know.'

Mrs Palmer smiled to herself. 'I accuse nobody, Miss Hibbert. I call only for consistency. If all the staff came to school *sui*tably dressed . . .' and she allowed her eyes to linger for a moment on the student teacher's jeans and Miss Hibbert's boiler suit. 'I suggest F U L L school uniform for the fifth year tomorrow, Mr Joseph, or home they all go.'

The head spoke timidly. 'But can we enforce it, Mrs Palmer?'

The deputy looked scornful. 'Certainly we can enforce

it, Mr Joseph. If it is enforced by all. By *all*, Miss Hibbert, or there will be no community project for fifth year dance.'

■

Two days after this Melanie was later than ever going into school. First she plaited the front of her hair into a gerbil's tail that fell forward across her forehead and down on to her nose. Next she did gerbils' tails that stuck out right round and across her head. After that she undid all the gerbils' tails to see what her hair looked like crinkly. Meanwhile she decided that the calf-length black pinafore dress with broderie anglaise petticoat that she got sent home in yesterday was yucky anyway and changed it for a football shirt, dungarees, thirteen necklaces, a beret and a lace bow tie.

She met Jasmine, Sangita and Jeanie opposite the school. Mrs Palmer had started getting really heavy about dress yesterday so they'd decided they'd only go into school if it was dance.

Jasmine had on red plastic trousers, a yellow sweatshirt with 'AHA' across the front, a bowler hat, rectangular sunglasses with red glass, lemon socks, black nail varnish and a chain across one hip, and Sangita a white satin dress, black patent shoes and long black lace gloves with the fingers cut out. Jeanie was wearing a clean white blouse and a navy blue skirt.

'Your *uniform*,' sneered Melanie. 'YUK!'

'I'm fed up,' flashed back Jeanie, 'with all this dressin' up all the time. *And* I'm gonna stick around for lessons from now on. I wanna REST!'

They were so late that the others (though not Miss Hibbert) were already in the studio by the time they got there. Jasmine was sniffing out what was new.

'Hey, who dis Rupert scarf, hee? It's yours, Mick?

You pay for it? How much?' She caught sight of the video. 'Hey, you! Do me this favour nah. Go and get the Michael Jackson video.' Petrovic went. She snatched Mick's scarf and tied it in a bow on top of her head. When Petrovic returned, she waved a hand. 'Set it up nah.'

Dave got it going for her and she watched for a few seconds. 'Right, us gonna do our own dance, OK? First of all it nods to the left. Den we're gonna jerk. Den up on your toes and gyrate.' She demonstrated.

Melanie got it straight off. 'Yeah, I get your drift.'

Sangita didn't. 'Come again! Come again!'

'Do your neck. Do your neck.'

'I say-ee! I jus' caught on!'

'I love that bit. That's the bit I love.'

'JASMINE SAMUEL!' Miss Hibbert stood in the doorway. Jasmine waved. 'Look here, Miss. Look! We do it just like him.'

'Who gave you permission to use the video? And WHAT do you think you've got on your backs?'

Melanie put her head on one side. 'Us clothes.'

Miss Hibbert pointed to the door. 'OUT, Melanie Fish. And Jasmine and Sangita. No more dance and no community project until you attend registration, attend assembly, attend all your lessons and WEAR YOUR UNIFORM.'

'Aw, Mi-iss!'

'I said OUT!'

They left.

■

Half an hour later they were back. They didn't fancy registration, assembly or lessons but they did like the idea of a week flashing round the community. Melanie's navy school skirt was skin tight and ended in a pelmet of pleats like a seal's flippers, Jasmine's had slits up the sides as far as the knee and Sangita's white blouse was rather inclined to frills, after the fashion of Princess Diana, but Miss Hibbert let that pass.

'What do we do first, Miss? In community week?'

'School for the last rehearsal on Monday morning. Then "The Glades" old people's home in the afternoon.'

'We don't have to wear us uniform when we go out, though, do we, Miss?'

Miss Hibbert gritted her teeth. 'You bet your sweet lives you do.'

■

On the way home Jasmine, Sangita and Melanie decided that the school had no right to insist on school uniform. Not when you were in the *community*. 'Tell you what,' suggested Sangita. 'We'll go in us uniforms to school, right? But when we've done at the old people's home we'll, like, put on us own stuff for goin' home, O.K.?'

'I've got this really cute outfit.'

'So've I.'

'Me too.'

'What is it, then, Mel?'

'Not telling.'

'Me neither.'

'Nor me.'

■

In the entrance to the old people's home was a comfort fund box and the results of the last money-making effort and prize draw. Old women crossed and re-crossed the hall, creeping between walking frames, muttering to themselves.

Melanie stared at the wispy hair and multi-coloured shawls, then whispered to Jasmine, 'A-ah, aren't they sweet? Know what? I reckon I'd be really good with old people.'

An old woman stared back at Melanie, whose hair was now as punk as a parakeet, and announced in a loud quaver, 'I don't know what they want to go makin' such a mess of thesselves for, I'm sure.'

A smiling nurse came to meet them. 'Hullo! I'm Mrs Sidebottom. The old folk have been looking forward to this *so* much.'

They had to change into their lycras right there in the entrance hall. This caused a lot of giggling as they stripped off using their skirts as tents. Melanie accused Dave of looking, and he went dead red.

At first the old people did seem quite keen on the entertainment. At least, they exclaimed in shocked delight when the girls shimmied on in their lycras for the Glenn Miller routine. But no sooner had they started the Chattanooga Choo Choo than the old woman who'd stared at Melanie in the entrance hall started shunting back and forth like a demented dodgem.

'What *is* it, Mrs Hepworth?' cried the nurse, still smiling.

'Sun's in me eyes,' complained Mrs Hepworth, and there was a prolonged refrain of 'Come over 'ere, love' and 'No, she'd be better off over *'ere*', from all her cronies.

The contemporary dance fared no better. Just as the Goods were locked in death throe combat with the Bads an old man shrieked at the top of his voice, 'Me legs! What about me legs?'

'What *is* it, Mr Reevie?' cried the nurse. The smile had dipped. The old woman with the sun in her eyes was still shunting like a steam locomotive and had thoroughly boxed him in.

But it was the Ruth Ellis that came off the worst. For one thing the nurse brought in cups of tea just as Miss Hibbert was outlining the story and the rattle of teacups was so loud that nobody heard a word.

'I don't know what this can be, I'm sure,' complained the shunter as Ruth Ellis lived it up with David Blakely/Dave Petrovic to the tune of 'Little Town Flirt'.

'I can't make this out, can you?' the shunter demanded of the nurse as Desmond Cussen/Mick Malone tried to seduce Ruth Ellis/Melanie Fish away from David Blakely/Dave Petrovic to the tune of 'Save the Last Dance for Me'.

'Do they want us to dance for them or don't they?' moaned Ruth Ellis to Desmond Cussen throughout 'Fun, Fun, Fun'. The old folk answered her by demanding second cups of tea, clattering their teaspoons and getting out their knitting.

'I-can't-stand-much-more-of-this,' Ruth Ellis informed David Blakely through a rictus grin in the middle of 'A Certain Smile'. He hoisted her into a particularly poignant lift. 'And you and me are finished, right?' she added poisonously, then gasped as she plummeted groundwards with all the grace of an overfilled sandbag.

From then on things got totally out of control. Desmond Cussen heard what Ruth Ellis had said to David Blakely and rightly assumed that the remark was not only directed at David Blakely in the dance-drama but at Dave Petrovic in real life. Ruth Ellis's over-hasty descent through the air confirmed his suspicions. So he was grinning manically as he handed Ruth Ellis the gun. She turned to shoot David Blakely. Petrovic seized the weapon as she turned. He proceeded to gun down Desmond Cussen and Ruth Ellis who resolutely refused to die. The old people suddenly sniffed out real drama and chorused 'Oh dee-ar!' in unison and Miss Hibbert stepped in.

The row was short and not very sweet. The crowd sat riveted throughout; even the shunter went rigid and at the end she led the old folk in their applause. 'That was very marvellous, wasn't it, Mrs Sidebottom?' she demanded of the nurse with a malevolent grin. Meanwhile Miss Hibbert was looking very very grim.

Melanie thought she might just go to the lavs to put on her cute new outfit, the way things had turned out. She reckoned she wouldn't emerge either until Miss Hibbert and the school bus could be guaranteed to have left the premises. Sangita and Jasmine felt the same way.

But although Melanie left it a full twenty minutes before she emerged in her black leatherette mini, black jacket with fringes, black pixie boots and black lacy tights, Miss Hibbert was still there. It was as if she'd been waiting on purpose, assisted by Jeanie Parkes, under the pretence of gathering up stray lycras and rogue leg-warmers into a sweaty heap. Melanie backed off fast when she saw her, but not before the other lav doors had burst open and there stood Jasmine and Sangita wearing . . .

BLACK LEATHERETTE MINIS, BLACK JACKETS WITH FRINGES, BLACK PIXIE BOOTS AND BLACK LACY TIGHTS! They took stock of one another out of the corners of their eyes and their faces fell.

Miss Hibbert started to swell. It was Jeanie Parkes who saved them. 'Least you can't complain this time, can you, Miss?' she demanded smugly, picking a thread of cotton from her navy skirt and shooting the cuffs of her regulation school blouse. 'Not now they're wearing their UNIFORM!'

Fergie Finds Out

'Dave Petrovic's party,' wrote Melanie in her 'Good Party Guide'. 'Medioca.'

Changes were rife at Davenport at this time. Not only had Melanie Fish given up Dave for Mick Malone, but Katerina Wainwright had given up Fergie Fish for Tez Tindale, Tez Tindale had given up Maria Wainwright for Katerina Wainwright, Maria Wainwright had given up boys and Dave Petrovic had given up hope.

Jeanie Parkes was also off boys – they weren't interested in poets, only in Ravers, it seemed, and she'd set up her own rock band to comment on this, with Candy Leedham on bass, Donna Hacket (drums) and Maria Wainwright (lead guitar). Jeanie wrote the lyrics and they all sang. They called themselves Dominant Jean and the D.N.A.s and their best number was 'If you can't join 'em, beat 'em'.

Oh, and Fergie Fish had given up Katerina Wainwright and Tez 'The Traitor' Tindale for investigative journalism and breaking.

'Watch me, Mel,' said Fergie, sprawled out on her bedroom floor. 'I reckon I nearly had it that time.'

Melanie looked up long enough to see Fergie heave his weight up on to his elbows. He began to tap round in a circle with his feet. She grunted and returned to her latest entry.

'Mel-a-nie!' Fergie had collapsed on to his bum now and was spinning round and round on the lino. He suddenly flipped over and lay flat on his stomach, panting. It didn't look like proper breaking to Melanie. All the lads in the fifth year were doing it and none of them looked like Fergie. He put her in mind of a stringy log of minced lamb at the Greek take-away, twisting and turning on a spit. She shook her head. 'It's no good, Fergie. It's not slick enough for the concert.'

Melanie had organized a concert for the following evening in the guide hut. It was in aid of 'Save the Smoking Dogs'. She'd seen a film about how dogs were given fags to see how many they had to smoke before they landed up stiff with their legs in the air. She thought it was the cruellest thing she'd ever seen in her life.

'Why do they call it "breaking" anyway?'

Fergie groaned. 'Because you can *break* somethin' doin' it. S'obvious. Dumbo!'

Melanie aimed a kick at him. 'I'm not surprised!'

The bed vibrated as Fergie flopped on to his back, ready to start the whole routine over again. Melanie remembered the way the light in the front room juddered every time he did it and how a crack was appearing right across the ceiling.

'Fer-gie?' she yelled over the noise of his crash landing after the flip. 'I don' reckon you should be doin' this, y'know!' He took no notice.

'Tizer Malone's party,' Melanie wrote next, selecting a red felt tip for this all important entry. 'SCRUMSHUS!' She carefully enclosed Mick's new name in a red heart and gave it an edging of pale blue lace.

Fergie thumped and flipped over again.

'FER-GIE! I s'll tell Mum!'

Fergie grinned and put his elbows on her bed, heaving himself beside her. She squealed and covered the latest Good Party Guide entry with her thumb.

'Let's have a look at it.'

'No-o! Gerroffit.'

Fergie fell upon her, tickling her till the book fell out of her hand. He snatched at it as she lay face down on the bed, gasping. He read the latest entry and pulled a face. Oh, no! Not Mugger Malone! You'd have thought she'd have learnt her lesson after Goliath Gillespie!

Mick 'Mugger' Malone was famous in Davenport for his leadership of the school mafia. The other members were Les Earnshaw, Paul Balogan and Carl Gregson. They stole out of handbags, threw flour round the lobbies, bent Mr Mortimer's aerial and let Miss Harvey's tyres down, then framed the other kids.

'What d'ya wanna call him *Tizer* Malone for, anyway? Mugger suits him much bedder.'

'Oooooooh, because when you're in love you're all, like, fizzy and bubbly and lovely and – *you* know.'

Fergie did. He didn't care to be reminded!

'Anyway, I think Tizer's a great name, don't you? After I started calling Tizer Tizer we called all the lads in our class after drinks. There's Coke Balogan, Shandy Singh, Guinness Gregson, Pepsi Pradhan . . .' She counted them off on her fingers. 'Anyway, Tizer supports "Save the Smoking Dogs", y'know, Ferg.'

Fergie looked unconvinced. The mafia – and that included Mugger Malone – smoked twenty a day and had told some of the second year that they didn't see why dogs should be deprived. And neither did the second years by the time their arms had been twisted through three hundred and sixty-five degrees!

He reached for his *Marvel* comic. But Melanie didn't

want to leave the conversation now they'd got on to Tizer Malone. 'Least, I think I'm in love with Tizer. Could be just infachuashun, I suppose.' She dived down the bed and moved in close to her dressing table mirror. She combed her blonde fringe as high as it would go and fingered the constellation of spots on her forehead as if she would read the fate of her love for Tizer Malone in their braille. She turned to Fergie. 'D'ya wanna know how it all began between Tizer and me? Our eyes met across a crowded maths room and . . .'

But Fergie had jumped up and was bouncing on her bed, launching himself in Melanie's direction and yelling, 'Is it a bird? Is it a cloud? Is it a plane? No, it's FLUSHMA-AN!'

Melanie buckled on to her fluffy pink rug, banging her knee on her dressing table. 'Sh-ugar! Jus' break it up, Fergie, will you? What's all this "Flushman" stuff, anyway?'

Fergie bounded up and down on the rug, grabbing upwards and yanking down on an imaginary old-fashioned bog chain.

'Flushman fights phoneys.'

Melanie staggered to her feet, rubbing her knee. '*I'm* not a phoney! Lay off it, Fergie, will you? Get lost. Go on. Scram. Leave!'

The phone started to ring. Fergie rolled towards the door but Melanie leapt across him. 'S'all right. It'll be for me. Bet you anythin' it's Tizer!' She rushed out, slamming the door. Fergie listened to her thumping down the stairs, two at a time. Then he crept out on to the landing. 'Roylston–430525–Who–is–that–please?' he heard her say in this dead stupid voice. She looked up and saw Fergie peering through the banisters. Her face took on an expression of exasperated rage. 'Phone-y!' Fergie mouthed at her before she shoved the front room door to with her foot. Fergie went back to her room and spent a minute or two going through her drawers but there was nothing new worth looking at so he went on into his own room.

He switched on the anglepoise over his desk and felt around under his papers for his eye-shade. He pulled up his swivel stool and squeezed his knees under the desk, half lifting it off the floor in the process. He'd had it since he was eight! He dragged open a drawer looking for his fags and stuck one behind each ear. He didn't smoke any more, not since he'd had a whole packet in four hours and been sick fourteen times. But he liked to keep a fag or two for sticking behind his ears. It made him look like a proper editor. When he grew up he was going to be a roving reporter and expose shady deals in high places. He'd find out who was selling arms to who and be made an O.B.E. for his services to world peace.

He pulled out issue two of his newspaper *The Foghorn*. At the top, underneath *The Foghorn* it said in capitals FLUSHMAN FINDS OUT. Underneath that was his favourite 'Did you know?' column.

Did you know?

1. That Mr Mortimer wears a chest wig?
2. That Mr Revitt (the Rabbit) calls the Remejul Department Legoland?
3. That a Remejul Department is for kids with Special Needs. Such kids need careful handling!
4. That Killer Kesterton called the Willows kids the Weeping Willows because they cried on the way to the dining centre. This was because Killer let on they have free dinners (KEEP QUIET ABOUT THIS).

Fergie rummaged among his socks and underpants and unwrapped the school log from his football shirt. He'd happened to spot it one day when investigating the school secretary's store room. It was covered in dust and clearly neglected and he reckoned the head wouldn't miss it if he borrowed it for a few days in the interests of investigative journalism. He thumbed through it for the bits he'd underlined.

5. That in 1918 out of twenty-five girls who attended the swimming baths regularly ONLY ONE learnt to swim?!

6. That during fire drill practice in 1939 the BOYS cleared the building in just one minute and the GIRLS took TWO MINUTES AND A HALF!

7. That on 6 June 1945 there was a Thanksgiving and Victory celebration. Each GIRL was given a card with the King's message and a victory hair slide and the BOYS WERE GIVEN AN ICE-CREAM SANDWICH EACH (HA! HA! HA!)

8. That Katerina Wainwright's a vampire?

9. That Tez Tindale's got verrucas?

10. That Melanie Fish is the ONLY SCHOOLGIRL in this city to be a ROYLSTON RAVER? Well done, Melanie!

11. That the versatile Fergie Fish will be giving an exhibition of CRACK BREAKING at the Save the Smoking Dogs concert tonight 7.15 p.m. in a guide hut near you.

Fergie paused lovingly. He liked writing the Did You Know? column better than anything else in the world. But the paper was due off the presses tomorrow. And when he'd finished the master edition he still had to copy it out another thirty-three times.

'NEWS IN BRIEF,' wrote Fergie feverishly. 'TAXATION TO BE PUT ON ALL TINNED GOODS. Said Mr Crick of Blitherington, "That just about puts the lid on it." VAMPIRE VICTIM LIVES TO TELL THE TALE. A shaken Mr Tindale of Bleedun-under-Werewolf told our reporter this morning, "Fangs ain't what they used to be." '

'THE ARTS,' scribbled Fergie.

'*Return of the Bog-Eyed Monster.*

The Bog-Eyed Monster Comes Back.

The Bog-Eyed Monster Rides Again.

Says our film correspondent Clancy Bathazard, "Not to be missed. These are all griping films." '

'INSIDE PAGES,' scrawled Fergie. He had to finish the master copy before Melanie came off the phone and remembered she was supposed to be overseeing his homework. 'COMPUTER GAMES by FOG-HORN. FOGHORN BINGO GAME, FOG-HORN HIS AND HERS, FOGHORN OTHERS, FOGHORN PERSONAL.'

'FOGHORN PERSONAL', Fergie's hand trailed crookedly across the page. 'Flushman seeks Flushwoman. Worthy partner. Home-loving and house-trained. Phone Roylston 430525 after office hours.'

A door slammed and Fergie could hear Melanie thudding back upstairs. He jumped over his bed and opened the door.

'So how was Mugger Malone?'

'It weren't *Tizer* Malone. It was flippin' Jeanie Parkes.'

'So what's with Dominant Jean?'

Melanie rolled her eyes. 'She said she wouldn't be in

the concert if Tizer was in it. She said she wouldn't share a gig with a fascist.'

Fergie grinned. That was good. He stored it up for *The Foghorn*. Did you know that Dominant Jean called the notorrus Mugger Malone . . .?

'It's all right you grinnin'. But no one'll come if she's not in it. She's dead popular at the moment – I can't think why! And Tizer's been practisin' his Freddie Mercury impersonations all week. Jeanie's gone dead warped, y'know, Ferg. She wouldn't have any lads at her party. It was dead boring and you should have seen the food! It was all, like, sesame surprise and budgie seed stew. I reckon since her dad left, the Parkes's have given up sex for the soya bean.'

Fergie nodded. Anything for a quiet life. But he didn't think Dominant Jean was *that* warped. In fact, she showed remarkably good judgement – for a girl. She'd happened to see him flogging the first edition of *The Foghorn* to some dim-witted first years for 25p and she'd been pestering him about when the second edition'd be out ever since. In fact, Dominant Jean was exactly the sort of woman he was looking for to share his investigative life. Someone with a show biz background'd be an asset.

Melanie remembered what her mother had said. 'Hey, Fergie, I hope you've been doing your homework.'

Fergie nodded with enthusiasm. Something about the violence of his nodding made Melanie doubt his word. 'C'mon, then. Let's see what you've done.'

Fergie dashed past her into his bedroom. He shoved *The Foghorn* out of sight. By the time Melanie reached his desk he'd opened his biology book and was scratching the date in Roman numerals. There were so many strokes and his writing was so spiky anyway that it looked like a squashed centipede semaphoring at the sky. As Melanie bent over him, Fergie got underway:

'A potato is a storage organ . . .'

■

The next day on his way to school Fergie happened to spot Dominant Jean turning right out of Baldwin Boulevard. She was stumping along at a great rate, carrying an off-cut of sacking with 'Swag Bag' printed on it and eating her dinner. Fergie had noticed that she usually ate it about twenty to nine on school mornings.

He waylaid her from behind a privet hedge, temptingly wafting the master copy of *The Foghorn* in front of her nose. He'd been having an admiring re-read of it as he ambled along.

'D'ya wanna buy issue two, Jeanie? 'S'just out. For the bargain price of . . .' he hesitated – she'd seemed really keen last time, 'for the bargain price of 20p.'

Jeanie sneered at him through a munch. 'No way.'

'O.K.' Fergie was about to make a V sign behind her head and bang back across the road when she said, 'I'll give you 5p if you like. Though that's 500 per cent profit margin on what it's worth.'

Fergie chose to rise above this observation. 5p in the pocket's worth a kick in the . . .

'O.K.'

Fergie rested his briefcase on his knee to unbuckle it. Jeanie pointed a greasy and agitated finger – he'd noticed before she seemed to be suffering from an advanced form of St Vitus' dance. 'That's posh,' she said, spraying crumbs.

'Yeah.' Fergie frowned into the sun. His mum would insist on buying it for him though he'd wanted a sports bag. He hated sport, of course, but at least with a sports bag you're not a marked man. Jeanie counted out five pence in ½ ps and Fergie handed her the thirty-third copy of *The Foghorn* by way of revenge. It looked dreadful. Even to his fond eyes it resembled a whole battlefield of centipedes expiring on a barbed wire fence. She peered at it for a moment, then turned her attention to the packet of sandwiches balanced in the top of the swag bag. She glowered down at them, lowered her nose and gave them a sniff. She picked one out, took a large bite and mumbled at Fergie through the mouthful.

'What's that you said?'

'These sandwiches are really awful.'

'They *look* really awful.'

'They are. They're really awful.'

Jeanie glanced up from the sandwiches and spotted a small middle-aged woman hurrying along clutching her reinforced shopping bag in front of her like a shield. She kept her head pointing straight in front of her so she wouldn't have to look at Jeanie and Fergie.

Jeanie stepped into her path and gave her a gruesome smile.

'Would you like one of these really awful sandwiches?'

The woman didn't say anything, but her eyes bulged as she stepped neatly into the gutter, then leapt back on to the pavement and charged on down the road, head straining forward like a constipated tortoise. Jeanie continued to take large gloomy mouthfuls. 'Chick pea and lentil,' she informed Fergie. 'Mum went on an "Improve your karma" course at the poly. Then she started giving me these.'

Fergie nodded as if this explained everything. Privately he didn't think they seemed to be making Jeanie Parkes *any* calmer. He'd never known such a jerky, unrestful female.

She dragged out a bag of wizened-looking raisins and poked them in Fergie's direction. 'Have a few.'

Fergie declined.

She peered at them dolefully and crammed some into her mouth. 'Well, they're better'n *nothing*, I suppose.'

Fergie thought that nothing would be a good deal preferable to those mangy-looking raisins! 'What do you eat for the rest of the day?'

Jeanie quickened her pace. 'Nothing.'

'*Nothing?*' Fergie took stock of her out of the corner of his eye. Then how come she was . . . well, rather on the ample side?

She was moving so fast now that he'd despaired of getting any praise for *The Foghorn* out of her before she reached the main gate. Suddenly she stopped and pinged *The Foghorn* with her finger. 'I want this for my file. For its anti-woman content.'

Fergie fell back three paces and gasped. But he *wasn't* anti-woman! Wasn't he requesting a Flushwoman in this very issue, to further his investigative life? And if she happened to be a shapely blonde who looked a little like one of the Ravers, well, he wouldn't be stand-offish. How come he was wasting his time on man-hating ghouls like Jeanie Parkes anyway?

'What this school needs isn't jokes and gettin' at the girls, y'know, Fergie,' continued Jeanie. 'Consciousness raisin'! That's what it needs.'

Consciousness raisins! Fergie stared at her. Those raisins had looked revolting! Besides, he didn't believe there were such raisins as *consciousness* raisins! Melanie was quite right – Jeanie Parkes *was* nuts.

She nodded at him and set off across the yard to the fifth year base. Fergie made his way into the shrubbery

on a short cut to where the first years hung out. He'd
make them pay for the scorn of Jeanie Parkes! And he'd
go to 'Save the Smoking Dogs' in an investigative
capacity and write a blistering critique on Dominant
Jean . . .

■

Dominant Jean and the D.N.A.s had the next-to-last slot
in 'Save the Smoking Dogs'. Melanie signalled to Fergie
in the wings and he switched on four spots. There in a
beam of rose alternating with baby blue and then another
beam of rose stood Candy, Maria and Donna, and with
her back to the audience, in a white spot, Dominant Jean
herself!

Fergie gasped.

Each D.N.A. was split straight down the middle like a
court jester. Half of their hair was curled and smothered
in ribbons like a butterfly bush; the other half was sleeked
to their heads like a greaser's. Half of their mouths glist-
ened with shocking pink lipstick and one eyelid each was
heavy with gold and navy eye shadow. The other was
blackened as if they'd been scrapping and what looked
like blood trickled from the other half of each D.N.A.
mouth. Each wore half a sugar pink sweatshirt stitched to
half an army camouflage jacket and one trouser leg
stitched to half a flouncy mini. One foot wore a glittery
sock and spiky-heeled shoe and the other, a Doc Martin.
Under the sugar pink sweatshirt arm each carried a life-
size doll and from the camouflage arm out poked a gun!

Then Dominant Jean turned round! She was dressed as
a ring-mistress in a red tailed coat, striped denims, high
black boots (made of dustbin liners), a T-shirt that said
'D.J. waives the rules', a top hat, a handle-bar moustache
and diamanté earrings with a rose between her teeth. This
she spat skywards as she cracked her circus whip, the

group started up, the guide hut began to vibrate and the
D.N.A.s broke into 'Don't Join 'Em, Beat 'Em' above a
heavy metal beat.

> *They say that girls are sweet and pretty*
> *They say that lads are tough and strong*
> *But get down to the nitty-gritty*
> *And see that they are WRONG WRONG*
>   *WRONG!*
>
> *We don't care for soft-soap roses*
> *From guys who pick us up in cars.*
> *It only leads to wiping noses*
> *While guys go out and prop up bars.*
>
> *Girls don't choose to bring up babies*
> *Lads don't choose to fight in wars*
> *They sell us on it when we're little*
> *Well, we shall make up OUR OWN LAWS!*
>
> *If what they tell you drives you crazy*
> *And their ropes tie you in knots*
> *There's one way you can defeat 'em*
> *Do not join 'em, BEAT 'EM BEAT 'EM!*
> *Do not join 'em, BEAT 'EM.*

And at every 'BEAT 'EM' Dominant Jean gave a
fine crack of her whip and the D.N.A.s jumped up and
down.

Fergie didn't like to admit it but he was very impressed!
Jeanie in drag put him in mind of Freddie Mercury in 'I
Wanna Be Free'.

The screams, catcalls and yells carried on long after
D.J. and the D.N.A.s had left the stage. Melanie came on
and did her jerky robotics dance in her lycra and dustbin

liner, but the crowd jeered, booed, threw things and screeched for Dominant Jean.

Fergie tugged the curtain shut and left Melanie to sort that one out. He made his way hastily backstage. He'd just hit on an amazing scheme for boosting circulation of *The Foghorn* one hundredfold!

When Jeanie came staggering past holding her moustache on with one hand and sweeping up the 'swag bag' with the other, Fergie placed an admiring hand on her arm. 'I'm here to make you an offer you cannot refuse, Jeanie.' He paused for dramatic effect and flicked out a cheque book headed 'Foghorn Account'. 'I hereby offer you joint editorship of *The Foghorn*. And you can use your half for anythin' you like.' Fergie smiled with fond indulgence and patted Jeanie's top hat. 'You can plug consciousness raisins or anythin',' Fergie waved an airy hand, 'anythin' at all.'

Jeanie looked at Fergie to see if he was serious. She decided that he was! She upended the swag bag and twelve Yorkie bars and four tins of diet Coke fell out. She pulled the rings off two of them and handed one to Fergie. Her eyes shone. 'To our *partnership*, then, Fergie,' leered Dominant Jean.

BREAKING GLASS

Brian Morse

When the Red Army drops its germ bomb on Leicester, the affected zone is sealed off permanently − with Darren and his sister Sally inside it. Immune to the disease which kills Sally, Darren must face alone the incomprehensible hatred of two of the few survivors trapped with him. And the haunting question is: why did Dad betray them?

YATESY'S RAP

Jon Blake

It was Ol's idea to play the Christmas concert. His second idea was to get a band together. A most unlikely band it turned out to be. Half of them couldn't play, most of them didn't like each other, and none of them had ever been on a stage. And then Yatesy arrived, with his reputation for being kicked out of several schools for fighting.

UNEASY MONEY
Robin F. Brancato

What would *you* do if you won a fortune? That's what happens when Mike Bronti buys a New Jersey lottery ticket to celebrate his eighteenth birthday. Suddenly, everything looks possible: gifts for his family, treats for his friends, a new car for himself – but things don't work out quite as Mike expects them to. A funny sensitive story about everyone's favourite fantasy.

THE TRICKSTERS
Margaret Mahy

The Hamiltons gather at their holiday house for their customary celebration of midsummer Christmas in New Zealand, but it is to be a Christmas they'll never forget. For the warm, chaotic family atmosphere is chilled by the unexpected arrival of three sinister brothers – the Tricksters.

THREE'S A CROWD
Jennifer Cole

How much fun can you have when your parents are away? No housework, no homework, a BIG party, and plenty of boys. Hey, who's throwing pizza around and where's Mollie disappeared to with that strange guy? (The first book in the *Sisters* series.)